DESOLATION RUN

DESOLATION RUN

Larry Lovan

Copyright © 2020 by Laurence Lovan

All rights reserved. No part of this book may be reproduced in any form or by any electronic or mechanical means including information storage and retrieval systems without permission in writing from the publisher, except by a reviewer, who may quote brief passages in a review.

First Edition

This is a work of fiction. Names, characters, places and events either are the product of the author's imagination or are used fictitiously. Any similarity to real persons, living or dead, is coincidental and not intended by the author.

ISBN 978-1-7349508-0-9

Cover design by Jennifer Gibson – www.JenniferGibson.ca

*Dedicated to
my wonderful wife, Wanda.*

ONE

It was no different than any other night, until Rebecca saw her father on TV.

The Black List Lounge had been a three ring-circus on speed all evening and they were short a waitress. The Road Raptors Motorcycle Club had invaded in force and occupied most of the floor space. Four rejects from the Sunset Strip—an Elvis, one Lady Gaga and two Madonnas—had taken refuge at the bar along with the usual bunch of boozers. The two Madonnas were parked at opposite ends, glowering at each other. Elvis was driving everyone nuts with his, "Thank yew vera much." That was when he could be heard at all over the roar of the jukebox someone had cranked up to the max. The bogus Happy Days Rock-Ola was loaded with Country Western and Classic Rock.

Rebecca hadn't had a break in six hours. If she had to listen to *Tequila Makes Her Clothes Fall Off* or *Born To Be Wild* one more time tonight, she was going to grab the owner's shotgun and blow the damn thing apart.

She threaded her way through the throng, holding a tray full of empty bottles and glasses in front of her. Someone snagged her T-shirt and held on. "Hey!" she yelled and jerked to a stop, managing not to spill her load.

A heavy-set man with a beefy-red face and looking like a reject from *The Sopranos* glared up at her. "There's no smoking in bars. I demand you tell those... people," he jerked his head in the direction of the pool tables, "to put out their cigarettes. My friend has asthma."

She looked where several bikers were shooting pool, most smoking, then back at the table. The guy's date was dressed in a tan pantsuit, trying hard to look like Ellen DeGeneres. He needed to try harder. His five o'clock shadow had hemorrhaged through his makeup. The guy coughed daintily and waved fingers in front of his face.

"Tell them yourself," Rebecca said, jerked loose and continued on. Freaking Hollywood. Wasn't her table anyway.

She set the tray down on the bar, leaned across and called to the bartender, "I need six more long-necks for those creeps at table five."

"Whatta they drinking?"

"Piss water."

The bartender nodded and dug in the ice chest for some Bud Lights.

"Rough night, huh?"

It was her sleaze-ball agent, Marvin Lewis, who'd shown up a half-hour earlier and parked himself on a barstool. Marv wore a chartreuse shirt tucked into a pair of lime green trousers and covered with a mahogany sports coat. He looked like a scrawny avocado. He'd been trying to talk her into doing a porno movie. It'd be a good career move, he'd argued, lots of exposure. He'd actually delivered that line with a straight face.

She ran a hand across her brow and back through her hair. "Normal bullshit, sales convention out slumming, can't keep their hands to their selves." She glanced at the TV above the bar and froze. Her father's face filled the screen. The eleven o'clock news was on but the sound had been muted. She couldn't have heard him anyway over the din, not that it mattered, his spiel never changed. The tagline read that Reverend Jonathan Spade was speaking at a fund raiser at the Los Angeles Convention Center. She'd missed which one of the candidates he was stumping for but could guess easily enough. Her father was in full Hellfire and Brimstone mode, his right hand slashing the air, face an angry scowl.

Her skin tingled, went hot and her breath grew short. Memories she'd suppressed seared her brain. Emotions threatened to spew out like a volcano. It'd been over five years since she'd last seen him— when he'd forced his way into her apartment and fractured her jaw. She gripped the edge of the bar to steady herself. How many times had she sat through one of his tirades? How many times had she been put in her place by that hypocritical son of a bitch?

"That your daddy?" Marv asked.

She looked at him. Her agent had a smirk on his face that reminded her of an opossum she once stumbled upon in the chicken coop.

"What an asshole," he said and chuckled.

She punched him in the mouth. She had no idea why she did it. She couldn't have agreed more with him. But she hit him anyway, as hard as she could. Maybe she did it because he had no right to call her father anything, having never met him. Or maybe because of the sudden realization that she was well on the way to becoming the person her father had condemned her to be. She'd been considering doing the movie.

"Help," Marv yelped as he staggered off his stool, a hand going to his injured mouth. "This crazy bitch just attacked me. Somebody call the cops." That was the last thing anybody in this bar would consider doing.

The bar owner hurried over. "What the hell you think you're doin'? You're fired, get the hell out."

"You owe me a week's salary," Rebecca said, having a hard time believing that punching someone in this dive was a firing offense. "I'm not leaving without it." She cupped her right hand in her left and held it tight against her belly and tried not to cry. She'd broken something.

"I owe you nothin'. Get the hell out."

"I'm not leaving without my money."

"That's it honey," one of the Madonnas hollered. "Don't take that shit off him. Stand up for your rights."

"Hey, she hit a customer. Fire her ass," the other Madonna yelled.

"Shut up, bitch," Madonna One said.

"Don't tell me to shut up, whore," Madonna Two said.

"Thank yew vera much," Elvis said.

Marv continued to yell that he'd been assaulted and if someone wouldn't call the cops, then at least call him a lawyer.

"You're a lawyer," several people yelled.

The bar owner spun toward him. "You don't need no lawyer," he said, took hold of the man's shoulder, gentle like, and gave him a lopsided smile meant to be reassuring.

Marv didn't want to be reassured. He jerked his shoulder away and spat a gob of blood onto the floor. His hairpiece, which was three shades of brown richer than his own hair, had been knocked askew and was in danger of coming off altogether. He dug his cell phone out of a pocket and fumbled with the keys. "Anybody know the number of that ambulance chaser on TV, Barry or Perry somethin' or another?"

"Forget the lawyer. Don't need no damn lawyer. I just fired the bitch. She's leaving."

"Not without my pay," Rebecca said, pushed between them and got right in the owner's face. She wasn't going to let this prick cheat her out of her money. She'd get her pay and begin her life anew in the morning, get her career back on track. She'd show her father.

The intoxicated throng at the bar continued to yell advice while the Sopranos reject stood and hollered that the cigarette smoke was choking his friend who had asthma.

Ellen gave another tepid cough.

A tall biker stiff-armed Soprano back into his chair and shouldered the bar owner out of the way. He spun Marv around, seized him by the collar and belt, then frog-marched him across the floor and out the door.

Rebecca watched them go. She had no idea why the biker had butted in but was glad to see her agent gone. She turned back to the owner, brushed some locks out of her face and continued to demand her salary.

At the bar, the two Madonnas spilled off their stools, met halfway and erupted into a hair-pulling, blouse-ripping, spittle-slinging catfight. Elvis tried to separate them while several grinning bikers crowded in to watch and egg them on.

The tall biker returned, alone. He stuffed something into his vest pocket and walked over. "Pay her what you owe her," he said and stopped a foot away from the owner.

The owner stepped back and turned to face the biker who towered over him. "I don't owe her nothin'. I'll be lucky not to be sued."

"Prick's gone and won't be back. Pay her, asshole."

Rebecca looked at the tall biker. He was lean, but well-muscled, his arms covered with tattoos. He was clean-shaven, unusual for an outlaw biker, and ruggedly handsome. He'd dressed in black Levis, boots, and a black t-shirt under a worn leather vest. The vest was covered with tags and patches—1%, FTW, and others. Above the right breast pocket a tag read *PRESIDENT*. Why was he helping her? No one ever stood up for her.

The owner started to protest again, but hesitated. He licked his lips and glanced around. It had grown quiet in the room, the catfight terminated thanks to a pitcher of beer being tossed on them, the jukebox run out of coin. The patrons at the bar watched wide-eyed while club members crowded forward in the obvious expectations of taking the joint apart. The tall biker gave the owner a nasty smirk as if to remind him of the drawback to owning a biker bar. It was patronized by bikers, most of whom were as stable as a shitload of nitroglycerin.

The owner turned, stepped behind the bar and hesitated again. Rebecca's breath caught. Surely he wasn't foolish enough to make a grab for the short-barreled, pump shotgun everyone knew he kept under the counter? He locked eyes with his assailant. The heavy moment, punctuated only by the soft whapping of the ceiling fans, ended when the owner caved and rang up *No Sale* on the cash register. He removed a wad of bills and started counting them out on the counter top. Rebecca breathed again. Apparently he wasn't into suicide. With a scowl, he pushed the bills toward her.

"That what he owes you?"

She flipped through them with her good hand, glanced at the owner, and stuffed the bills into a pocket of her shorts. She looked at the biker and nodded.

He stared down at her, his nut-brown eyes so hard and cruel just moments before now looked amused. After a long moment's scrutiny he said, "C'mon, run you to the ER, get your hand looked at." Without waiting for an answer he turned for the door.

She started to bristle at what sounded like an order but then took a deep breath and followed him. After all, he had helped her get her money.

TWO

Rebecca trailed Johnny out the bar and across the dark parking lot, past some more bikers and their women who watched them go by. She knew who he was even though this was the first time he'd come in while she was working. The other waitresses were always talking about Johnny, president of the Road Raptors MC. Her workmates were infatuated with him, even the married ones—especially the married ones. Bradley Cooper, Chris Pine, Scott Eastwood, were some of the ways they described him.

She'd seen him stroll in an hour or so earlier. He was hard to miss, tall enough to play for the Lakers. Tall and lean, carrying himself like he owned the place. He'd sat at another girl's table which was fine as she had no desire to fight over who was going to wait on him. She had no idea why he'd decided to involve himself in her affair.

"See your hand," he said and turned to face her.

She held out her right hand, cupped in her left. Despite the faint light cast by the nearest lamp pole, it was obvious she'd broken a bone. Her hand was red and badly swelled.

"Yeah, it's broke. The hell was that about?"

She stared into his eyes. How do you tell a stranger you just realized your life was going to shit, becoming everything you'd swore it wouldn't? Why would you tell him? "My agent wanted me to star in a porno movie," she said instead.

He grunted. "You'd be good at it."

Anger replaced pain. She released her wounded hand and launched a slap at his face with her left, but he caught her by the wrist and laughed. "Already broke one hand tonight, wanna break the other too?"

"I'm a serious actress, not a whore."

"Yeah? What movies have I seen you in?"

She jerked her wrist free and didn't answer his question.

"What I thought."

"I've appeared in commercials and done bit parts on several TV shows." *Yeah, bit parts, nothing but crowd filler with no lines. Only that, after five long years, which is why I waitress in dumps like this.* She shook her hair about and stood straighter. "I've done some live theater, plays."

"Admire a person with scruples. Too many people sell themselves short. C'mon." He led her to a group of parked motorcycles. They stopped alongside a large, black, customized Harley Davidson. In the hazy light, she could barely make out the club emblem painted in ghostly gray swirls on the gas tank. The bike had chrome forks, black finished engine, exhaust and mufflers as well as a butt-sprung seat that curled over the shortened rear fender.

Johnny mounted, jerked the bike upright and nudged the kickstand into place with his boot. "Climb on."

She shook her head. "I can't afford the ER."

"Your agent's picking up the tab," he said and patted a breast pocket.

"He is? Why would he do that?"

"Convinced him it was the Christian thing to do."

"Isn't he Jewish?"

Johnny shrugged.

She didn't want to get on the bike. Her life was screwed up enough. The last thing she needed was to be in debt to a biker. But her hand hurt like the devil. Something needed to be done for it.

"C'mon, it won't bite," he said with a smile. Thin lips that could have been cruel turned roguish. Brown eyes that could freeze, melted. A man's all too-knowing face transformed itself into that of a playful youth when he smiled.

It was Johnny's smile that finally convinced her to climb on the bike.

THREE

The bike erupted into life with a primeval bellow when Johnny slammed his foot down on the starter. Rebecca had ridden on the backs of motorcycles before, but never anything like this monster. She could smell its stench of scorched metal, burnt fuel and blackened oil. She could feel its might pulsating between her legs. Currents of barely controllable, maniacal power thrummed through her thighs into her sinews. They penetrated her very being. She wrapped her arms tightly around Johnny's chest. This wasn't a machine, it was a beast, awakened from its slumber and demanding to know by what right they sat astride its back.

She had to hold on with her left hand and right forearm as she couldn't tolerate putting any pressure on her injured hand. Johnny must have realized that. He took it easy on the ride. Normally Road Raptors rode like maniacs. They were real outlaw bikers. And some of them were nothing but animals, especially the one they called Magoo. She'd become all too familiar with his leers and sexist remarks while working at that dive. He always picked one of her tables to sit at and referred to her as, "Hey, baby." He sounded like Beavis, or was that Butthead? Whichever, she found him incredibly annoying. But what could you expect from someone who relied on

MTV for his pick-up lines. At least he kept his hands to himself. So she smiled and did her job, always careful to keep the table between them.

It was lucky she sat up higher than Johnny or she wouldn't be able to see. Still her eyes barely cleared his shoulder. His dark hair blew into her face, tickled her nose and cheeks, caused her to blink. She leaned back a bit. The wind roared past her ears competing with the growl of the engine. She could just make out the top of his colors from the glare of headlights—a grinning Raptor skull with blood dripping from its muzzle. Embossed on a flaxen arc above the skull, in obsidian letters, was ROAD RAPTORS. She knew another below read SO CALIFORNIA.

She turned her head, rested her cheek against his shoulder and caught a hint of an aftershave she couldn't place, a heady aroma of musk—strong and earthy. She breathed in deeply. Johnny must have cleaned up before going out tonight. His brothers could take a lesson from him. She snuggled in tighter against his back, the tension ebbing out of her muscles, and watched the traffic blow past. Pleasant warmth flowed through her veins. The sharp pain in her hand subsided to a dull ache. The chopper was a beast, but Johnny had tamed it. She wouldn't care if the ride lasted for hours. Johnny wasn't concerned with lane lines or traffic controls, mundane things like that. Speed limits were nothing but suggestions. He rode with an abandon and ease befitting a medieval knight on his steed. All too soon they arrived at the hospital.

*

Once at the ER, Rebecca was told to take a seat and a doctor would get to her when he could. Johnny went over to the cashier's window, said something and passed the cashier a business card along with a wad of money he took from his breast pocket. She saw him nod her way and the cashier lean out to take a look at her. Then he came over and told her he had to split.

She thanked him for his help. "Anytime," he said with another boyish smile, turned and sauntered away. She watched him go, suddenly sorry to see him leave. Apparently he was just a decent guy, helping her out. Decent guys were few and far between.

She took a seat in the waiting room and suffered in silence. She was used to being by herself and no stranger to suffering. Still, couldn't they at least give her a shot of something to ease her pain? But they ignored her.

The waiting room was a jumble of humanity, a fallen tower of Babel, competing with squalling infants, scolding parents and moans of pain. A young, olive-skinned child ran over and leaned against her legs, looking up with large, inquisitive eyes. She managed a weak smile. The child's mother jabbered something and he took off, joining another group of youths who were busy clambering back and forth over an empty chair. Pretty soon one of them did a face-plant on the tile floor, rolled over and sat up, his face scrunched up like a prune. Once, he succeeded in sucking in enough air, he began to scream at the top of his lungs. A large woman, wearing an ankle-length, brown dress with a black scarf tied over her head, got up and waddled over to him. She jerked the child up by an arm, shook him a couple of times and yelled at him in a language Rebecca thought might be Russian.

The woman dragged the squalling kid back to a chair and shoved him into it before resuming her own seat and then ignoring him. In the chair next to the child sat a burly, gray-haired man dressed in khaki pants, sandals and a filthy, white wife-beater. His hair stuck out from his head in clumps. Sweat trickled down his face and large forearms. It glistened in his chest hair that billowed out above his undershirt. He stared straight ahead, oblivious to the child. Every now and then he let out a loud groan. Rebecca found him harder to take than the bawling kid. If one was in the ER, it was because you were in pain. No need to announce it to the whole world.

She looked away and tried to concentrate on the idiot box hung from the ceiling near the far wall, hoping her father didn't come back on. The color had been fiddled with making the people on it appear orange. One woman's red dress glowed as if it was radioactive. The TV was tuned to CNN, but the sound was off. Rebecca soon tired of trying to read those poorly typed words that flashed by at warp speed. All they talked about was other pain and suffering anyway, an unending litany of disasters large and small.

She closed her eyes and tried to rest, but rest wouldn't come. An image, dreamlike in its vividness, kept invading her consciousness—the feel of that iron monster between her thighs, the scent and look of its master. It was no wonder the other waitresses fought over who was going to wait on him.

She shook off that thought. She'd been fired and Johnny was gone. And that was for the best. She had no time for another relationship that wouldn't go anywhere anyway. There were several casting agencies she'd listed with, besides the dirt-bag agent that'd cost her the waitress job. She'd get on the phone in the morning and work them, take control of her career and get it back on track. That hate-filled, cold-hearted, son of a bitch who'd sired her wouldn't destroy her. She wasn't the worthless whore he'd condemned her to be. She had value. She had worth as a human being. She'd prove him wrong. If only to herself.

*

When Rebecca was finally seen, X-rays confirmed the break, a fractured bone in the side of her hand, behind the pinkie. The doctor splintered her hand and encased it in a cast that reached above her wrist. Only her fingers from the middle knuckle protruded from the front. He wrote her out some prescriptions and discharged her.

The exit from the treatment room led back through the waiting area where she was surprised to find Johnny sprawled in a chair. *When did he come back? Why did he come back?*

He looked asleep but as she approached him, he said, "Fixed up?"

She held up her cast in way of answer.

"Cool." He stood and said, "C'mon." He led her over to the front desk. "What's your name?"

"Rebecca."

He shook his head. "Too long, call you Becky."

"Suit yourself."

A receptionist was filling out an insurance form on another patient. "Mind if I borrow this?" Johnny said, and snatched the ink pen from the woman's hand. She snapped her head up and started to say something but thought better of it after getting a look at him.

"Wanna be first to sign your cast." He took her cast in his right hand and wrote, *Johnny pres LA chapter Road Raptors MC. Becky keep your fist tight next time you punch someone.* He handed the pen back to the tight-lipped clerk who grabbed it away.

Outside a fresh breeze blew, stirring up empty fast-food wrappers and discarded newspapers, temporarily chasing away the smog. The sun had crested the eastern horizon and sent elongated shadows across the parking lot. Rebecca couldn't remember ever seeing LA this quiet and deserted. But she was seldom awake at this hour. And if she was, she was probably headed to bed.

"Hungry?" Johnny said.

"Hardly." Tired was more like it.

"Well I am. C'mon, buy you breakfast."

Outlaw bikers weren't known for being Good Samaritans. No doubt Johnny expected something in return for all his help. A wave of heat swept through Rebecca's body and her muscles tensed. There was little doubt what he expected in repayment. She needed to put a stop to this now. She opened her mouth to tell him no thanks, but the words died when she spotted that beast he rode, leaning on its kickstand, chrome forks gleaming in the early morning light. She imagined again the feel of that monster between her thighs and the thrill of the ride. It would save her bus fare.

They rode to some greasy hole in the wall of a diner, where she discovered she did have an appetite. Fried eggs, sausage, bacon and hash browns with biscuits and gravy, white, buttered toast—a cholesterol nightmare, but absolutely delicious, washed down by about a gallon of coffee.

Afterward, Johnny ran her home to her apartment and pulled to a stop on the lot, by the main door. He set both feet on the ground and let the bike idle.

Rebecca slipped off the side of the bike. *Okay, this is where the payback is supposed to come.* "Sorry, I can't invite you in," she said, not sure what sort of reaction to expect.

"Hell, I wouldn't invite me in either," he said with that killer smile, and she almost changed her mind.

She watched him roar off the lot, probably waking everyone in the complex, and listened until the sound of his engine was swallowed by the growing din of an awaking city. Then she went inside, totally at a loss as to what this biker was all about.

When Johnny showed up later that night, with some takeout and a six-pack… he did get invited in.

FOUR

Juggler sat at the undersized table in the kitchen of the house trailer, drinking a beer straight from the can. He'd like a glass but hadn't been able to find one. Apparently these shit for brains used the plastic trash they brought home from McDonalds, or found alongside the road.

To call this dump a pigsty would be to flatter it. The living room carpet was caked with all sorts of dried crud. There were holes in the walls and the curtains ripped. Empty beer cans and wine bottles littered the floor along with plastic bags, clothes, underwear and dirty diapers. Supermarket tabloids, porno mags, fast food wrappers, syringes, full and dumped ashtrays covered the few tables. He'd shoved a pile of it, along with unopened mail and empty pizza boxes, onto the floor to make room at the table. The place had the rank, sweet stench of a garbage dumpster.

Scattered about the floor were small piles of dog shit the bitch was too lazy to clean up. She had one of those little, yappy dogs. It'd yapped and made a lunge for his legs when he'd first come in and he'd booted the mutt halfway down the hall. The dog let out a yelp that sounded more like a scream and hobbled into the back room to hide.

"There was no call for that," the bitch had said, so he'd backhanded her across the mouth. Now she was collapsed in the far corner of a filthy couch, her snot-nosed brat held tight against her side. She watched him, fear in her eyes along with a touch of hatred. But fear was the dominant emotion. The right side of her jaw was swelling and turning purple. Witchy, premature gray hair, hacked off at the shoulders, frizzled out from her head. She looked like she had a bad case of eczema. She sniffled and wiped her nose with the back of a hand.

What a skank, Juggler thought, and sipped his beer.

Chico had called about twenty minutes earlier to say they were on their way and that everything was cool—which meant that everything was cool. If it hadn't been cool, he'd have said everything was okay or fine, anything but cool. In that case, Juggler would have bailed out of here fast. Trailers were nothing but a death trap. He'd only chosen this place because it was well-insulated from any prying eyes, stuck back here in the hills by its lonesome. Still, he was taking no chances. A Glock rested on the table near his right hand, concealed under an upside down pizza box he'd torn the lid off of.

The growl of a pair of approaching motorcycles filled the trailer and their headlights lit up the small kitchen window. He slipped his hand under the pizza box and gripped the automatic. The bikes came to a stop and he heard the sounds of dismounting and footsteps on the wooden stoop. The door opened and the man Chico had brought entered the room. He was skinny, dressed in grimy jeans, olive drab t-shirt and a leather cut. The man took a couple of steps in, ran a hand across his chin and looked around. When his gaze fell on the bitch something halfway between a smile and a smirk crossed his face. He nodded at her but she ignored him.

Chico stuck his head in, looked at Juggler then backed out and closed the door. Chico would keep watch outside.

Juggler released the gun and stood. He pulled a clear plastic baggie, containing several rocks of crank, from a side pocket and tossed it at the bitch. The bag landed at her feet and she snatched it right up.

"You never saw us and we were never here," he said. "Tell anyone different and you and your brat are dead. Now get your ass in the back room and shut the door."

The woman rose without a word, took the child by an arm and shuffled down the hall. The man stepped aside and watched her go. He watched until the door banged shut, then turned back, a leer on his face but it quickly faded.

Juggler sat and motioned for the man to join him. "Grab a beer from the fridge and get me another."

The man nodded in reply and wandered over to the refrigerator. He opened it, reached in and turned his head to the side. "Jeez, fuck. Whatta they got in here, a dead cat?"

"Wouldn't surprise me."

The man fished out two cans and shoved the door shut with his hip. He sat one in front of Juggler and popped the top on the other. His hand shook noticeably and sweat beaded his forehead.

"Have a seat," Juggler said. "Elwood, right?"

The man nodded, pulled up the only other chair and sat. He was having a hard time meeting Juggler's eyes. His gray eyes darted back and forth between Juggler and the front door. He licked his lips again. The back of his hands were as red and raw as the bitch's face.

"You know who I am?" Juggler said.

Elwood snorted. "Jeez, yeah. Everyone knows who you are." He hadn't tasted his beer. Instead he held the can on the table with both hands and continued to look away.

"Chico tells me you're not happy with your club."

"Jeez," Elwood said, looked around again, then at Juggler. "That fuckin' Bill. Treats me like shit. All of 'em do. That motherfucker. A couple a weeks ago a bunch of Coffin Fillers jumped my ass and beat the shit outta me. You think he does anything 'bout it? Fuck no. He meets with their president and talks. Talks! Tol' me he negotiated a settlement. Whatever the fuck that means." He took a quick drink of his beer and returned the can to the table.

"No shit," Juggler said, trying his best to sound sympathetic. "Man, that sucks."

"Damn right it does," Elwood said and swiped some sweat off his face with a forearm. "Fuckin' asshole."

"Someone jump one of our people, they answer to me. And I don't negotiate."

Elwood's eyes flicked back to Juggler's, then away. He nodded and took another swallow of beer. "Wish I rode with your club."

"Well… we're always looking for new blood."

Elwood's eyes came back to Juggler's again and stayed there. "Jeez, you like serious?"

"Yeah, Chico tells me you're a good man. Shame to waste someone like you on a pussy club like that." He picked up his beer can, tilted it toward Elwood, then took a swallow. He set the can down and smiled.

"Jeez, Chico said that?" Elwood took another drink of his beer, his Adam's apple worked up and down. "Guess I'd have to go through all that prospectin' bullshit again," he said and looked away.

"Maybe not. There could be a way around that." That got Elwood's attention and he looked back at Juggler. "There are some people we really don't like. You ever kill anyone?"

Elwood's eyes changed. The fear ebbed out of them and they grew dull, distant. "Yeah," he said, barely above a whisper.

"Who?"

"In Iraq. Greased a bunch of them cocksuckers." He took another drink of his beer and banged the can back down. "You think they give me a fuckin' medal for it? Fuck no. Goddamned orficer wanted ta try me as a war criminal or somethin'. Said I murdered some civilians. Civilians my ass. Cocksuckers pick our pockets during the day and cut our throats at night." He took another drink of beer. "Sergeant… he took care of it for me. Sarge was a good guy," he added softly and stared at his beer can.

"Well that's kind of who I am, the Sarge who looks after the guys. Anybody stupid enough to fuck with one of us is not around long enough to make the same mistake twice."

Elwood nodded. "Who you want me to kill?"

Juggler told him.

Elwood's eyes flew open wide and he sat up straight. "Jeez, fuck! How the hell would I get at them?"

"Leave that to me. I'll set the whole thing up. All you got to do is pull the trigger."

Elwood looked around the room again as though searching for a way out. "Why don't you have one of your men do it?"

"Because I want Bill and his club to take the fall for this."

"Whatta bout me? Everyone will know I did it."

"Not if you don't leave any witnesses. And afterwards you change patches and then no one will ever fuck with you."

"Jeez, I don't know," Elwood said and shook his head.

It took Juggler nearly ten minutes to convince Elwood to accept the job, which saved his life. If he'd refused, Juggler was ready to kill him where he sat. Saved three lives as the bitch and her kid would have to go too, along with their fucking dog. *The man's a hero.* Juggler couldn't stifle a smirk at that thought.

They stood and shook hands. "Glad to have you in the club, brother," Juggler said. He hugged the man and patted him on the back. When he released Elwood, he retrieved the Glock from under the pizza box.

"Shit! What's that for?"

"This?" Juggler held the gun up between their faces—barrel pointed at the ceiling, and examined it. "This was in case someone other than you and Chico came through the door." He stuffed the weapon in his waistband behind his back and smiled at Elwood. "C'mon, let's get out of here."

Elwood followed Juggler to the front door. When they got there he paused and looked down the hallway. He scratched his chin and turned to Juggler. "That your old lady?"

Juggler reached for the knife in the scabbard on his hip. He was going to cut this ignorant fuck's throat. Somehow he managed to restrain himself—somehow. Through clenched teeth he said, "Fuck no, she ain't my old lady."

Elwood nodded and a sly grin curled the corners of his mouth. "Chico's?"

"No. Her man's dead. Blew his ass up cooking crank. Burned down half a city block."

"Widow huh? Jeez, wonder if she's lonely?"

Juggler couldn't believe what he was hearing. "You saying you want to fuck her?"

"Yeah, you mind?"

"Why the fuck would I mind? You want to fuck her, go fuck her."

Elwood grinned broadly and started down the hall. Juggler fought off another irrational urge to kill him. Instead, he called out to his back, "When you're done give her ten dollars."

Elwood stopped and turned around, brow wrinkled. "Ten bucks?"

"I know that's nine more than she's worth, but she's got a kid to feed."

Elwood pulled a greasy wallet out of a rear pocket, opened it and counted his money, twice. Finally he put it back, shrugged, turned and continued down the hall. Juggler watched him enter the back room, before leaving the trailer. He felt like he needed a shower.

The night had grown cooler and was about as dark as it could get. Stars filled the night sky. No moon. He paused for a moment to look at the celestial display. You never got a view like this from the city. Smog must have drifted out to sea. He took a deep breath of fresh air.

"Everything hokay boss?" Chico said. He was waiting by the bikes, a darker shadow, identifiable only by the glow of the joint he was smoking.

Juggler took the joint out of Chico's mouth, took a long drag on it and handed it back. "Everything's fine." He mounted his Harley. "You did a good job, brother."

"Where he at now?"

"He's fucking that skank."

"Oh shit." Chico laughed and climbed on his bike. "Man got no taste."

They fired up their bikes and blasted out, Juggler taking the lead. *Yeah, man got no taste, or brains. That pathetic fuck fried his long ago. He's too brain-dead to see the obvious.*

What he had to do next was get Ducky and Tramp to go along with his plan. He had no intentions of presenting it to them as his plan. What he'd do is mention it as a happenstance, a chance encounter he'd stumbled into. He had no doubt they'd take it and run with it, in the direction he wanted them to go. If necessary, he'd steer Ducky with a few well-placed comments—comments, not suggestions. Let Ducky think he was the one who'd devised the scheme. The arrogant, paranoid club president of Satans Kin was easy to play, as long as you didn't overdo it. Subtlety was the key.

Juggler had no intentions of ending up in a shallow grave in some dirt field somewhere.

FIVE

Rebecca sat on a wooden chair at her dining table. The bare heel of one foot rested on the edge of the seat, her other leg dangled down. She took a sip of her Diet Coke. Another perusal of the want ads didn't improve them any. She'd copied and pasted the most likely openings onto a new file she'd labeled *shit job openings*, but none of them were remotely nearby. It didn't matter. Until her hand healed she couldn't wait tables anyway. Maybe by then something would turn up. If not, she might try going back to that last dive and see if she could kowtow low enough to get her old job back. She powered off her laptop and closed the lid.

The doctor had told her the cast would remain on for three weeks—only twenty more days to go. Her hand ached, a dull, constant throb. She'd filled the prescription for the antibiotics but without health insurance or a drug prescription plan, that had hurt worse than the break. The pain pills she'd passed on. Aspirins would have to do. Even with insurance she wouldn't have filled that prescription. She'd seen far too many people screw themselves up with drugs, including doctor-prescribed meds. Some of those people had been quite talented, although you'd never know it now. She was from the Midwest, small-town

Missouri. She'd stick to wine and beer, along with the occasional joint, just to be sociable.

The morning and most of the afternoon she'd spent on the phone, calling the casting agencies she was listed with. They'd scored her a couple of small roles in the past. She'd all but worn out the zero key on her cell phone punching it to force her way past the robo-menus and get a human to talk to. Only to be put on eternal hold with the bad elevator music, in the hopes she'd grow sick of listening to Barry Manilow and hang up. Several times she was disconnected. But she called right back and stayed with it. None of the agencies had anything for her at this time, but they'd keep her in mind. It was disappointing but she wouldn't let it discourage her. Today was Thursday. She'd call them again on Monday. In fact she'd start calling every Monday and Thursday. If nothing else, maybe one of them would tire of her calls and find her something.

She needed a new agent. Hopefully word wouldn't get around about her punching the last one. A large, dog-eared paperback of agent listings lay on the table. She'd bought it at a used book store, thumbed through it and identified some possibilities. It was too late to visit any of them today, but she'd hit a couple tomorrow and see if she could sign with them. And she wouldn't stop with just a couple. She'd visit every agency she could find until she landed one. Someone had to have work for her.

She'd appeared in several small theater plays and would audition for more. The plays didn't pay squat but you never knew who might be in the audience. If nothing else, another play would give her something to update her website with. Meanwhile, she needed to eat and pay the rent, so she'd continue to wait tables... somewhere.

The smoke detector chirped for the umpteenth time. It needed a new battery. It competed with the drip from her kitchen faucet to see which could be the most annoying. Her landlord said he'd put her on the maintenance list and would get to them ASAP. That had been three weeks ago. Not to be left out, the wall clock tocked off the seconds. When had it become so loud?

It was after seven. Was he coming tonight?

She glanced at her left hand and shook her head. To prepare for tomorrow's agent visits, she'd decided to paint her nails. Now all her toenails and the nails on her right hand were bright red. The nails on her left hand weren't. She'd discovered too late that she couldn't grasp the little brush with her injured hand. Dumb, just dumb. She'd have to locate the polish remover.

Last night Johnny showed up at her door and she didn't have the heart to turn him away. Besides, he'd brought dinner, a large pepperoni pizza with cheesy bread and a six-pack of tall boys. They'd eaten the pizza, gobbled the cheesy bread, and killed off the six-pack while watching a movie on TV. She'd wondered if he planned to get her drunk, but as he drank four and a half of the brews himself, apparently not.

He'd sat on one end of her second-hand, artificial leather sofa, recently purchased through a Rent-to-Own, his long legs stretched out in front of him. She'd sat on the other end, her legs tucked under her. Johnny said hardly a word all evening, other than to comment on her many plants. He said they gave the room a pleasant smell. "Smells alive," was how he'd put it. He'd stayed on his end of the couch and behaved himself. He hadn't even tried for a goodnight kiss when leaving.

For some reason his indifference irritated her. What the hell, normally first dates consisted of fending off groping hands and all too eager lips. She was an actress/waitress so she had to be easy right? Did he find something wrong with her? Maybe that hadn't been a first date.

The clock had ticked down to nearly seven-thirty. Johnny wasn't coming. She might as well fix something to eat. The freezer revealed a pair of tasteless, frozen, lean, mean diet meals—Chicken something and Shrimp De-Lite. Beneath them resided a slightly-more-tempting, ice-encrusted, TV dinner, Pot Roast and Paste. Other than that there was a plastic freezer bag containing some leftover meatless lasagna. Frost had invaded the inside of the bag and transformed that delicacy into a miniature Siberian landscape. She'd open a can of soup.

There came a rap on her door and she all but ran to the peephole. It was Johnny. And he held a bucket of KFC in one hand and another six-pack in the other.

She took a quick check of her reflection in the wall mirror, brushed at her hair, inhaled deeply and forced herself to count to three before opening the door. "Hey," she said.

"Thought you might need dinner again," he said with his irresistible grin.

"Thanks, c'mon in. I'll get plates."

Johnny set the bucket and beer on the small, round table and hooked out a chair with a boot. He sat and watched as she stretched to reach into the upper cabinet. Her cheapo, Wally World cropped tee rode up and pulled tight. She wasn't wearing a bra, too much of a hassle to fasten one-handed. She snagged a pair of plates and set one in front of him.

"Interrupt something?"

"What?"

He nodded at her left hand.

She looked at her hand and felt her face go flush. She managed a weak smile. "I get three-fourths the way done then..." She held up her right hand.

"Where's the nail polish?"

"On the counter."

He picked the little bottle up, shook it and unscrewed the top. "Sit down."

She looked at the bottle, licked her lips and slowly sat in the next chair. Johnny scooted his chair in front of her and took her left hand in his right. She'd noticed he was left-handed.

"I'll try not to make a mess," he said and flashed another roguish smile. His eyes sparkled.

Johnny had large hands with long fingers. Her hand looked lost in his. She could feel the rough calluses on his palm and sense the raw power in his grip even though he cradled her hand gently. Brow furrowed, he leaned forward and deliberately brushed the polish onto her thumbnail. He'd cleaned up again. His hair looked soft and full, smelled fresh. The aroma of the same aftershave she'd noticed before wafted up to her—earthy, masculine. She felt herself grow warm and squirmed a little in the chair.

"Oops," he said and glanced up. "Not as easy as it looks."

"You're doing fine."

With the skill of an artisan, Johnny slowly applied the blood-red ink to her nails. She could feel the brush caress her fingertips. It was getting stuffy in the room and she was having trouble getting her breath. Her heart beat faster. She watched as he dipped the brush into the vial, turned and carefully, with small strokes, worked the brush across her next nail. He glanced up and smiled once more, then turned back to his work.

Finger followed finger. After completing all five, he replaced the brush, blew on her fingertips and sat back. "Best not quit my day job, huh?"

She stared at her hand, looked up, and got to her feet. She bent a knee and slipped her leg onto his thigh, leaned forward, wrapped her arms around his neck, and brought her lips to his. His arms went around her back and pulled her onto his lap without breaking the kiss.

Johnny's lips were rough, unyielding, demanding. She slipped her tongue between them and he pulled her closer. A surge of heat pulsed through her veins and she kissed him harder. Something moved beneath her, pressed against her bottom. She should end this now… but it had been so long since she'd been with a man, if that term even applied to her last lover. Self-centered prick was more like it.

Johnny stood, cradled her in his arms and carried her to the sofa. He sat, lay back and pulled her on top of him. Her knees straddled his waist, lips still locked. He ran his hands up her back, beneath her shirt. His fingers flowed smoothly across her flesh, tingling. She sat back, took hold of her shirt with her left hand and pulled it over her head.

Johnny rose on his elbows, struggled out of his leather vest and t-shirt then dropped them onto the floor.

Rebecca ran her hand through the hair on his chest, tinting some of it red where it brushed against her nails. She'd thought every male in LA shaved their chests. The actors all did. But they were about make-believe. Johnny was real. She leaned forward and nuzzled his chest hair. He had a small, silver ring in his right nipple. She licked his nipple, took the ring in her teeth and tugged gently.

Johnny moaned, ran his hands down her back, over the swell of her hips, beneath her shorts and grasped her rear. He squeezed her cheeks and pulled her tighter still.

She shifted her lips back to his, her breasts pressed against his chest. His hardness now poked her belly, throbbed. She slipped off and stood beside the couch. She rolled her hips as she slid her shorts and panties down then flicked them away with a flip of a foot. She unhooked his belt and unzipped his pants. He raised his hips as she tugged his jeans and boxers down to his knees.

Rebecca climbed back on, again straddling his hips. She shook her head sending her dark curls swirling about. Her breasts jiggled, the nipples swelled hard. His hands went to her waist as she leaned forward and her lips found his once more. She felt him enter her and pushed down hard with her hips. "Oh yeah," she murmured. Conscious thought abandoned her, banished by the sensual pleasure that flowed through her body. She worked her hips faster, in rhythm to his thrusts.

With hormones kicked into overdrive, it didn't take long to reach their destination.

*

"Wow," Johnny said, sometime later, still breathing hard.

Rebecca lay on her side in the crook of his arm. She smiled, ran her hand across his chest and worked her fingers through the dappled hair. She held her hand up and examined it. The nail polish had run and smeared her fingers, staining them red. Shame to have wasted all his precise work—he'd just have to do them again.

"Wow," he said once more. Johnny lay with his other arm bent under his head. He hung off the sofa from the knees on, pants around his ankles. "Afraid dinner got cold."

"Who needs dinner?" She rose on her elbow and looked at him, his eyes shifting to hers. "After last night I was beginning to worry I must resemble your sister or something."

He grinned. "Playing it cool."

She moved her lips close to his ear. "From now on, play it hot," she said, and tickled his ear with her tongue. His grin grew, as her left hand drifted across his belly.

SIX

Magoo popped the tab on a Stag, tilted his head back and didn't come up for air until he drained the can. He let out an explosive belch, crushed the can in one huge fist and chucked it at a passing motorist. The crumpled can skimmed across the hood of a Cadillac Escalade and ricocheted off the windshield causing the driver to slam on his brakes. Before the SUV skidded to a full stop, the driver got a look at his assailant and switched his foot back to the gas pedal. This he stomped on harder than he had the brake, causing his vehicle to chug a couple of times and backfire, before catching and roaring off with a squeal of tires.

"Thas it, run you pussy," Magoo shouted at the fleeing vehicle.

Several club members laughed. "Magoo, chill out," Clean said.

The Road Raptors MC had gathered on the parking lot of a failed restaurant, just off the interstate, waiting for their president to arrive. In response to Clean's comment, Magoo repeated the process but missed the Beamer convertible he launched his next can at.

"C'mon, man," Clean said, "someone's gonna call the pigs you keep this up."

Magoo wandered over to them. "Where the fuck is Johnny?"

"He'll be here," Wild said, noting a mixture of beer, sweat and possibly drool glistening in Magoo's beard.

"Man, ever since Johnny got that new old lady of his he can't be depended on for shit," Dirty Dan said and flicked away a half smoked cigarette. "He needs to dump that bitch."

"So tell him," Wild said. "Or you want me to pass that on?"

"Hey man, that's just between us," Dirty Dan said, eyes wide. He ran a hand across his chin and looked around to see who else heard him, then back at Wild. "Don't go tellin' him that. Was just my opinion."

"Keep your fucking opinions to yourself."

"Yeah man, don't go tellin' him."

Magoo staggered back to the edge of the lot, unzipped his fly and proceeded to piss into the street. An approaching van in the curb lane swerved to its left to avoid his stream, nearly side-swiping a car in the next lane. That car locked up its brakes, skidded and spun, ending up in the center turning lane, facing back the way it'd come from. Other brakes squealed as more cars slid to a stop and horns blared. Magoo raised a fist and extended his middle finger in the general direction of the racket.

"Jesus, Magoo!" Clean yelled and looked to Wild for help. "Do something man."

Wild lay on his bike, back against the sissy bar, boots crossed at the ankles on top of the headlight. He'd removed his cut and draped it over the top of the bar. Sweat soaked the sides of his muscle-tee under each arm and the shirt felt plastered to his back. "Whatta you suggest?"

"I don't know. You're the VP, think of something."

"Already have."

"Yeah?"

"Yeah, think I'll wait for Johnny."

Clean stared at him for a moment, shook his head and walked off, muttering to himself.

Johnny was the only one who could handle Magoo, the only person Magoo would listen to. Although Clean did seem to have some influence with him. Whether that was a good thing or not, Wild hadn't decided yet. He wasn't sure where Clean was coming from. Clean didn't always jive with the club.

Magoo was two hundred-ninety pounds of tattooed mean. Normally drunk, usually stoned, he wasn't the sort of individual open to reason. As tall as Johnny, Magoo had long, ratty, brown hair that hung halfway down his back, and an unkempt beard that Wild kept expecting to see something crawl out of. He looked like someone you'd see come screaming out of a dark forest with a two-handed sword, ready to take Caesar's head off.

Johnny needed to get here. Dirty Dan ran his mouth too much and his brain too little, but he was right. It didn't look good for the Pres to ignore the club—particularly for a woman. That could lead to a loss of influence. And there were club members who'd like nothing better than to move the pair of them out of the leadership roles.

Wild swiped a wrist across his brow. *Fucking parking lot's an oven.* Johnny was bringing Becky with him on this run. Wild couldn't see anything good coming from that. He'd never seen Johnny so hung up over a bitch before. Usually it was the other way around. While Becky was attractive, she wasn't anything special. She had a great ass and legs, but if she'd agreed to do that porno, she'd need to see a plastic surgeon and get her tits pumped up. Not that there was anything wrong with her rack, just wasn't porno queen size, double D whatever. Yet Johnny had gone completely nuts over her. The last couple of weeks he'd spent far more time with her, than he had with the club. Just two nights before, Johnny had blown through church then cut out. Normally, he hung around afterwards, shot the shit and slammed a few brews with the brothers.

That especially didn't sit well with Johnny's former squeeze, Sheva. Sheva didn't like being moved off the back of Johnny's bike. Wild was letting her ride on his today, which presented its own problems. Club VP, he'd be riding on Johnny's right for this run. Normally, Johnny would be running in the right-hand position of the front row with their road captain on his left. But two nights before, their road captain had gone over the high side when he'd taken a curve too fast and slid into a guardrail. He'd totaled his bike and nearly himself. With Sinbad in the hospital, Johnny had decided to double as road captain for this run. That moved Wild's bike up a row. Bitch-packing Sheva, he'd have to be careful to keep a good distance between them. He wouldn't put it past that crazy bitch to reach over and shove Becky off the side of Johnny's bike at about ninety mph, if she thought she could get away with it. And Sheva's judgment wasn't the best.

Magoo tagged another car, but this one made no attempt to stop. Wild wasn't concerned about someone calling the pigs. In this neighborhood, it'd be a low priority call, a call they'd take a couple of hours to respond to in hopes everyone was gone when they arrived. What had him concerned was that Magoo was getting trashed. A late start, they'd be pushing hard down the highway. The last thing the club needed was a biker who didn't have complete control of himself.

He knew firsthand what that could lead to. Several years before, he'd ridden with another club. They'd been roaring down an interstate in their standard two-abreast formation when someone had passed out, screwed up or just lost control and dumped his bike. Twelve bikes ended up wrecking, most in the pile-up, but several had veered off the highway and down an embankment. Three bikers and one old lady died. Two more ended up in wheelchairs for the rest of their lives. Wild had been seriously injured, breaking a leg and shattering his left shoulder. The pins that now held his shoulder together caused it to stick up an inch or so higher than his other shoulder—which is how he ended up with the name Wild. The wreck marked the end of that club. When he prospected with the Road Raptors, Sinbad decided that with his hunched shoulder and blond hair, he resembled Klaus Kinski in that old Eastwood western, *For A Few Dollars More*. So Sinbad called him Wild and it stuck. As biker names went it wasn't a bad one, better than most. He'd always been a bit wild.

He shook his head. Johnny needed to get here. They were running way the hell late.

SEVEN

Rebecca sat quietly behind Johnny, trying to recover from the shock of having the patrolman pull right up to their rear tire before cutting loose with his siren. It'd nearly scared her to death. She had the uneasy feeling that if Johnny hadn't pulled right over, the patrolman would have rammed them.

They were stopped on the shoulder of a busy boulevard, sweltering in the early afternoon heat, while the cop took his time writing out the citation in his air-conditioned patrol car. She wasn't sure why Johnny was getting a ticket. They hadn't been speeding, despite running late. And they were wearing helmets, half helmets anyway. Skid lids, Johnny called them. The ticket had something to do with his bike. She could sense Johnny was really pissed and fighting to maintain control, his body tense. Heat radiated off him and she doubted the temperature had much to do with it.

She wore Johnny's colors over her leather riding jacket. He'd explained earlier that the only time a woman was allowed to wear colors, which just to confuse things were also known as his patch, as well as his cut, was when they were on a run. It was important to always show the colors on a run. The club wanted the whole world to know who they were. You didn't cover up the colors with a female body, no matter how attractive that body was. Once they reached their destination she'd have to return them to him. She wondered if she hadn't been showing the colors, would they have been stopped?

That they were running late wasn't her fault—well, not really. She'd been ready to go when Johnny showed up. He'd taken one look at her in her leather chaps over jeans and leather jacket, leathers he'd bought for her, thrown her over his shoulder and carted her straight to the bedroom. It took some doing to get undressed, what with her cast, then back into the chaps and his cut, but it had been worth it.

Of course then she'd had to get dressed again, after a shared shower—another delay—and now here they were stuck on the shoulder. She felt a bit queasy, but whether from this predicament or the soapy water she'd inadvertently swallowed, she couldn't tell.

The past two weeks had not produced any acting jobs. But she'd concentrate on the positives. She'd visited several agencies and left a copy of her portfolio at each. The one play she'd auditioned for had resulted in a political correct version of, "Don't call us, we'll call you." But she'd heard of another local theater that was holding auditions for *Ten Little Indians* next week. Getting time off from work to do a play was always a big hassle. Usually she ended up quitting her job to do the play. Not a problem at the present.

There wasn't much point in contacting any agencies over the three-day weekend. It was doubtful any would be open or taking calls if they were. So she'd accepted Johnny's invitation to join him on the club's Memorial Day Run. If something did come up she could be reached on her cell phone. Also, Johnny said there might be some actors, directors or even an agent hanging around the campgrounds. For some reason bikers seemed to attract that crowd.

Johnny had been spending most nights at her apartment, sometimes not arriving until late. He'd been encouraging her in her quest. They'd gone out to eat a few times and caught some movies, but mostly they hung out at her apartment. He fixed the drip in her faucet and replaced the battery in the smoke alarm which she'd been too stubborn to do—determined to wait on the super. When they did go out, he stayed away from biker hangouts and left his cut in her apartment. She had no idea what he did for a living, but always had plenty of cash. He mentioned something about painting customized bikes.

The cop got out of his car and swaggered back to them.

Johnny scribbled his name on the ticket, snatched his copy and said, "Thanks a lot, dickhead."

That sent the patrolman's hand to the grip of his automatic and his face turned red. "You better watch your mouth, punk."

Johnny didn't respond, just stared at the man until he turned and walked back to his squad car.

"Was that wise?" Rebecca whispered. "Calling him a name."

Johnny snorted. "Used to be you talk to a cop like that, he'd beat the crap out of you, run you in and book you for resisting arrest. Pigs are all afraid someone's filming them now. Too many of them have made it onto the news. Long as there's possible witnesses, they have to eat that shit."

"Won't he remember it?"

"Fuck him." Johnny spit, fired up his bike and wrenched it back into traffic.

Ten minutes later they rolled onto the lot where the Road Raptors waited. Rebecca didn't like the looks she drew from the club members, especially the women. She particularly didn't like the hard stare she got from one woman with long, straight, jet-black hair. The woman was tall, slender and dressed in black leather pants and a short leather vest. She'd gone sans a t-shirt and her vest looked like it was about to rupture as it strained to contain several pounds of implants. No one was that overly endowed. The woman had more skin with ink than without, along with lip, eyebrow and nose rings. She glared at Rebecca for several minutes before tugging on a jacket, small helmet and climbing on the back of a bike. The rider gunned the bike towards them and stopped on Johnny's right, while the rest of the club's bikes exploded into life, the sound deafening.

"Ready to roll?" Johnny yelled to be heard over the din.

"Born ready," the rider said through clenched teeth.

"Somethin' wrong?"

"You're late."

"Got stopped by our favorite pig."

"Musta took his time."

Johnny stared at him for several heartbeats. Johnny's neck muscles tightened and he straightened up taller on his bike. Rebecca had seen the other biker at the Black List, but never waited on him. He had ice-blue eyes, blond hair that hung halfway to his shoulders and wore the vice-president tag. Johnny had told her that the club VP was called Wild. "He did," Johnny said at last. "That a problem?"

Wild held his stare for several more moments then shook his head slightly. "He's a prick."

"Yeah, let's roll."

Wild nodded in reply.

The club wheeled off the parking lot, nearly forty bikes in all, two abreast, with a pair of three-wheelers and two breakdown trucks bringing up the rear. Johnny and Wild led the bikes up an on-ramp to the interstate, and kicked them in the ass.

EIGHT

The Road Raptors blasted down the highway, monopolizing the passing lane. Black leather, Levi's, boots, custom chrome, paint and steel, heavy metal thunder—they ran like they owned the road. They rode only American made Harley-Davidsons, FXRs and FXRTs with a few classic panheads and flatheads mixed in, each remade in the image of its owner. They blew past vehicles that refused to cede them their lane, on both sides of the cars, scant inches away, flipping off the drivers as they roared by. The highway patrol turned a blind eye to them. It was one thing to pull over a single biker, quite another to corral the entire club. The amount of effort required and the resulting hours of paperwork were hardly worth the few busts for outstanding warrants they'd garner. The club was headed for the ranch where they'd join several other clubs for the long Memorial Day weekend. It'd be a weekend of partying, boozing, brawling and hopefully working out a few issues, preferably with nobody dying.

The interstate the club traveled was six lanes of rough, sun-baked concrete, three lanes each way with dusty, littered, ochre-colored gravel shoulders. A wide swath of clay loam and dying sagebrush served as a median. The sparse vegetation did little to block the sudden gusts of hot, arid wind that swirled across the road carrying debris and grit with it. Flashes of painfully bright light reflected off bumpers and windshields.

Rebecca's legs were baking beneath the leather chaps. She noticed few of the bikers wore them. Some wore leather pants, others just jeans. Many of the men were bare-chested under their cuts, their heavily tattooed torsos baked brown. Her hand felt slick under the cast and the itching was about to drive her crazy. Thank God it'd be coming off in a few days. Yesterday the itch had been so bad she'd jammed a pencil under it and worked it back and forth in an attempt to get some relief.

She rode with her arms around Johnny, astounded at how fast the club went and how close together the bikers rode. It reminded her of images from old war movies of planes flying in formation. She glanced at the bike on her right. The black-haired passenger wasn't riding with her arms around her partner. Instead, she lounged against the sissy bar with her arms at her side and looked bored. Her long hair billowed out from beneath her small helmet like streamers. The woman turned her face toward her, but Rebecca couldn't see her eyes behind the dark pair of sunglasses she wore. She chided herself for not thinking to bring a pair of her own. The sun's reflected glare blinded her, forced her to squint.

She didn't think that woman much liked her and had no idea why. They'd never met. She loosened her grip on Johnny and slid back a couple of inches on the seat to get comfortable. She didn't make the mistake of leaning back against the sissy bar. Johnny's bike didn't have one. Wild's companion watched her for a few more moments then turned away.

She'd never met a man like Johnny. Her previous relationships had all been aspiring actors with a schizoid screenwriter tossed in. To a man they'd been shallow, insecure, needy, hyper. Except the screenwriter who was certifiably nuts. Johnny was different. Johnny was strong, competent, independent and in charge of his life. Johnny was solid. If she had to describe him in one word it'd be cowboy. Not the clichéd white-hat cowboy but the loner—Gary Cooper. Clint Eastwood. Despite the insane speed they were rolling at, she felt safe riding behind him.

If my father could see me now, he'd be convinced his prophesy had come true. Well it hasn't. I'm not a whore. I'm riding with Johnny, not the club. We're just going camping for the holiday weekend. That's all. And why am I explaining myself? Why should I care what my father or his God thinks?

Still, ever since that day five years ago, she'd wondered if her father's God had turned a completely deaf ear to him. Certainly her life hadn't turned out the way she'd envisioned. There'd been no starring roles in movies or TV. No co-starring roles either, only those commercials and crowd scenes. And there hadn't been any of them lately, just that offer of a porno movie. She couldn't believe she'd actually been considering it, under a stage name of course. Randi Times or…

No, she wasn't going to go there. There'd been too much self-pity. It'd been a moment of weakness brought on by her lack of success and the crappy jobs she'd had to take to survive. But she was back on track now. And all in all, the last five years had really been a pretty lame form of eternal damnation. More like incessant disappointment.

She glanced to the right again. That motorcycle had gotten a lot closer. The black-haired woman on the back was staring at her again. Was it her imagination or was the woman leaning toward her? Maybe she wanted to say something. Rebecca started to lean her way when Wild looked over, saw how close together they'd drifted and eased his bike back to the right. The woman continued to stare but now sat straight up. Most likely she had been all along.

*

The club ran north for several hours before cutting off onto a bleached, two-lane blacktop that headed east. A quarter mile down that road they pulled off at a truck stop, full of big rigs, to gas up. While the bikes refueled, Rebecca took the opportunity to buy a cheap pair of sunglasses and use the restroom. The ladies room was full of biker babes but their lively conversation ceased abruptly when she entered. In a silence so heavy she thought it would crush her, she waited her turn in line. She could sense everyone watching her. She tried a couple of smiles but got only glares in return except for the weak smile she got from the emaciated woman who exited the stall in front of her.

Back outside the bikes were lined up on both sides of an island using the same two pumps. They didn't shut either pump off until all the gas tanks had been filled, including the two pickups. Then Johnny went inside and paid the bill for the entire club.

Once back on the blacktop, the club didn't let up any as the road was mostly empty straightaway. They eventually slowed when they came to a small town. Rebecca didn't catch the name of the hamlet, but that didn't matter—she had no idea where they were anyway. It was an old town, well into its latter stages of existence, a miserable looking place. The berg was dirty with littered trash everywhere, no greenery and the rusting hulks of old cars decorating several yards, many up on blocks. The houses themselves showed the effects of decades of neglect and indifference. Faded, peeling paint, torn screens, broken windows patched with cardboard. Many houses barely looked inhabited, except for the satellite dishes nestled on the roofs.

The downtown area was no better. Most of the buildings were vacant with boarded-up or empty storefront windows. Only the bars and liquor stores appeared to be thriving. The town was occupied primarily by Hispanics who Rebecca figured were field laborers. Years of toil, worry and pain were deeply etched into their faces. Almost to a person they ignored the club as though they were accustomed to seeing bikers pass through.

The county sheriff did watch them go by. He stood outside his headquarters, next to his squad car, thumbs hooked into his belt under his ample gut. Their image reflected from the mirrored sunglasses above his handlebar moustache. What B-movie lot had they gotten him off of?

After rolling through the town, the Road Raptors went another half dozen miles or so then turned onto a dirt road. They held their speed down to about thirty as the road was very dry, and they kicked up a lot of dust. Rebecca looked to the rear and discovered many of the bikers had pulled bandanas over their mouths and noses, which enhanced their image as outlaws. Thank God she rode in the front row.

They continued along this road for several miles before turning onto an even narrower dirt lane. The lane was really just two tire ruts worn into the hard, baked earth. They crossed a dry creek bed and ran up a steep rise between two barren hills. Upon reaching the crest, Johnny pulled to a stop. Rebecca peered over his shoulder. In the valley below sat a large, ancient, one-story wooden structure with a covered porch on one end and a tin roof. If this was the ranch it wasn't a working ranch. She couldn't see any horses or livestock. No corrals or barns.

At least a couple of hundred motorcycles were gathered around the grounds, mostly in groups, along with a few cars, pickups and SUVs. The party had already begun. People were all over the place, bikers and their ladies. A pair of riders spun their bikes in circles near the porch, apparently seeing who could kick up the most dirt. Their dust cloud drifted away from the building toward a small lake off to one side. Several gnarly trees grew up around the lake and she could see more bikes parked beneath them. These bikers didn't appear to be mingling with the others but stood in a group in front of the trees.

Johnny must have spotted this crew at the same time she had. He jerked up straight and strained his neck for a better look. After nearly a minute's scrutiny, he sat back. "Damn!"

NINE

Johnny said something to Wild that Rebecca couldn't make out, and they were rolling again. They rode down the slope—the tracks curved first one way than the other—and entered the ranch under a wooden pole set atop a pair of stone pillars. Two rusty hooks dangled where there'd once hung a sign. The club slowed to a crawl and paraded past the ranch house. Most of the other bikers and women yelled greetings, waved beer cans and tooted their horns. The bikers gathered in front of the trees didn't call out greetings. Instead they stood, hands at their hips or arms folded across their chests, and scowled. They looked to be all men. Rebecca didn't see any women as Johnny led the club in a slow, almost insolent loop past them.

They continued back to the ranch house where Johnny stopped his bike and killed his engine. Rebecca tugged off his cut and handed it to him. She slipped off the side, laid her jacket over the seat and stretched, while he pulled the vest on.

Several bikers approached on foot. One tossed Johnny a can of beer as he climbed off the bike. Johnny caught the can one-handed, popped the top with a spray of foam and downed a large swallow. He swiped his mouth with the back of a hand. "Thanks, man, needed that." He took another drink, turned toward the club by the trees and grimaced. "Fuckin' Doctor, let anyone in."

"No shit," answered one of the bikers who had his own president tag on his cut.

"You know these cocksuckers gonna be here?" Wild said and joined them.

"No."

"What's Doctor up to?"

"Doctor?" Rebecca said.

"Yeah, owns the ranch," Wild said, glancing at her. "Was used in a lot of old westerns last century. Inherited it from an uncle or somethin'"

"Varmint doctor," Johnny said. "Veterinarian."

"Fucker's been hooked on more shit than most rockers," Wild said and nodded toward the porch steps.

An obese man wearing house slippers slowly hobbled across the porch toward them. *He must go four-hundred pounds,* Rebecca thought, *and he's not even six-foot tall.* Thinning, long gray hair, knotted into a ponytail, looped over one shoulder of a pair of bib overalls covering a flannel shirt despite the heat. It was impossible to gauge his age, face a bright crimson, heavily lined and covered in ashen stubble.

Doctor stopped at the top of the steps. "Johnny, Wild," he said between wheezes.

"Why didn't you tell me Satans Kin would be here?" Johnny said, not trying to cover the anger in his voice.

"'Fraid you wouldn't show if'n I did. They want to make peace. Come on up here. Let's talk."

"Johnny!" a voice called.

They spun in that direction. A pair of bikers had left the group by the trees and walked their way. One wore the president's tag, the other the VP. They stopped and the president held up his hands at shoulder level, fingers splayed, a greasy smile on his face. He had slicked back, black hair and a thin mustache. The VP was shorter and built like a fireplug. Rebecca couldn't tell where his neck stopped and his head began. A large, blue death's-head had been tattooed on the top of his bald head.

It had grown deathly still. Rebecca looked around. Everyone had stopped where they were and watched the scene at the steps. She felt a chill. Her heart rate increased. A hot breeze blew dust in a swirl around the feet of the two bikers. It looked like a showdown. All that was missing was a score by Ennio Morricone. A dozen yards behind them another biker moved a few feet to the front of the rest of their club. He had buzz-cut white hair, bad skin and unblinking dark eyes that held all the warmth of a shark.

Someone took Rebecca by an elbow and yanked her backwards. "Get in back," he growled.

She was shuffled through the club brothers who all edged forward. A couple had chains dangling from their hands. Another held a tire iron. She caught the glimpse of a knife. The women were gathered in a group behind them. Some gripped beer bottles by the neck, twitching, eyes-wide, straining to see over their men, while others scampered about gathering up rocks. *What the hell is going on?*

She skirted around to the far end of the line so she could see. Johnny and Wild strode forward to confront the Satans Kin leadership. Johnny got very close forcing the Satans Kin's president to look up. There couldn't have been an inch of space between Wild and the vice president's chests, locked in their own stare-down. The club behind them moved several steps closer and held their own make-shift weapons. The Road Raptors stepped forward too, bodies tense, shifting about, rolling their shoulders and necks, trying to get loose. To her right, more clubs gathered. *Whose side are they on? Are there any sides?* She could feel the electricity in the air, the silence deafening.

Her stomach began to churn and she was desperately thirsty. *This can't be happening. We just got here.* Not a western showdown, more like a scene from *Braveheart*, armies massing for battle while the leaders parlayed between them. *Oh God, is Johnny going to negotiate or pick a fight?*

The only person who didn't look wound tight was the white-haired biker. He remained in front of the Satans Kin club, his heavily-tattooed arms folded across his chest, weight on one hip. It was as though he was watching a sporting event. He wore the Sgt at Arms tag.

The Satans Kin's president glanced toward the clubs forming to their side, then back at Johnny, his simpering smile never left his face. "This what you want Johnny? We came to talk. But this what you want, we're ready. Your call."

Johnny didn't answer.

A line of geese swept by overhead, no more than thirty feet off the ground, headed for the lake, oblivious to the tense scene below them. Their honks sounded like rifle shots in the silence and Rebecca flinched. No one else paid them any mind, every eye fixed on Johnny. She watched the geese circle about and then settle out of sight behind the Satans Kin club.

Johnny still hadn't answered. The heavy moment seemed to last a lifetime. Finally he jerked his head in the direction of the porch.

The Satans Kin president's smile widened and his teeth showed.

They turned and walked toward the steps.

TEN

It was as though someone let the air out. The white-haired biker turned, waved once at his club, and they returned to their camp under the trees. The other clubs dissolved back into party mode as quickly as they'd abandoned it, their leaders joining the gathering on the porch. The Road Raptors remained by the ranch house and their bikes but split into small groups.

Rebecca took a couple of minutes to get her breath under control and heart rate back to normal. *Did this just happen? What have I gotten myself into?* She wanted to ask Johnny what was going on but knew better than to follow him. Instead, she eased up to a gathering near the steps. She recognized some of the bikers from her time at the Black List Lounge, Dirty Dan and another who had to be Clean. His completely bald head and gold earring were a dead give-away.

"Fuckin' assholes," a biker she'd heard called Animal said. Or maybe that was just a description of him. He was the Road Raptors' Sgt at Arms and looked like another character out of a bad B-movie, dressed in grimy jeans with a stained, black and yellow Killer Bee t-shirt under his cut. He wore a sweaty wet, red and white print do-rag on his head and clinched a half-smoked cigar in his teeth. "Ruint our entry."

"Man," Dirty Dan said, "I keep tellin' ya what we need to do to make a real entry."

"Oh knock it off you fuckin' pervert. Thas all bullshit anyways. Never happened."

"It did."

"Bullshit."

"What never happened?" Rebecca said, unable to stop herself, curiosity trumping caution.

They turned and stared at her, not liking being interrupted by a woman, even if she was the president's woman.

Clean's eyes flicked toward the porch then quickly back to hers, his lips twisted in a smirk. "In the seventies, college pukes runnin' around naked—"

"Streaking," someone said.

"Yeah, streaking. Numb Nuts here wants us to believe some club, brothers and old ladies both, rode into one a these meets werrin' jus their boots."

"Bullshit," Animal said again.

"Naw, man, it really happened. My ole man was ridin' with a club and seen it. Really got the party goin'"

"Yeah, it would," Clean said and laughed.

"Well, I don't give a fuck if'n it happened or not," another biker said. "I ain't riding my bike bare-assed for anyone."

"Got that, brother," Animal said.

"So, like the ride?" Clean said. He was the first club member other than Wild to talk to her.

"I did. I can't believe how fast and close together you ride."

"Jus part of bein' a biker. Sets us apart from civilian shit-heads that think they know how to ride."

"Bunch a pussies," Magoo said, joining the group and standing uncomfortably close behind Rebecca.

She felt her flesh grow hotter, stood up straight and took a deep breath. She should have bought a pair of sunglasses with those little mirrors in the sides. Too many unpleasant things were slipping up on her lately.

Johnny came back. "Animal, find a campsite by the bluffs. Want 'em at our back. Far away from here as we can get." Not waiting for an answer, he took Rebecca by the arm and steered her away.

"Johnny, what's happening?"

"Gotta meet with some people. Ladies gonna make a beer run. Join 'em."

She wasn't sure if he was telling her or asking her. It certainly sounded like an order. She started to bristle but then thought better of it. If he was going to be tied up in a meeting, she didn't want to hang around out here with Magoo breathing down her neck. "Okay."

Johnny led her over to the breakdown trucks. One was a battered, rusty, red and white Ford F150 with a busted grill, dented hood and bumper. The other a fairly new, gray Chevrolet Silverado.

"Becky's gonna ride along."

"Well, she's not riding with us," a dishwater blonde in jeans and a denim shirt with the sleeves cut off said. A multi-colored tattoo covered most of her right arm. "Our cab's full."

Johnny jerked to a stop. The two women with the blonde looked really uncomfortable and eased away from her. They looked at each other and one shook her head slightly.

"She can ride with me." It was the painfully thin brunette who had smiled at Rebecca in the restroom earlier. The woman stood on the driver's sill plate of the F150, looked over the roof and waved—a hesitant smile on her face.

Johnny's face darkened and his muscles tensed. The blonde continued to meet his gaze but her two companions were now busy examining the ground at their toes.

"I don't mind riding in the Ford," Rebecca said.

Johnny hesitated, then stalked abruptly to the Ford and jerked on the passenger door handle. The door opened with a bang and a loud creak, revealing a dusty, sepia-colored interior. Dirty, yellow foam had infiltrated its way through the shredded cloth seat. In one spot a chunk had been torn out exposing rusty springs. Johnny nodded at the driver. "Foxy Roxy," he said as Rebecca climbed in. He faced the driver. "Take good care of my lady."

"Hey, will do," Roxy said. "I been wantin' to meet her." Roxy had shoulder-length hair, similar to Rebecca's, and tattoos on each of her thin biceps.

Johnny slammed the door, slapped the cab once and walked away.

*

Roxy maneuvered the Ford down the dirt lane about a hundred feet behind the Silverado, bounced over the ruts and talked non-stop. She swiped her forehead with a wrist. "AC crapped out. Piece of shit. Probably cost more to fix than this heap's worth." The muscles on her upper arm brought her tattoos to life as she wrestled the steering wheel.

Rebecca searched around unsuccessfully for a latch for her shoulder harness. It appeared that mechanism had exited the vehicle along with the missing hunk of seat. Roxy hadn't bothered to fasten hers. Both air bags had been duct taped back into their holders.

"Tiny's gonna shit when he hears 'bout that."

Rebecca gave up her search and tried to hang on. "Tiny?"

"Flo's old man. No one talks to the Pres like that."

"Why'd she do it?"

"She's pissed. Johnny wouldn't let her ride."

"On his bike?"

Roxy shook her head. "Naw, on her own." She glanced over. "On short runs, the club usually lets old ladies who have bikes and can keep up to ride them. Don't know why Johnny nixed it on this run. Flo always rides. Hey, what a shock to find Satans Kin here. Wonder why Doctor invited those assholes? You only get in by invitation. Some club tries to crash the party, they get their butts whipped fast."

"I heard him tell Johnny something about them wanting to make peace."

Roxy snorted. "That'll be the day." She drove over a large bump causing the truck to bounce, and Rebecca nearly struck the roof. "Shit, sorry. Didn't see that one for all the fuckin' dirt Flo's throwin' up."

"Do you think there'll be trouble?"

"Don't know." She glanced over again and shrugged. "Probably not. None of the clubs like Satans Kin. They stir up some shit with one club, they'll end up facing them all. Hear you're an actress."

Rebecca nodded. "Johnny said there might be some movie people hanging around the camps"

Roxy laughed. "Yeah, pornos. Those creepy motherfuckers are always lurking about, looking for new talent." She laughed again.

Shit. I should have known.

"Sheva and some of her pals have done pornos."

Rebecca grimaced and looked out the side window.

Roxy picked up on it. "Hey, I agree, that's not acting. I mean, how much talent does it take to spread your legs, play with yourself and blow a bunch of dudes?"

The women returned to the same dismal town they'd passed through earlier where they had to hit several bars and liquor stores to load up both trucks. The other clubs had gotten there before them and pretty much cleaned things out. Few businesses wanted to completely exhaust their stock.

Flo purposely ignored Rebecca while the trucks were being loaded. Her two passengers followed her lead. Only Foxy Roxy prattled on.

The amount of beer being loaded was staggering, a couple of hundred cases at least.

Flo paid for the beer with a roll of hundreds she kept tucked into her bra. "Well, I guess that will have to do for tonight," she said with a smirk.

*

"How do they cool all this beer?"

"They don't," Roxy said, still managing to hit nearly every bump and pothole. "Hey, warm beer isn't bad. Better than no beer."

"I don't think Flo likes me."

"Oh, she jus doesn't know you yet. Johnny should have brought you around so's we could get used to… I mean meet you."

Rebecca shook her head. "I don't think any of them like me, and some of them are kind of scary."

"Hey, no one's gonna mess with the Pres's old lady. Johnny'd kill them if they did."

"Is that what he'd do?"

"Fuckin' A."

"So no one will mess with me?"

"Hell no, you don't need to worry 'bout that." Roxy paused for a moment and chewed on her lower lip. "Might be a good idea to steer clear of Sheva though."

"Sheva? Which one is she?"

"Tall, thin, long black hair, fake boobs out to here. Lotta crap in her face."

"She was riding on Wild's bike."

"Yeah, that's her."

"What's she got against me?"

"She and Johnny used to hang some."

"His old lady?"

"Naw, not really. At least not officially. But Sheva liked to act like she was and lord it over the rest of us."

"And what am I?"

"You? You're Johnny's old lady," Roxy said as though the answer was obvious. She took another quick look at Rebecca.

"Officially?"

"Yeah."

"How can you tell?"

"I don't know, you jus can. No one in their right mind's gonna mess with you."

No one in their right mind. Well, that significantly limits things. "So, I'm Johnny's official old lady and Sheva's his former unofficial old lady?"

"Yeah, somethin' like that."

"No wonder she doesn't like me."

Roxy snorted. "No shit. You might want to stay clear of her when Johnny's not around. Sheva's totally mind-fucked."

ELEVEN

They left the trucks near the ranch house where a prospect was assigned the job of guarding the beer. Roxy grabbed them each a can. Rebecca sipped hers as they walked away, not yet convinced that warm beer was better than no beer. Johnny was still in his meeting.

Loud music and cheers blared from the direction of the lake so they drifted over there to check it out. A makeshift plank stage had been erected across the backs of a trio of pickups. Half a dozen barefoot women, clad in tees, bikini bottoms or jeans, were on it dancing to the music. They were really getting down and a large crowd of bikers had gathered to watch and urge them on.

"Can anyone get up there and dance?" Rebecca said after watching them for a few minutes. She loved to dance and the girls were having a lot of fun. It might be a way for her to fit in.

"You don't want to get up there," Roxy said.

"Why not?"

"Watch."

A biker with a long, scraggly goatee and a huge beer-gut, toting a large plastic bucket, climbed on stage. He held the bucket above his head and paraded behind the dancers and the audience redoubled their cheers. He started at one end and proceeded to pour water over the front of each dancer's tee. The women faked surprise but it was obvious they'd been expecting this as none of them were wearing bras or made any move to leave.

"A wet t-shirt contest?" Rebecca said.

"For starters."

She glanced at Roxy, who nodded at the stage. The women's shirts were soaked, making them nearly transparent. Each dancer was well-endowed, either from nature or a plastic surgeon.

Shouts of, "Take it off! Take it off!" filled the air. In response, one dancer whipped her soggy tee off, swung it around over her head a few times and launched it into the crowd. The remainder quickly followed. Now dancing topless, the women picked up the tempo to see who could jiggle the most. "More! More!" the spectators urged and the women obliged. One by one they shed their lower garments until they were all dancing nude. Cell phone cameras flashed all about.

Rebecca wrinkled her forehead and her eyebrows scrunched together, a sour taste in her mouth. *What is this nonsense?* She turned to leave, but as she did, shouts of, "Sheva! Sheva!" erupted all around her.

She turned back and there the woman was, long hair, tattoos and facial piercings, undulating onto the stage. Sheva made her way to the middle, in front of the other women who continued to dance. She didn't bother with water. Instead she leaned forward, popped open her vest and released two of the largest breasts Rebecca had ever seen. These she wiggled at the audience which went wild. Then with a start, Rebecca realized Sheva was looking straight at her. Sheva cupped a breast in each hand and wagged them at her.

The sour taste was replaced by a burning in her throat. Rebecca spun on her heel and left.

*

Roxy scurried after Becky, caught up, and they returned to the ranch house. The meeting was still going on. The occasional shout could be heard, but there was no gunfire, no chairs being busted and no one had been tossed through a window or door, so maybe they were working things out. Doctor had parked his fat bulk upon a dusty, green sofa on the porch near the front door. One side of the couch was propped up with a cinderblock, slanting it toward his end.

Even though it was late afternoon, it hadn't cooled off any. They sat down on a bald patch of earth, shaded by the building, near the steps to wait. Well away from the yard hydrant which was getting a lot of use. It was the only source of clean water for the bikers. A standing pool of muddy water had formed about its base and people sloshed back and forth through it to fill up bottles and jugs, wet bandanas, or bend over for a sip. *Someone ought to attach a hose to it.*

Becky shoved her hair behind her ears and wiped her brow. The edges of her lips were turned down and her forehead wrinkled. She clasped her hands around her legs, pulled her knees tight against her chest, rested her chin on them and stared at nothing. She hadn't said a word since leaving the stage area.

"Hey, that dancin's for show only," Roxy said, wanting to cheer her up. "Those gals all got husbands or boyfriends. No one makes 'em get up and dance. They do it because they like it."

"Like it? Dancing nude?"

"Yeah, some gals get turned on strutting their stuff. Kinda cool to watch the guys get all worked up."

"Have you ever done it?"

"Well… couple a times. But I don't have the bod for it. Really sucks to have some asshole yell to put your fuckin' clothes back on."

Becky gaped at her, then broke into laughter.

Roxy laughed with her. "Yeah, nobody wants to see a scrawny bitch like me. They want to see Sheva's fake tits. If I had money, I could get mine done."

"Don't," Becky said and placed a hand on her arm. "Don't ever do that. Don't sink to Sheva's level. You're better than that."

Roxy was touched. No one had ever told her that she was better than someone before. Most people just ignored her—or put her down. Even her nickname was a put-down. It just happened to rhyme with Roxy. She really liked Becky and wanted to be her friend. She'd hang around her as much as she could and fill her in on what she needed to know. Maybe they could become best friends.

Caught up in her daydreams, she failed to notice that the show had ended. Sheva, who'd changed out of her vest into a black t-shirt, with a couple of her friends tagging along, was headed their way. When Sheva spotted them, she quickly switched positions with the women on her left, which would leave her passing closest to Becky. Sheva carried a plastic cup full of beer. When she drew next to Becky, she showed off the acting ability that had relegated her to porno movies by doing a terrible imitation of a stumble and dumped the cup's entire contents onto Becky.

"Hey!" Roxy yelled and looked up, eyes and mouth wide open.

"Sorry… tripped," Sheva said with a sneer and continued on, her two companions tried unsuccessfully not to laugh.

"You did not! You did that on purpose!"

"Watch your mouth Roxy," one of the women said. "She tripped." The three walked on, now giggling.

Sheva flipped the cup over her shoulder. It bounced a couple of times and rolled to a stop at Roxy's feet.

Becky hadn't said anything. She sat, mouth wide open, arms held out from her side and looked down at her clothes. Beer ran off her face in rivulets. Her T-shirt and top half of her jeans were soaked. She jerked her head up as Sheva and her smirking friends sat down some thirty feet away to watch.

"She did that on purpose," Roxy said and kicked at the empty cup. She got on her knees and tried to brush the beer off her new friend's clothes. Becky pushed her hands away, stood and stared at the trio watching them. Then she turned and hurried away.

"Where ya goin', hun?" one of the women called after her.

"Oh boo-hoo," the other said overly loud. "Bet she's runnin' to Johnny, to protect her from the big, bad biker girls."

"Fuck him," Sheva said.

Roxy glared at them, then scampered after Becky. Becky wasn't looking for Johnny. Becky went straight to the beer stash.

"Hey, we gotta another wet t-shirt contest goin' on?" The prospect guarding the beer said.

Becky ignored him, grabbed a can of beer and one of the red plastic cups Flo had bought for the women. She popped the top, carefully emptied the contents into the cup, tossed down the can and started back.

Roxy's breath caught. *Oh, God no.* She sure hoped Becky wasn't planning to do what she was sure Becky intended to do. She should stop her. Sheva was crazy mean. But she was only a mama. What right did she have to tell the Pres's old lady anything? Gnawing at her lower lip and grasping her arms by the elbows, she trailed after Becky.

Sheva and her friends were busy talking and didn't notice Becky's return. She strode right up to them. "Hey!" When they looked up, Sheva got the full cup of beer right in the face. "Sorry, but I tripped too."

Sheva yelled and spluttered in response, rocking backwards, waving her arms.

Becky stared at her for a moment, then turned and walked away, pitching the cup aside.

Roxy was so stunned—she almost didn't get the warning out. "Look out!" she managed to shriek.

Becky spun around to find an enraged Sheva right on top of her. Sheva slammed into her and tried to grab her by the hair. Becky lost her balance and they both went down in a heap of tangled legs and flailing arms.

"Cat fight!" went up a yell and everyone nearby rushed over to watch.

"We've got to help her," Roxy yelled, but Flo appeared at her side, snagged an arm and held her back.

"She gonna ride with us, she's gonna have to learn to take care of herself."

"But Sheva will hurt her."

Flo shrugged in response.

On the ground the two women rolled about, yanking, clawing and punching at each other. They wrestled their way into the muddy pool of water by the yard hydrant, struck it hard enough to shake the galvanized pipe. Becky spun onto her belly to get to her knees. Sheva clambered on top of her, shoved her face into the water and tried to hold it there. Becky got a handful of the woman's hair, yanked down hard, elbowed her in the ribs and slipped out from under her.

She came up gasping and spitting. Sheva pounced back on her and they rolled out of the pool. Mud clung to their bodies, matted their hair. Wet slime streaked their arms and faces. Their shrieks and yells mingled with the cheers and laughs of their audience. Sheva got past Becky's guard and left three jagged scratches across a cheek. Becky fought back as best she could but was no match for Sheva, who was stronger, faster and more experienced at this sort of thing and managed to overpower her. Sheva's two enormous breasts proved to be weapons all their own, nearly crushing the breath out of her.

"Fuckin' bitch… cocksuckin' cunt," Sheva yelled, sucking in air. Filthy water trickled off her chin as she straddled Becky's waist. "Cause Johnny's hot for your ass you think you can steal him away?" She breathed heavily, chest heaving, lips pulled back, her teeth bared. "Think you're a fuckin' actress? By the time I'm done, you'll only be acting in horror movies." Sheva pulled a butterfly knife out of a rear pocket and flipped it open. "Let's see how bad Johnny wants you after I carve my initials in your whore's face?"

"Sheva, no!" Flo yelled, and she and Roxy started for them, but Sheva's two friends intercepted them.

"Stay out of it," one of them said.

Sheva glanced over at them, an insane gleam in her eyes. It was only a moment's pause but it proved one heartbeat too long. Becky got her right arm loose and swung with all the force she could muster. Her cast smashed into the side of Sheva's skull with a loud, *thonk*. Sheva's eyes rolled back into her head, and she collapsed forward onto Becky, the knife spinning out of her hand.

Becky shoved the inert woman off and scrambled to her feet, trembling, her breath coming in loud gasps. She bent forward, hands on her knees.

"Holy fucking shit," one of the spectators said. "I think you killed her."

"What?" Becky said, still struggling for air.

"I think the bitch is dead."

On the porch, Doctor had bestirred himself and wandered over to watch. He harrumphed, struggled down the steps and across to where Sheva lay motionless.

"She's not dead is she?" Becky said, her voice sounding like a plea.

Doctor toed Sheva a couple of times in the ribs with his slippered foot. "Yep, she's dead."

The color drained from Becky's face but before she could faint, Sheva let out a low moan and squirmed a bit.

"No wait," Doctor said, quickly revising his diagnosis, "she's alive." He turned and waddled back to the porch, stopping halfway up the steps, to rest a moment and wheeze.

"Good catfight," someone said.

Doctor glanced his way. "Been better if'n they'd both been nekid," he said.

TWELVE

Roxy pulled Rebecca back to near where they'd been waiting and got her seated again.

"Jesus Christ! Jesus Christ! You just kicked Sheva's ass!"

"What?" Rebecca mumbled, never taking her eyes off a still very sluggish Sheva, who rolled onto her back with a loud groan. She couldn't believe she'd just been threatened with a knife and was still having trouble getting her breath as adrenaline pounded through her veins.

"You kicked her ass," Roxy said, squatted and tried to wipe some of the mud and grime off Rebecca's face with her hands.

"She had a knife."

Sheva's two friends knelt beside Sheva and tried to get her into a sitting position. They got her halfway up, lost their grip on her mud-slimed figure and she crashed down on her back. One of them looked Rebecca's way and snarled. "You goddamn bitch."

"Hey, watch your mouth," Roxy said, "or she'll give you some of the same."

The duo eventually got Sheva up into a slouch with her head sagging onto her chest. She rolled her head around a couple of times and brushed at it with a hand. She looked from one woman to the other, a blank expression on her face, eyelids twitching, pupils dilated. After several minutes, her friends pulled Sheva to her feet. With one companion on each side, and her arms over their shoulders, they helped her stagger off. Rebecca watched them until they disappeared into the crowd.

"How's your face?"

"What?" Rebecca reached for her cheek.

"Here, don't touch that," Flo ordered and knelt beside her. "You'll get dirt into it." Flo held a wet cloth and proceeded to clean off the wound.

"You're Flo."

"I'm Flo."

"That short for Florence?"

"It is, but my last name's not Nightingale, hold still."

Flo swiped at the scratches a couple of more times. "That's not bad. They'll scab over and peel off. In a couple weeks, they'll fade away altogether. Handle yourself pretty well for an actress. Must be your time as a waitress."

Rebecca didn't answer, simply sat quietly and let Flo administer to her.

Several other women joined them and formed an arc in front of her. They smiled and nodded. "Way to go Becky," one of them said. "Kicked that rotten cunt's ass good."

Flo finished dabbing at Rebecca's cheek and stood. She looked at Roxy who watched her intently. "C'mon, let's get her over to the trucks and get her cleaned up." Roxy nodded and helped Rebecca up.

"Grab a couple of buckets of water," Flo said to one of the other women, then looked back at Rebecca. "Got a first-aid kit in one of the trucks. We'll spray some antiseptic on those scratches. God alone knows what kind of filth is under Sheva's fingernails."

*

Magoo watched through an alcoholic fog as the bitches led Becky away. He'd been hanging around the beer stash when he'd seen her rush up, fill a cup with beer and hurry off. He'd followed and watched the fight. Not many things impressed him. One that did was the ability to win a fight. After all, that was the whole purpose of a fight, to win it, didn't matter how. In a fight you used any weapon at hand… he paused and thought that over. He snorted out a half-laugh/half-grunt. *Any weapon a hand, thas funny. Becky used a weapon a hand. Busted that big-titted cunt's head with it. Little bitch is lot tougher than she looks.*

That thought led him to ponder how unfair life was. Why should Johnny get all the hot bitches? Johnny was supposed to be a friend. They'd known each other since they were kids. You'd think Johnny would toss one his way once in awhile. And he'd seen Becky first, working at the List. He wasn't as smooth with bitches like Johnny, but he'd talked to her a couple of times, even left her a tip. She'd smiled at him. It wasn't right for Johnny to cut in on him, not right at all. A real friend wouldn't do that. He needed to do something about it. What he wasn't sure, but he'd think of something.

He drained his beer, belched, crushed the can and let it drop. He turned and headed back to the beer stash. He'd get another. Beer always helped him think better.

It'd be his twenty-seventh of the day.

THIRTEEN

When the meeting broke up, Wild followed Johnny onto the porch. They were the last to leave the room. He knew Johnny was watching to see if Ducky, the Satans Kin president, spoke to anyone on the way out. Ducky had done most of the talking in the meeting, sounding like one of those assholes you saw on TV every couple of years, running for office. He'd even used words like. "Getting off on the wrong foot," and, "Mending fences," bullshit like that. What the fuck? Someone write him a speech? Johnny hardly said a word, instead listened to the other presidents list their complaints. It hadn't been that he didn't care. It was just Johnny's way. Wild knew Johnny would remember everything said and who said it.

Neither Ducky, nor his VP, Tramp, spoke to anyone. They hustled down the steps and back to their camp.

Doctor hefted himelf off the sofa. "How'd it go?"

"Good," Johnny said.

Doctor studied Johnny for a moment, squeezed him on the shoulder, nodded and then went inside and pulled the door shut.

They wandered over to the edge of the porch, near the steps, and leaned against the wooden, upper rail. They each placed a boot on the lower rail which creaked noticeably under their weight. A fat spider had built a web in the corner of the nearest post, where it joined the roof. He'd already snared one fly.

Johnny ran a hand over his sweaty forehead and back through his hair. The stuffy room had been stifling. "Wadda you think?" he said softly.

"It sucks. That asshole's being too agreeable." Wild kept his voice low as well.

Johnny nodded once in reply.

"Think they'll try anything here, in front'a the other clubs?"

Johnny shook his head slowly. "Who the fuck knows? Half those shitheads live on crank and peyote. Tell Animal, no contact between the clubs."

"Right."

He wanted to ask Johnny where he thought Doctor fit in. But before he could, Clean bounded up the steps, stopping on the next to last one. "Ya missed all the fun."

"Aw, shit, what happened now?" Wild said, unable to keep the disgust out of his voice.

"Your new old lady and Sheva got into it," Clean said, looking at Johnny.

"What?" Johnny jerked his foot off the rail and stood straight. "Where's Becky?"

"Flo, Roxy and some others got her over at the trucks, cleanin' her up."

Johnny shoved past Clean and went down the steps two at a time.

"Hey, man," Clean called at Johnny's back, "Sheva got the worst of it."

"She did?" Wild said, now unable to keep the surprise out of his voice.

"Hell, yeah. Becky busted that big-titted slut in the head with her cast. Sent her off to la-la land."

"What the hell were they fightin' 'bout?"

"Don't know. Johnny'd be my guess." Clean let out a smirk. "Got to chuckin' cups'a beer at each other, then into a wrestlin' match in the mud over by the pump. Sheva pulled a shank and Becky unloaded on her."

"She what?" Wild said, his voice dangerously low.

"Smacked her in the head—"

"Not Becky, you asshole, Sheva! What's this shit 'bout a shank?"

"Oh, Sheva pulled a blade—"

"And what the fuck were you doin', watching?"

"Well… thas how I know what happened."

"So's you were jus' gonna stand by with your finger up your ass while that crazy bitch carved up the president's lady?"

"What…? No, oh hell no. I was rushin' over to break it up. But before I could, Becky took care of it."

Wild stared at him, not buying any of his horseshit.

Clean looked around and back at Wild. He shrugged and mumbled, "Happened really fast."

"How bad she hurt?"

"Don't know, man. Might have a concussion or—"

"Not Sheva, you fucking moron, Becky! She get cut?"

"What, ah… no. Sheva raked her cheek with her claws is all."

"You sure? She didn't get cut?"

"Naw, man."

"Where's the shank?"

"I got it." Clean dug in a pants pocket, pulled out the knife and tossed it to Wild.

Wild flipped it open. The knife had a five-inch blade and was razor sharp. *That stupid, fucking bitch. What'd she think Johnny'd a done had she cut Becky? Probably used the shank to open her own throat. What a fucking mess. He'll go ballistic when he hears about the knife. Bad enough we get here and find this Goddamned Satans Kin. Now we gotta deal with this stupidity too.*

He decided he'd have to handle this one himself. It was a distraction Johnny didn't need. Johnny had to keep his mind on the club this weekend. He'd have to move fast. Once Johnny heard about the shank… "You're sure she didn't cut Becky?"

"Naw, man, never got the chance. Probably bluffin' anyways."

Wild wasn't buying that either. "I'll hang on to this," he said, closed the knife and slipped it into a pocket.

"Sure, how'd the meet go?"

"Johnny wants you to know, he'll tell you."

Wild brushed past Clean and hustled down the steps. He needed to find Sheva fast, not that he gave a damn how bad she was hurt, but he needed to get her out of sight for a while. Also, he wanted to make sure she and those tramps she hung with weren't planning any revenge. He'd make it clear what they could expect if they tried something. If there was anything left of them after Johnny got through, he'd turn it over to Dirty Dan to have his way with. *That oughta discourage anyone, even porno queens.* He grimaced at that thought.

FOURTEEN

Rebecca sat on the open tailgate of the Silverado, wrapped in a blanket, feet crossed at the ankles. She swung her legs back and forth, unable to sit still. What if that lunatic had cut her, slashed her face? Goodbye acting career. Then when she checked the condition of her cell phone, which had survived, she discovered she couldn't get service here. An agency could be calling her with a good part, and she'd never know. *Fat chance of that.* But it could happen. She wondered if she could convince Johnny to take her home. Not likely. He'd forgotten all about her anyway. She'd really screwed up, coming on this run. Nothing to do now but see it through.

A couple of women had built a small bonfire nearby. Roxy, and she believed the other woman was named Brandi, had impaled her clothes on sticks and were waving them over the fire in an attempt to dry them, while smacking them with another stick to knock the drying mud off. Hadn't she seen that in a movie? A stiff breeze kicked up, fanning the flames. She hoped they didn't set her clothing on fire. She had no desire to become one of Dirty Dan's wet dreams.

She ran a hand over her wet hair. Flo had dumped a bucket of water over her head to wash the mud out, then given her a blanket to wrap up in. At least that had finally cooled her off some.

Flo sat down beside her and the tailgate settled a couple of inches lower. She handed her a cup of beer. "Here, you spilled your last one," she said, with a faint smile.

"Thanks." Rebecca took the cup, sipped and grimaced. *Warm beer, right.*

"I'm not going to try and tell you what to do," Flo began, obviously picking her words carefully. "No one likes to be threatened with a knife."

"She was going to use it, wasn't she?"

Flo hesitated for just an instant. "Yes."

Rebecca took another sip.

"I don't know if you realize the temper Johnny has. Make a big deal about the knife—he's liable to hurt Sheva bad. I mean real bad."

Rebecca turned and stared into Flo's pale-blue eyes. *I should care?* Flo's forehead wrinkled and her lips drew into a thin line. She had a long, narrow nose like Meryl Streep, angled off to the right near its tip, like it had once been broken. Her cheeks took on a slight, red hue. She was a bit older than the other women and more intelligent. Rebecca could see that in her eyes.

"Sheva did get the worst of it," Flo pointed out.

Rebecca broke eye contact and looked at Flo's right arm. This was the first good look she'd gotten at Flo's tattoo. It apparently ran across her back and went all the way down the outside of her arm onto the back of her hand. The tat was different shades of gray, green and yellow. It looked reptilian and ended in bone-colored claws on the back of her fingers.

"Johnny won't hear about the knife from me as long as she doesn't come looking for a rematch," she said, wondering why she was doing this.

Flo took a deep breath and exhaled. Her eyes grew warmer and a small, but genuine, smile curled the corners of her lips. "Good." She patted Rebecca's leg.

"Becky!"

"Here comes the man now." Flo nodded his way.

Johnny drew to a stop in front of them. "You all right?"

"Fine."

"What happened?"

"I got into a fight with your former old lady."

"What?" Johnny shouted, his face darkening with rage. "Who told you that bitch was my old lady?" His gaze fell on Roxy who visibly wilted under it.

"It was Sheva told her," Flo quickly said.

"Did she?"

"Yes," Rebecca said, stunned by the way he'd looked at her new friend and the fear she saw in Roxy's eyes.

"You know Sheva," Flo said. "Always tryin' to act like the top dog."

"Sheva was never my old lady."

"That's what they told me."

"Then why did you call her that?"

"Because I'm pissed." Rebecca hopped off the tailgate, clasped the blanket tight around her and shook her hair free. "You go off and leave me alone for half the day to be attacked by that maniac, claiming I'm stealing her old man away. And all those directors you told me about… they make pornos."

"Don't they make other kinds too?"

Rebecca rolled her eyes.

Johnny glanced around and back. "Goddamn it, been kind'a busy."

Rebecca didn't respond.

"Didn't expect to find Satans Kin here. Had to look after the club. Hear you handled that bitch on your own."

"Kicked her ass," Roxy said.

"And made some new friends," Flo added.

Johnny glanced at the bonfire where Brandi was still waving Rebecca's pants over the flames. "What happened to your clothes?"

"Sheva baptized me with beer."

"She do anything other than claw your face?"

"No."

Out of the corner of her eye she saw Flo smile again. "Might have a few bruises here and there," she added. "No big deal. You done with your meeting?"

"Need to speak to the other presidents, one on one."

"You mean you're going to leave me alone again?"

"No… you come along."

"Can we wait for my clothes to dry or would you rather I just put my leathers back on?"

That got a smile out of Johnny and the tension visibly eased out of him. "We wait," he said.

FIFTEEN

Sleeping bags, camping gear and some beat-up coolers had been loaded haphazardly in the pickups before they left the city, which is why it took both trucks to haul the beer. Rebecca got dressed while Johnny told Flo and the prospect guarding the stash to take it over to the campsite Animal had picked out. What he actually said was, "Get this shit over to our camp. Me and Becky'll be along."

With her clothes more or less dry, but stinking heavily of beer, she set off alongside Johnny, who altered his normal stride so she wouldn't have to hustle to keep up. She doubted anyone would notice the alcohol stench. All around them, bikers were spraying one another with beer and pouring it over each others' heads. It was probably as close to cologne as many of them ever got.

The sun sank into the western horizon and the temperature dropped. Each club built a large bonfire in the area they'd staked out and their club members gravitated toward it. The onset of darkness, combined with over-consumption of beer, drugs and God knows what else, brought the boys out to play. Fights popped up everywhere. They were of short duration and she figured that within minutes, the opponents would be best of friends once more. At least until one of them looked the wrong way at the other again.

The fights were easier to take than the open nudity and sex. Women were having trouble keeping their clothes on and the men their zippers zipped. At one camp she spotted a topless woman on her knees performing oral sex while several more bikers waited in line. And this just feet from other partying club members who appeared totally oblivious of it. At another stop, she saw a couple on the ground doing what couples had been doing ever since Adam first laid eyes on Eve. A crowd had gathered to watch and urge them on.

Over the years she'd attended some "Hollywood" parties. But there the debauchery was shunted off to a bedroom, or confined to the swimming pool. Not so in your face. She stayed close to Johnny.

Two things quickly became apparent. First, the other clubs intended to let the Road Raptors take the lead in dealing with Satans Kin. She wasn't privy to the discussions Johnny had with the other presidents. But she found a spot where she could watch them. Body language, along with scraps of conversations she picked up from others, made it clear that the Road Raptors would call the shots.

The second thing—everyone wanted to get a look at the bitch that'd kicked Sheva's ass. How ironic, she'd become a celebrity. This certainly wasn't the sort of notoriety she craved or wanted. Worse, she got the feeling that some of the younger biker babes were sizing her up, maybe with the intentions of having a go at her. If beating Sheva was a big deal, beating the woman who had bested her would be too. This was one title she had no desire to defend, but knew she dare not show any weakness. Bikers fed on that. Time to go into actress mode and hope no one called her bluff. One fight a day was plenty.

At the Storm Troopers camp, one woman said, loud enough to be overheard, "She don't look like so fuckin' much."

Rebecca did a slow turn toward her. With weight on her left leg and hand on hip, she let her cast dangle by her side. "You got something to say to me bitch, say it to my face."

That brought a bunch of "Whoas!" and whistles from people nearby.

They glared at each other. The woman wasn't backing down. Rebecca felt her muscles tense and her breath come fast. The biker babe was heavily inked, about her height but a lot heavier. She looked Rebecca up and down and an evil sneer curled her lips. The club president, Kaiser Bill, walked over and gave the woman a hard, one-handed shove. "Get the fuck outta' here you dumb bitch. They're our guests."

He turned back to Rebecca. "What you got in that thing, lead?"

"Just my hand." She covered her relief with a frown and tried to look disappointed as she watched the other woman slink off.

Kaiser Bill roared with drunken laughter. He stood nearly as tall as Johnny and pushed Doctor's weight. But there was a lot of muscle backing up the flab. He wore a ridiculously under-sized, over-ornamented, silver helmet with a spike on the top. He'd liberally decorated his cut with medals that looked to her like crossed, black chalices, outlined in silver, and hung from red, white and black ribbons. She squinted at one. It had a swastika in the center.

"Iron crosses," Kaiser Bill said proudly and pulled one closer to her face. "Fuckin' Krauts highest medal."

She nodded in understanding even though she had no idea what he was talking about or why he'd wear German medals. If Animal looked like he'd climbed out of a B-movie, this guy looked more like one of those cartoonish bikers she'd seen in some Sixties beach movies she'd binge watched one wet weekend. There were swastikas painted on some of the bikes and even a couple of Nazi flags flying from poles. Was this club a bunch of neo-Nazis or just neo-assholes? If the former, she figured her father would fit right in, given his views on the Jewish religion.

While Johnny and Kaiser Bill held their discussion, she noticed one biker taking a lot of interest in them. He was skinny, sweating heavily and constantly scratching at scabs on his hands. When Johnny looked over, the guy quickly looked way. She found his behavior rather odd, but then the whole crew was odd.

They spent a half-hour or so at each stop, drank a beer, shared a joint and declined anything stronger. She did take a drink from a wineskin the Coffin Fillers passed around. Home-made Dago Red they called it. Paint stripper, she figured a chemist would analyze it.

Unlike the Road Raptors, most of the other clubs had some non-members hanging around, mostly male. *Groupies?* After she got done choking down the bathtub vino, and while Johnny was busy with the club president, she was approached by a middle-aged man. The guy wore designer jeans, very expensive Nikes and an open-necked, red shirt with a leather vest. A gold chain necklace with a crucifix contrasted with his tanning-booth torso. Bald on top, he had medium-length salt and pepper hair on the sides and a pair of dark-tinted, wire-rimmed Raybans.

"I understand you're an actress?" he said.

"Yes, I am," she said, suddenly tired and hoping this jerk didn't ask what movies she'd been in. The warm beer, first and second-hand pot, and the lack of food were catching up with her. She felt light-headed and wondered if Johnny was about finished and ready to return to their camp. She hoped the club had brought along something edible to eat.

"Name's Martin Raymond." He handed her a business card he slipped out of a wallet. His nails had been recently manicured. "I run an exclusive talent agency," he said with an oily smile. "Call me when you get back in town. Might have something for you."

Great, just what I need, another opportunity to do a porno. She started to tell him to stick his card up his ass but thought better of it. The tough girl role was getting tiresome. She stuffed the card into a pocket. She'd toss it in the fire later.

"Call me," he said again as Johnny came over, slipped his arms around her waist from behind and nuzzled her neck.

"Ready to go?" Johnny said, ignoring the man.

"Born ready."

*

Serenaded by yells, shouts and drunken laughter, and dodging any stray, wasted bikers who came zombie-ing out of the dark, they made their way along a narrow, gravel road. The grit crunched under Rebecca's feet. A chill wind swept through the trees and she shivered. She moved nearer to Johnny's side and he slipped an arm around her shoulders, pulled her closer.

"Will you tell me what the problem is with Satans Kin?" she said.

"Ducky Dunston," Johnny said flatly.

"Ducky Dunston?"

"Club pres, piece of shit. Used to be a Road Raptor. Fucker pulled a shank on me once."

"A shank?"

"Knife. Beat the holy shit outta' him. Should'a shoved that shank up his ass."

"So that's the problem."

Johnny hesitated. "Part of it... pretty sure the asshole was dealing."

"Drugs?"

"Yeah, violates club rules. No dealing. If someone wants to score something for their own use, long as it don't become a problem, fine. But no dealing. Feds catch one brother dealing—they'll try and tie the rest of the club in on a RICO. Ain't worth it. Our lawyer's rich enough already."

For some reason, she felt he wasn't giving her the full story. There had to be a reason for pulling a knife, didn't there? Or did there, thinking back to her fight with the psycho bitch, Sheva. Still, she had the uneasy feeling Johnny was worried and keeping something from her. He seldom spoke this many words at one time. But apparently he'd said all he intended to say. She'd ask Roxy to fill in the rest.

They arrived at their camp to find it pretty much like the others. Stoned and drunk club members staggered about, some in danger of toppling into the fire. Everyone was talking too loudly—or not at all. Magoo looked catatonic, seated on the ground and staring into the fire. He rested a can of beer on one knee. Every now and then he'd hoist it to his lips.

Some of the women had shed their upper garments and stood around, drinking, laughing and being fondled. A few more had misplaced their bottom garments as well and danced around the bonfire in naked ecstasy, accompanied by a CD player that blared out the same Country Western and Classic Rock the Black List featured. *Someone raid the jukebox?* At least she didn't see anyone on their knees giving head. But she didn't look too hard.

Roxy spotted her and hurried over. She held a paper plate containing a blackened steak and some coagulated baked beans. "Here," she said and handed Rebecca the plate. "I saved you some dinner."

Rebecca took the plate and glanced at Johnny.

"Go ahead," he said with his killer smile. "Need to check on some things. Be back."

She nodded in response, sat on a nearby log with Roxy and dug in.

*

Wild stood well back from the fire, drinking a beer, and watched the women dance around it. He hoped none of them stumbled into the flames. It'd happened before. He had a wet blanket and a couple of buckets full of water near at hand. He hadn't mentioned it to Johnny, knew he didn't need to, but Satans Kin wasn't bitch-packing. A sure sign they were up to something.

"Hey, man," a retiree said and slapped him on the back.

"Good to see you."

"Not missing this," he said and wandered on.

Ex-club members, who'd left in good standing, were always welcome on the holiday runs. There were several retirees on this run, as well as a couple of Nomads. The Nomads were loners, club members who hadn't hung their patch in any chapter. He sort of thought of them as being like mountain men, who just got together occasionally to party. They had to be tough to survive on their own. He was glad to have the extra bodies with them.

Off to his side, he spotted one of the retiree's wives eyeing him. She had to be twelve, fifteen years older than him. He couldn't recall her name. Her heavy breasts were scarcely contained by the skimpy bikini top she wore that hung nearly to her navel. In fact, one pink nipple was peeking over the garment. A substantial roll of flab, muffined out above the waistband of her too-tight jeans. She tried to bat her eyelids at him but was so shit-faced it looked more like a nervous tic, which caused him to grin.

She took that as an invitation, sashayed over and plastered herself against his side. "Hey, baby," she said and tried to kiss him.

He turned his head away, not trusting where her lips had been. The sour smell of her breath gave him an unpleasant clue.

"Waas'a matter, baby? Don't you like me?" she said, rubbed her hand up and down the front of his pants and squeezed the bulge there. "Ah see, you do like me."

"Crazy 'bout you," he said, fending off another kiss. Christ, he was actually getting turned on. She reminded him of a middle-aged woman who'd lived on his block, back before he dropped out of school. What a crazy, perverted bitch she'd been, taking advantage of a fifteen-year-old boy while her hubby worked. Not that he'd minded. Nor had his pals. That old gal had a large, soft ass and loved it doggie-style. He often wondered what had become of her.

He looked around for something he could bend this woman over. They'd skip the foreplay. Instead, he saw Johnny look his way and nod towards the trucks.

"Hang on, gotta take a leak," he said and peeled her off him.

"Want I should come along and hold it?"

"No," he said and swatted her on her rump. "Don't run off."

He joined Johnny.

"Everything okay?" Johnny said.

"So far. How's it with the others?"

"Waitin' on us."

Wild snorted. "Figures."

"Who you got watching them?"

"Animal. I'll spell him in a bit."

Johnny nodded and looked around. "Seen that bitch, Sheva?"

"I seen her."

"And?"

Wild snorted again. "Gotta lump on her head the size of a damn egg. Your little gal really unloaded on her."

"Good." Johnny glanced around again. "Need to speak to Tiny. Then be off over there with Becky." He nodded in the direction he intended.

"Got it."

"You better get back to Loretta before she passes out."

"Probably be an improvement."

Johnny snickered and left.

As he watched Johnny leave, he realized he'd slipped a hand into his pants pocket and grasped Sheva's butterfly knife. He pulled the knife out and looked at it in the dim light. *Guess Johnny still hasn't heard about you. Be hell to pay when he does, especially since I didn't tell him. Nothing I can do 'bout that now.*

He started to return the knife to his pocket but then got a better idea and walked over to his bike. He'd laid his riding chaps across the seat. The leather chaps had reinforced knees with extra padding. A seam on the inside, above his left knee, had come unraveled, forming a sort of pocket. He stuffed the knife in there and tossed the chaps back over his bike seat. It seemed like as good a place to store the shank as any. He turned and headed back to Loretta.

SIXTEEN

Clean struggled along in the dark, stumbled over rocks, roots, uneven ground—his own feet. He didn't like the great outdoors, especially at night. Fuck that shit. Too damn many things lived in the woods that came out after the sun set, skunks, mountain lions, fucking bats. *Good evening. Let me sink my fucking fangs into your fucking throat.* It wasn't just animals, but snags that'd trip you up, limbs that'd claw at your eyes, and those goddamned fucking spider webs hanging from branches that kept settling on his head like hair nets. He was constantly wiping them off and could feel things skittering across his bald pate. *Motherfucking spiders.* He hated motherfucking spiders.

Off to his right, something yipped and howled. He stumbled to a stop, his heart thumped in his chest. He'd left his piece in his sleeping bag which he'd buried in the back of the F150, just in case they got stopped by pigs on the run. He'd heard this howl earlier, before he snuck out of camp. Someone had said it was a fuckin' coyote. Someone had said it was fuckin' Bigfoot. Maybe it was Bigfoot fucking a coyote—or the other way around. Whatever the hell it was, it sounded a lot closer now. He moved on, as fast as he could. He was already way late.

That he was late couldn't be helped. He'd had to wait until everyone settled down or got too messed up to notice him leave. The last thing he wanted was for someone to see him go and ask about it later. He could lie and say he was visiting another club, but this late? And what if someone checked? No reason anyone should, but what if they did? How'd he explain away the lie? It was smarter to be careful and not take any unnecessary chances.

Then to complicate matters, he'd had to loop around the area he'd seen Johnny and that new, hot bitch of his slip off to earlier. Stumble over them in the dark, kick her in the ass, step on her tits or something, and Johnny'd kill him.

So he bided his time and had just been about ready to slip off when he'd noticed Wild had disappeared. Where the hell had he gone? One minute he'd been tending the fire and the next he'd been replaced by Animal. Running into Wild in the dark would be worse than Johnny. The nosey prick had to know everything. Hopefully the son of a bitch had just gone to take a dump. But when Wild hadn't returned in half an hour, he couldn't wait any longer. He slipped away and promptly got lost. It took quite awhile to figure out where he was and which direction he needed to go.

An hour after leaving camp, he found himself nearing his destination. At least he hoped that huge, dark shadow that loomed in front of him was the ranch house. He tried to move quietly while he approached the building from what he took to be the rear, as per his instructions. When he drew close, two darker shadows detached themselves and moved to intercept him.

"You Clean?" one of the shadows said and blocked his way.
"Yeah."
"You're late. Come alone?"
"I'm alone. Forgot my GPS."
"Fuckin' smart ass. Raise your arms."

"Why?"

"You shut the fuck up mano and jus' fuckin' do it," the second shadow said.

He raised his arms and felt himself patted down. "I'm ticklish."

"Shut the fuck up," the second shadow said again.

"Clean is clean," the first shadow said with a snort and stepped away.

"You wait here."

He could barely make out the second shadow as the biker hurried over to the building and rapped once on the door. The door opened with a scrape of wood catching the sill and the guy said, "He's here."

"Send 'em in," a voice said.

He was escorted over and shoved inside when the door swung open wider. He stumbled on the stoop but kept his balance as the door slammed shut behind him. It was darker inside the building than outside and the air foul with cigarette smoke. He bumped his head against something hanging from the ceiling that jangled in protest.

"You're late," Doctor said.

"Hey, man, had to wait until they settled down… then I backtracked a couple of times to make sure no one was followin' me," he lied, to impress Doctor.

Doctor wasn't impressed. "Got lost most like."

Doctor opened a second door and entered a dimly-lit room. Clean followed him into what was the kitchen and jerked to a stop. The room was full of Satans Kin.

"What the fuck is this? 'Sposed to be jus' me and Ducky."

"Shut up," Tramp said. He was sprawled in a worn, chrome-framed chair and looked really pissed. "Frisk his ass."

"Your men already did."

The club Sgt at Arms, that freak Juggler, stepped forward and jerked his hands up each side of Clean's torso, forced his arms into the air, and began searching him.

Juggler was certainly one creepy motherfucker. Tall, lean with wiry muscles, arms sleeved out with tats and hair the same color as Johnny Winters and his albino brother, cut short. But he had dark eyes, not pink—nasty dark eyes that looked like they belonged on a clothing store dummy. They were eyes that took everything in and gave nothing away. His face was badly pockmarked. He must have had a shitload of zits as a teenager. Clean had an almost overpowering urge to ask him, *what's par for your face?* He managed to squash that impulse. Juggler hadn't gotten his name for his ability with bowling pins or tennis balls. It was said he could open a throat in less than a second. He only spelled his name the way he did to confuse civilians and pigs. The bikers all knew what it meant. And most of them couldn't spell well enough to know the difference anyway.

Juggler took his time and Clean turned his head to avoid the man's foul breath. *Jesus, what the fuck did he have for dinner?* Juggler finished his search by squeezing his crotch. "Want I should cough?"

Juggler ignored him and backed away. "He's good."

"Where the fuck you been?" Tramp said. "Youse 'sposed to been here hours ago."

"Like I told Doc, had to be careful. Didn't want no one following me. Ducky here?"

Tramp didn't answer, instead continued to glare at him.

He stood in the middle of the room for several minutes while nobody spoke. There had to be at least a half-dozen Satans Kin here and they had all the exits covered. He began to feel very uneasy. His mouth went dry and he couldn't swallow. Sweat trickled off the back of his head and ran down his neck. He glanced around. The kitchen was a pigsty. Greasy, faded wallpaper the color of snot, torn in several places and patched with newspaper, covered the walls. Tacked here and there were pages torn from jerk-off mags, heavily smudged. The stove was filthy and the sink full of food encrusted plates. The place stank of fried food, stale beer, vomit and farts. An ancient refrigerator kept making a noise that sounded like someone muttering, "Screw you," over and over.

A knock came on the back door and Doctor left the room. He quickly returned. "They swept the perimeter and didn't find anyone. He came alone."

Swept the perimeter? We in the damn army?

Tramp didn't respond, just continued to glower at Clean as if weighing options. The only other sound came from a wall clock ticking down the seconds. After several more uncomfortable moments, Tramp stood, brushed past him, opened an interior door, stuck his head out and said, "Fucker's here."

Tramp stepped aside and Ducky entered, buckling his belt. Ducky nodded to the room he'd left and one of the bikers slipped in. Before the door slammed shut, Clean heard some whimpering. Ducky must have had company. The asshole had an appetite for young, teenage girls and word was that the Kin were heavy into sex-trafficking, as well as drug running. Well, wasn't any of his concern—leastways, not yet.

Ducky had to stretch to make six-foot, even with boots on, and was of average build. The guy had to have been fucking insane to have challenged Johnny that time. Lucky for him Johnny hadn't killed him. Ducky wore black leather pants and his cut over a buttoned-down, white dress shirt. *Prom night?* He had slicked-back hair and a thin mustache with a patch of whiskers under his lower lip. He looked like a beaner but didn't sound like one.

Ducky smiled broadly, crossed the room, arms wide, and hugged Clean like a long-lost brother. Then patted him on the back, turned him loose and stepped back, continuing to smile, but with lips only. Ducky's brown eyes were hard and cold. "Beginning to think you weren't gonna' make it. Having second thoughts?"

"No." *And if I did, I sure as shit wouldn't tell you.*

"Good. Sit." He motioned at the chair Tramp had been seated in.

Clean filled it and watched Ducky closely who sat opposite him, leaned forward, arms on the table, fingers interlocked and continued to smile. He couldn't tell if that smile was meant to reassure him or intimidate him, maybe both.

When it became clear that the Satans Kin president wasn't going to start the conversation, Clean cleared his throat and said, "So… how ya gonna' waste Johnny?"

SEVENTEEN

The eastern sky brightened, lighting Clean's way who hurried to get back to camp before he was missed. He stuck to the road this time as that was the surest way of finding the campsite. He shivered, but only partially in response to the drop in temperature. What had he gotten himself into? Ducky was one crazy-ass son of a bitch. He was afraid the Satans Kin president had watched too many episodes of *Sons of Anarchy*.

Ducky's plan for dealing with Johnny and Wild was simple enough that it might work. It depended on being able to lure the two into another meeting. The meet would be with Ducky and Tramp only, with Doctor there as an impartial witness. The meet would be held during the day at the ranch house to queer any suspicions the Road Raptors might have. To prevent confrontations, both clubs would remain in their campsites until the meet ended. A sure sticking point with that asshole Wild, but that was Ducky's problem. Security would be provided by one of the other clubs that the Road Raptors trusted. Their job would be to keep the clubs in their camps and protect the ranch house.

He shook his head. What the hell? That shit was straight out of a movie, *The Godfather* or something. But it was an odd-ball enough approach that Johnny just might go for it. Ducky wouldn't tell him which club he had in mind to run security or how he'd convince Johnny to accept them.

What Ducky did tell him was that he had a mole, whatever the hell that was, in the other club. The mole would be hiding in the ranch house and once the meet was under way, would burst into the room and blow both Johnny and Wild away. To make it look good, the guy would fire a few more rounds into the walls, shots that had supposedly been aimed at the other three occupants but missed. Since the mole was a member of the club providing protection, he should be able to slip away in the ensuing confusion. That would pin the assassinations on the club providing security and help keep suspicion away from Satans Kin.

The mole was a long time member of the other club who wanted to join Satans Kin. This would be his initiation into the club—or so he thought. The dumb shit would head for a rendezvous point where he'd be dealt with and disposed of by Juggler. No way could the guy ever wear a Satans Kin cut after this. That'd give the whole scheme away.

With Johnny and Wild out of the way, Clean could assume the leadership role. As president, his first move would be to end the prohibition on drug dealing. Ducky knew there were several club members who didn't like the rule. With Satans Kin as partners, they could squeeze out the other clubs and take over their turfs as well, adding the bikers they wanted and getting rid of the rest. This would give them the secure base, manpower, and with the drug money, the backing they needed to expand nationwide and compete with the major clubs. Ducky has some large balls.

It was at this point that Ducky left the lane of reality and veered head-on into oncoming traffic. To help Clean assume power, Ducky had a list of several Road Raptors who would have to go.

"Go?" he'd said. "Go where?"

Ducky handed him a list, scrawled on a scrap of paper. "Juggler will handle it. We got a shipment of Uzis from our friends down south and he's dying to try them out."

He glanced at Juggler. That psycho didn't look like he was dying to do anything. In fact, the guy looked like the fucking Sphinx. Didn't he ever blink?

He read the list and nearly shit. This crazy bastard planned to gun down better than a third of the club. What the hell did he expect the cops to do? Sit around and play with their dicks? A couple of killings here could be concealed—had been in the past. Start blowing people away with automatic weapons though and it'd be like World War Three. No way could that be concealed. The pigs often had a squad car parked on the dirt road and occasionally flew over in a chopper to keep an eye on them. And here lately there had been talk of camera equipped drones being spotted. One club claimed to have shot one of the fucking things down with a shotgun. Man, if they cut loose with automatic weapons, the pigs would freak. They'd bring in the state cops, FBI, ATF, goddamned Homeland Security and anyone else with a badge. No, only Johnny and Wild needed to die.

He'd argued long and hard, assuring Ducky he could garner the needed votes without him thinning out the club and bringing down more heat. Ducky eventually gave in.

Then that ass-wipe Tramp opened his hole. "Fine, but Magoo's got to go. Cocksucker's too unstable and him and Johnny go way back."

Clean had been forced to argue just as hard for Magoo's life. Magoo's support was crucial to his ability to gain control of the club. But he didn't want Ducky to know that. So he'd pointed out how invaluable Magoo would be to their joint venture and assured

Ducky he could control him. If Magoo became a problem, they could deal with him then. He finally convinced Ducky to leave Magoo be as well.

The Road Raptors' camp should be just around the next bend. He left the road to slip into the site from the brush. While he paused to listen, he wondered if there was more to those proposed shootings than just to help him get elected. Could it be that Ducky wanted to cripple the Road Raptors? Was Ducky's real goal to drain off the club's strength and leave him a butt boy to Satans Kin rather than an equal? That dirty son of a bitch. That was it. He'd have to keep a close watch on that sleazy prick for any signs he intended to alter their agreement. It would be just like Ducky to try and hit him with a fate accomply, or whatever that frog term was. Bastard!

Right now he needed to get back to camp and figure out a way to cover his ass—in case Ducky's plan for Johnny went to shit.

EIGHTEEN

Rebecca awoke to find a grinning, but blurred, Foxy Roxy squatting beside her, holding a steaming cup in both hands. She blinked her eyes several times to try to clear them and brushed the hair off her forehead. She rolled her head to the side and rose up on an elbow. That half of the sleeping bag was empty.

"Seen him and Wild headed off somewheres," Roxy said. "I brung you a cup of coffee."

She blinked her eyes a couple of additional times and sat up. A lightning bolt of pain, centered somewhere behind her eyes, rewarded that effort. "Oh God, my head," she mumbled and brought her hands to her face. The sleeping bag slithered off her shoulders to her waist. "I drank too much yesterday."

"This'll help," Roxy handed her the metal cup.

"Thanks." She took a sip and grimaced. The coffee was strong enough to fuel the Harleys. She took another sip and glanced around. A few club members wandered about, looking like extras from the set of *The Walking Dead*. She doubted they'd ever gone down for the night. Empty beer cans, trash and clothing littered the area around the smoldering bonfire. A strong, ammonia-like odor caused her to nose wrinkle. Christ, couldn't these people go into the woods to pee? The camp was surrounded by stunted, spindly trees and ashen-colored sagebrush. A light breeze blew away the last of the night's chill bringing the promise of another blowtorch day.

She'd survived day one. Now to get through the next two, hopefully with no more fights.

"You know, you ain't supposed to pass out or fall asleep the first twenty-four hours of a run," Roxy said.

"You're not. Why?"

Roxy shrugged. "I don't know. You just ain't."

"Who made up that stupid rule?"

Roxy shrugged again. "Don't know. But if you do, you're liable to wake up to some asshole pissin' on you, or worse."

"Worse?" She felt her skin crawl.

"Seen biker's boot sprayed with lighter fluid and set on fire. Dog shit placed in their hand and their nose tickled with a leaf. Crap like that."

Completely grossed out and left speechless by such juvenile nonsense, she took another sip of coffee and realized she was flashing the entire camp. She tried to grab the edge of her sleeping bag with her right hand but couldn't close her fingers on it. Flustered, she looked for somewhere to set her cup down.

"Here." Roxy took the near end of the bag and pulled it back over her, tucking the end under an arm.

"Thanks." She squeezed her arm tight against her side. Her head continued to throb.

"Flo's got some breakfast going, over by the trucks. You wanna get dressed and grab some before it's all gone."

"Yeah… okay… right. Oh God, my head. Where are my clothes?"

Roxy gathered them up, handed them to her and she got

dressed while still inside the sleeping bag. Roxy watched, grinned and wrinkled her turned-up nose.

"What?"

"Nothin'. Most old ladies ain't so modest."

"I noticed." She finished dressing, crawled out of the bag, located the hiking shoes she'd worn, shook them out and pulled them on. When they stood up, she let out another groan.

"Head again?"

"No, my back. It's stiff." She leaned back a couple of times from the waist with her hands on her hips, then from side to side.

"Not used to sleeping on the ground."

"Guess not." She continued to stretch. "So you didn't get any sleep?"

"I cheated and caught a couple of hours in the cab of the Ford. Figured with the doors locked, I'd wake up if anyone tried to get in and mess with me."

"Weren't you with your old man? Who is your old man by the way?" She covered a yawn with a hand and faced Roxy.

"No one—and everyone. I'm a mama."

"A what?"

"A mama. Means I'm club property and anyone who wants me can have me."

"What the hell?" Her breath caught and her mouth fell open.

"Hey, it's not so bad. The Road Raptors are my family. They look out for me. So I pay 'em back the only way I can. I'm not much in demand anyways. Few brothers other than the prospects get that desperate, but some of them are kind of cute. Mostly I get stuck doing the crap jobs like club laundry. Wash the brothers' underwear. Gross."

She shook her head, this was too much to absorb so early in the morning. They started walking. "Are there many mamas?"

"A few."

"Sheva. Would she be...?"

Roxy snorted out a laugh. "Yeah, Sheva's a mama, but don't ever say that to her. She's kinda' reserved for the club founders and officers."

"Like Johnny."

"Hey, Johnny was never serious 'bout that bitch. But he's a man and she was available and more than willing. Don't sweat the past."

Just the present. "What about an old lady? What if some biker wants to get it on with her?"

"Won't happen. Old ladies are property of their old man."

Property? Her skin crawled again and heat flashed through her veins. *Property? What the fuck, I'm nobody's property. Something my father refuses to accept. Him and that damn church of his.*

"Someone try to mess with a brother's old lady without his permission," Roxy continued, "he'll get stomped and tossed outta' the club."

"Without his permission?"

Roxy shrugged once more. "Some guys are into threesomes, foursomes and moresomes. But the old lady would have to agree. At least in this club. Johnny's funny 'bout that."

"And mamas?" She looked at Roxy again while they walked.

"We're always agreeable. I jus' hope Dirty Dan never takes a liking to me. You know why they call him Dirty Dan don't ya?"

"Because he doesn't bathe?"

Roxy barked out another laugh. "That's a good one. He probably doesn't. But that's not how he got his name. It's because he likes to do it dirty. Back door, if you know what I mean. Problem is he's hung like a damn horse. Even a porno queen like Sheva, who'd probably do a horse if it was in a movie, has a hard time taking him that way. I do my best to keep him turned off me. I mean, hemorrhoid city."

"That's disgusting."

"Yeah, hurts too. Let's get some breakfast. Hey, Flo, any left?"

Flo glanced their way, nodded and picked up a couple of paper plates. She knelt in front of some cast iron skillets on a portable camp stove and started ladling food onto the plates. The left side of Flo's face was badly swollen and purple, her left eye black and nearly closed.

"My God!" Rebecca said and jerked to a stop, "What happened to you?"

"Ran into my old man's fist," Flo muttered, not bothering to look her way.

"What? Why?"

Flo's head jerked up and she glared at Rebecca.

"Becky," Roxy said, took her by an arm and turned her aside. "What goes on between a biker and his old lady is nobody's business but theirs."

"What? Look at her." She pulled away and turned back to Flo. "Does Johnny know about this?"

"Becky, I'm telling you. This is none of our business. Drop it."

"But—"

"No buts. Sit down and let's eat."

They sat, but she continued to stare at Flo. This wasn't right. What were these bikers... cavemen? "This isn't right, Johnny—"

"Johnny won't do nothin'. It's none of his business either. Leave it alone."

Flo walked over and tossed a plate full of scrambled eggs and fried bacon onto Rebecca's lap, splashing some onto her jeans. "Eat your damn food and listen to your friend." She tossed the other plate onto Roxy's lap, turned and walked away.

NINETEEN

Wild did his best to match the pres's long strides. Their boots kicked up dust on the arid roadbed, which was really just two tire tracks the width of Doctor's Hummer. Gravel had been dumped on ruts to keep them from washing out in the winter rains, which hadn't come now for several years. Their camp was a good quarter-mile from the ranch house.

"Who brought the message?" Johnny said.

He shook his head. "Some greaser. Never seen him before?"

"Beaner?"

"Yeah."

"Damn."

The very first run the Road Raptors had gone on was to this ranch. He'd been a prospect then and his sponsor, Johnny, the VP. The Buzzard, Buzz for short, had been president. The club had returned every Memorial Day weekend since. There had been the usual bullshit problems—brawls, knifings and drug overdoses. One year a club member in the Coffin Fillers MC, his mind fried on crank, decided two of his brothers were DEA agents and shot them, killing one. But this was the first time a club like Satans Kin had been allowed in. He hated Satans Kin. He hated anyone involved in drug trafficking.

Several years before, a drug dealer in a pimped out cage, fleeing gang-bangers the asshole had shorted, splattered his older brother all over an intersection. The piece of shit's lawyer worked out some sort of plea bargain with the worthless courts and six months later, the druggie, having settled with the gangstas, was back in business. A short while later the pigs found the dealer stuffed in the trunk of his Caddy, a dozen hypos stuck in him. Apparently the detectives never got a line on the blond biker the dealer had last been seen talking to, and chalked it up to a mob hit. Leastways that's how the newspaper reported it.

The Road Raptors' prohibition on drug dealing had been the main reason he'd prospected with them.

Some loose earth shifted beneath his foot and he nearly lost his balance. Johnny grabbed his arm to steady him. "Shit, thanks." *God, this place sucks.*

The club had been considering finding a new location for the first run of summer. The ranch had never been an Eden, but with the drought the state was locked in, each year this dump had gotten drier, dustier and hotter. The only real plus was that it was private property and well off the highway, away from prying pig eyes. He shook his head. Too bad Johnny hadn't located another destination.

"There he is," Johnny said.

At the base of the porch steps, Tramp stood, fidgeting and smoking. He was easy to spot with the head tattoo. Wild's muscles tensed and heat flushed through his body. Tramp was small by biker standards, no more than five-eight, but solid and a handful in a fight. Like many small thugs, the prick made up for his lack of size by being overly aggressive and ruthless. Tramp wore a belt made from the drive chain of a Harley. It made for a handy, and potentially lethal, weapon. The greatest advantage being there were no laws prohibiting wearing a chain for a belt. Tramp also had on steel-toed boots and metal-studded riding gloves.

They strode to a stop in front of him. "What the hell do you want, asshole?" Wild said.

Tramp flicked away his cigarette, squinted at Wild for a moment, his brow wrinkled, eyes nearly invisible, then turned to face Johnny. "Ducky wants a private meet, jus the four of us with Doc as a witness." When Johnny didn't respond, he said, "He wants to work out our problems."

"Nothing to work out," Johnny said. "You stay the fuck off our turf."

"Yeah, we get that. But we need to lay down exactly where those boundaries are so none of our people stray over into them—or yours into ours. And we need to discuss some compensation for those recent stompings. Some of our peoplc got hurt."

"So'd some of ours," Wild said.

"So maybe it's a wash. But we need to hash it out."

"Where do you want to hold this meet?" Johnny said.

A snotty grin formed on Tramp's face. "Right here. Anywheres else we'd need to rent a derrick to tote Doc there." He grunted a laugh. "Ducky wants to meet today, while it's still light. He also thinks we should keep our clubs in their campsites while the meet is going on."

Lava shot through Wild's veins. "Like hell!" He stepped closer to Tramp and pointed toward the lake. "Your people are right over there while ours are way the fuck over there." He waved in the opposite direction with his other hand. His face was inches from Tramp's. He could feel and taste the man's hot breath.

Johnny slipped a hand between them and pushed him back a few inches. "Wild's right."

Tramp licked his lips and glanced around. "All right, so youse move yours in some, but no closer than ours. And they stay together while the meets on."

"How the hell do we guarantee that?"

"Ducky thinks we should get one of the other clubs to guard the ranch house and keep our clubs apart."

"Yeah? Which club?"

"Hangmen."

"Fuck that," Wild said.

"What's wrong with them?"

"Nothing, except you suggested them."

"So who do you want?"

"Coffin Fillers."

"Bullshit, and for the same reason."

Wild glared at him, wanting nothing more than to tear the shit apart.

"Okay," Johnny said. "We're gonna run out of clubs. Storm Troopers."

Tramp ran a hand across his chin and licked his lips again. "Ducky really wanted the Hangmen. Have to run this by him and see if'n he'll go with the Storm Troopers or not."

"It's the Storm Troopers or no meet."

Tramp looked at Johnny and grinned but with his lips only. "Guess that leaves us no choice. Six okay?"

"Make it four."

"In a hurry, huh? Okay, four it is. And to prove we're on the level, we'll let you contact the Storm Troopers to set security, okay?"

"Fine."

"Don't be late." Tramp turned and walked off. No handshake had been offered or expected.

They watched until Tramp angled behind the ranch house and was lost to view.

"What the hell?" Wild said. "You buying this shit?"

Johnny shook his head. "Something's wrong." He lit a cigarette and continued to stare in the direction Tramp had gone. After nearly a minute, "C'mon, let's talk to Kaiser Bill."

*

Juggler leaned against a tree and watched Ducky fiddle with an Uzi Machine Pistol like he had some idea what he was doing with it. The gun was one of a half dozen they'd bought from that psychotic fuck, Rubio, their contact with the Tres Rojos drug cartel. It was a wonder Ducky hadn't blown his damn head off yet or accidentally mowed down half the club.

He still couldn't believe that idiot had nearly queered the whole plan last night by adding that shit about eliminating half the Road Raptors club. Clean might not be too bright but at least he'd enough sense to argue Ducky out of that nonsense, maybe. More likely Ducky still intended to go through with it after the assassinations. *We'll see about that.* If nothing else it unnecessarily alerted Clean to just what a sleazy weasel Ducky is. He shook his head and wondered if Ducky was beginning to see the obvious. Clean had about as much chance being elected the next Road Raptors president as either of them did.

What he found most interesting though, was how hard Clean had argued for Magoo's life. What's going on there? Could Clean have let Magoo in on this? Not likely. Magoo had the IQ of a turnip at best, and was Johnny's oldest friend. He had no idea what was going on in that club but couldn't visualize Magoo ever being part of any plan to harm Johnny.

Tramp stalked into camp and headed their way. Ducky sat on a stump, using another tree trunk for a back to his throne. He looked up as Tramp came to a stop in front of him. "Well?"

"It's on for four today."

"And security?"

Tramp grinned. "Storm Troopers. You had that figured."

"Great. Who suggested them?"

Tramp's grin grew. "Johnny."

"Fucking A!" Ducky laid down the gun, stood and squeezed one of Tramp's shoulders. "Good work, brother."

"I left Johnny on his way to talk to that tin Hitler. Any chance he'd refuse?"

"That ignorant Hun? No way in hell. Old Bill will piss himself in his eagerness to take this on. He'll see it as proof he's our equal. The asshole's always felt none of the other clubs took him seriously."

Tramp snorted. "Wonder why?"

Ducky laughed and faced Juggler. "Get word to our mole it's on for four today."

He nodded and turned away.

"Hey, cum-head," Tramp said. "You're sure that prick can shoot straight?"

He turned back and took a step toward Tramp. "Get the shit outta your ears. I told you, guy was a sniper in Iraq, better than thirty confirmed kills. I've seen his ribbons and medals."

"Yeah, and I can go to an army surplus store and get all the shittin' medals and ribbons I want."

He took a couple of steps closer, letting his hand dangle close to his knife sheath, a familiar tingling in his limbs. "You sayin' I don't know my job?" he said softly. "Want I should bring him over here and have him shoot a used rubber off that lump between your shoulders?"

"Why you fuck—"

"All right, enough!" Ducky said and stepped between them.

"I can bring him over if you want."

"I don't want that cocksucker anywheres near our camp. Someone see him here would give the whole thing away. Jus be sure he's hidin' in that ranch house come four."

"He'll be there."

TWENTY

Johnny stood at the edge of their camp and gazed at the ranch house in the distance. All he could see from here was the tin roof. A thin curl of smoke rose from a chimney. *Must be a cooking fire, in this heat.*

Kaiser Bill hadn't been able to shed any light on what Satans Kin was up to, but was more than willing to handle security. Bill promised no one would disturb the meet and he'd see to it their clubs stayed apart. Instead of easing his concerns, Bill's optimistic assurances just served to fuel them. Bill was okay, despite the Nazi nonsense, probably didn't even know what a Nazi was, just wore their shit to piss off people. Johnny wasn't sure how capable Bill or his club was. He'd have preferred the Hangmen handle security. But since Ducky had been the one to suggest them, Wild had been right to refuse.

He couldn't shake the feeling he was missing something. He played the whole talk with Tramp back in his mind. It didn't feel right. Ducky was capable of any type of treachery, yet what could he hope to get away with in broad daylight, in front of the other clubs? Then there were those rumors that Satans Kin had connections with a Mexican drug cartel. Lots of money in moving drugs, as well as young girls for sex. He grimaced. He'd heard those rumors too. The two went hand in hand. Money means power. Hell, Ducky wasn't going to discuss boundaries. Ducky intended to offer them a deal, or threaten them—most likely both. *Should have killed that piece of shit when I had the chance.*

What was Doctor's part in this? He had to have some role in it. Buzz had never trusted that prick. Doctor only looked out for Doctor, Buzz had warned him more than once. He toyed with the idea of paying him a visit and see if he could sweat, or beat, something out of the fat bastard. But with nothing to go on he'd be groping in the dark. Also that would alert Doctor and Satans Kin that he was suspicious. Best for now to let them think they were fooling him.

He rubbed his temples and yawned. What dumb shit had come up with the rule of no crashing for the first twenty-four hours of a run anyway?

He'd lain awake all night, holding Becky in the crook of his arm, watched her sleep and listened to her soft breathing. No one would dare fuck with her while he was there, stupid rule or not. He wished to God he hadn't brought her along. But the Memorial Day Run seemed to be the perfect time to introduce her to his lifestyle and her to the club. The holiday run was usually a good time. He knew he had to either bring her into the club or stop seeing her, and he wasn't about to stop seeing her. Not only was she beautiful, she was smart, feisty and fun to be with. Her throaty, sultry voice never failed to excite him even though he figured it was just a part of her actress gig. He'd noticed that when she got really pissed her voice got higher.

Christ, had he fallen in love? What the fuck.

He felt her presence before he heard her—a whiff of her fragrance, a sense of no longer being alone. He felt his heart beat faster and he stood straighter. He waited for her to encircle his waist with an arm. When she didn't, he turned to face her. She stood a couple of paces away, weight on one hip, arms folded across her chest and a scowl on her face.

"Am I your property?"

"What? Oh… that's jus a biker word. Means hands off." He paused for a moment and shook his head. "Never much liked it. Don't use it."

"So I'm free to leave if I want?"

He stared at her. *What the hell?* "You want to leave?"

"No," she said after a couples of moments. "Not particularly."

"Then what's the problem?"

She didn't answer.

Jesus, women. He shrugged. "You're free to do whatever you want. No one owns you."

"Good." She stepped over, slipped her hand behind his head, rose up on her toes and pulled his lips to hers. After breaking their kiss she smiled. "Why so glum, still worried about Satans Kin?"

"My job to worry, I'm the pres."

"The buck stops here."

"Not if it gets spent first."

She laughed at that.

"Know what I need?"

"I can guess," she said with an impish grin.

"Well you guessed wrong. Need to clear my head. Wanna go for a ride?"

"Sure, where?"

"Wherever the bike takes us."

*

Rebecca donned her riding leathers while Wild and Johnny argued.

"Who are you taking with you?" Wild said.

"Becky."

Wild rolled his eyes and let out his breath. "Which club members?"

Johnny didn't answer.

"You can't go by yourself. There's been bikers coming and going all morning. A bunch of Satans Kin rode out earlier."

"Be fine, need to clear my head. Run into trouble I'll call."

"You check your cell phone lately?" Wild held up his phone. "No bars. We can't get service in this shithole."

"Need you here."

"Then take someone else along," Without waiting for an answer, Wild turned and surveyed the camp. "Animal, pres wants to go for a ride. Grab your bike and keep him company."

Animal nodded his head and hustled over to his bike.

Wild turned back to Johnny who scowled but said nothing. Animal's bike fired up and he gunned it over to Johnny's stopping on his right. Animal wore a helmet that looked to Rebecca like an old leather football helmet. Or maybe what World War Two tankers wore. She climbed onto Johnny's bike and seated herself behind him. She glanced around as he started the bike and spotted Roxy, standing by herself, looking forlorn. She tapped Johnny on the shoulder. "Can Roxy come with us?"

"What?" He swiveled to face her.

"Roxy. Can she come along?"

Johnny glanced at Roxy then at Animal who'd been listening to the exchange.

Animal grinned, removed his cigar, turned and waved. "Hey, Foxy Roxy, park your bony ass right here," he said and patted the seat behind him.

Roxy's lips split into a big grin and not bothering with any riding leathers, ran over and climbed on.

"Here," Flo yelled and tossed her a small helmet, which Roxy caught, pulled on and fastened the chinstrap. Then they were rolling with Johnny in the lead and Animal right behind.

*

Sheva watched the entire sickening display from a pair of stunted trees she'd taken refuge behind. Johnny hadn't come looking for her, but she'd been staying out of his way just the same. Her temper often got the best of her. She knew she shouldn't have pulled a shank on that little bitch. She also wished she'd cut the cunt's throat with it—cut her fucking head off. She hoped an eighteen-wheeler would snuff them all and leave their ripped-apart bodies strewn all over the highway, like a heard of deer that had been run over.

She stepped out into the road and watched them disappear around a bend. Several yards in front of her, Magoo stood watching them too. After a few moments, he walked over to the beer stash, hefted a whole case onto a shoulder and wandered off.

TWENTY-ONE

The bikes hung a right at the blacktop, away from Dismalville as Rebecca had dubbed the town, and ran side by side with Johnny near the centerline. It was mid-morning and warming up fast, but pleasant enough riding in the open air. Even getting smacked in the face by the occasional insect didn't spoil it. What was it Roxy had said? *You can always tell a happy biker by the bugs in his teeth.* She smiled at that but kept her lips closed.

They ran near the speed limit, not pushing it like they had the day before. Traffic was light. The occasional van or SUV full of wide-eyed children went by, along with pickups and cars of all description—cages, the bikers called them. They passed a few groups of bikes headed the other way. Johnny and Animal acknowledged one-percenters but ignored civilian bikers. The citizens were easy to spot, bundled up in neat black leather, wearing dark-visor, fishbowl helmets and riding garbage wagons. Either that, or kids in shorts and T-shirts, but still sporting Star Wars headgear.

A trio of speed demons on crotch rockets blew past them from behind, doing about ninety on a blind curve. The idiots had to lean their bikes so far over to hold the curve their knees nearly scraped the pavement. No doubt they each had a hard-on over how they'd just shown up the big, bad bikers. Animal flipped them the bird.

After about twenty miles they cut off onto another road that ran up into some large hills. They passed an old beater station wagon, full of immigrant farm workers, struggling up an incline and leaving a cloud of blue smoke in its wake. The land here was greener with tall pine trees growing right up to both shoulders. The trees cast a picket fence of light and dark across the road.

They crossed a river and turned onto another paved road that led into a state-maintained campground. In single file they slowly rolled past RVs, trailers and tents that jammed the grounds to overflowing. At the end of the campground, they headed down a gravel lane, ignoring the *Maintenance Vehicles Only* sign. They followed the lane to a bend in the river where they pulled to a stop under some tall trees at the river's edge and dismounted. Everyone stretched. It had grown hotter. If they were going to be here very long she wanted to get out of her leathers.

Animal pulled off his cut, draped it over the handlebars and stuck his helmet on the headlight, then wiped sweat with his do-rag. He tugged off his boots and socks, letting them lay where they fell. Still wearing his Levis and grimy, yellow and black-striped T-shirt and with his cigar clenched between his teeth, he waded out into the river and sat down. Only his head remained above the water. "Ahhh...," he moaned in relief.

Roxy stripped off everything, revealing more tattoos, including the club patch on her right butt cheek. With a whoop of joy, she ran past them and leaped into the water landing near Animal and splashing him good. She popped up behind him and shoved his head under the water. Animal came up spluttering, discarded his ruined cigar and went after her. He caught her, hoisted the squealing woman over his head and tossed her as far as he could. Roxy landed with a big splash, got to her feet and waded back. Upon reaching Animal, she leaped onto his chest, wrapped her arms around his neck, her legs around his waist, and planted a kiss on his lips as he went over backwards, arms pinwheeling. Their heads resurfaced and their laughter filled the air while they continued to wrestle about.

"Wanna join 'em?" Johnny said. Not waiting for an answer, he began to undress.

It'd been years since she'd skinny-dipped. Not since her early teens. Sometimes in the summer, when it got really hot, her mother would take her and her siblings to the river where they'd disrobe and splash about. That would be when her father was out of town saving souls somewhere. His calling demanded a lot of sacrifice and travel. Her mother taught them all to swim. And even though there were swimming holes closer to their home, her mother always took them to the same spot. It was the place her father held old-time river baptisms. These excursions were some of the few occasions she could ever recall seeing her mother smile.

She looked around. About thirty yards downriver, a couple of shocked fishermen stared at them. From the other direction a group of canoes floated their way. The canoes were full of high school-aged kids in baggy swim trunks and conservative bikinis. Their shepherd, in a wet, white tee over a dark, one-piece suit, crouched precariously in the lead canoe. The woman wore a tan ball cap and shaded her eyes with a hand. She looked as shocked as the fishermen.

"Come on in," Roxy called and waved at her.

"What the hell," she said and quickly shed her clothes. She took Johnny's offered hand and, side by side, waded into the river.

TWENTY-TWO

Helen Richards-Dubois, middle-aged youth director for the First Baptist Church of Cantrell, California, and wife of Pastor Lucius Stanford Dubois, was horrified. She was chaperoning a group of graduating high school seniors. They were on a final, spiritual retreat before heading off to summer jobs and college in the fall. What kind of depraved sex orgy were they drifting into? Righteous indignation replaced shock. She stood to scold the shameless trash and the canoe wobbled beneath her. But her sense of outrage evaporated when she spotted what she took to be a pair of "chopped hogs" parked on the shore. *Oh my God, bikers!* She'd heard there were some lurking in the area. How many more of the brutes were about? Head pivoting this way and that, she yelled for her charges to paddle for all they were worth and stay as close to the far bank as they could. Most of them ignored her. The boys especially were content to let the current carry them slowly past this Bacchanalian treat.

Roxy waded toward the floaters and stopped a scant half-dozen yards from the nearest canoe. The water here was shallower, barely reaching halfway up her thighs. "Hi," she said and waved, smiling broadly. "How y'all doing?"

A couple of kids gave tentative waves in return.

"Don't look at her!" Helen yelled. "And paddle. Paddle!"

"What's your hurry? This is a great place for a swim. Wanna join us? My friends won't mind."

"Hurry, hurry," Helen yelled.

"Where y'all from?"

"Cantrell," a slender, wide-eyed blonde in a turquoise bikini, sitting in the front of a canoe, said. Her partner, a sun-burned pink, heavy-set boy in paisley swim trunks, removed his paddle from the water and gaped at Roxy, an idiotic grin on his face.

"Oh yeah? We're from LA."

"In God's name, paddle!" Helen screeched. She swiveled her body from side to side, simultaneously trying to watch both shores and her charges. Her movements became so frantic she tipped her canoe, spilling herself into the river. She came up spluttering and spewing water, latched onto the side of her canoe, and tried to right it.

"Here, I'll help you," Roxy said and started wading that way.

"No! Stay away!"

"Hey, I jus wanna help. I can swim as good as a goddamned fish. How deep is it over there? Are you in trouble? Don't worry, the women all say I'm really good at mouth to mouth, although my tongue kinda' gets in the way. Maybe I ought to call the guys. They're real studs. They'll get on each side and have things straight in no time."

"No!" Helen blurted, between mouthfuls of water. She hooked an arm over the back of the canoe and tried to paddle with her other and kick with her feet.

"Suit yourself, your funeral." Roxy turned back to the canoes. "Hey, you're kind of a stud yourself," she said to a red-headed, freckle-faced boy who gawked at her. "What's your name?"

"Tom—Tommy," he stuttered.

"I'm Foxy Roxy. You ride a Harley, Tom—Tommy?"

"No."

"Oh, too bad. I've been looking for an old man. I know how to treat him real good." She slowly ran her tongue around her lips. The redhead quickly paddled on.

Roxy laughed and continued to wave at the kids while they drifted by. Several waved back and a few waved at Rebecca, mistaking her holding her cast over her head to keep it dry for a wave.

Rebecca squatted in the water so her breasts were covered. Skinny-dipping was one thing but flashing a bunch of high school kids was too outrageous for her. Not so Roxy, who stood with her legs shoulder-width apart, hands on hips and faced the floaters. Johnny and Animal sat in the water and enjoyed the spectacle.

A pair of canoes paddled over to the up-ended one and a duo of boys jumped in to help Helen before she drowned. One boy, either accidentally, or accidentally on purpose, ended up with a hand on her rear end. She let out a howl when he shoved her up into the canoe once they'd righted it. Johnny and Animal laughed and applauded.

The last canoe floated by. With a final wave, Roxy turned and waded back, a grin on her face. "You see that one kid grab a handful of that old bitch's ass? Bet that's the first time anyone's laid a paw on it in years. Surprised it didn't give her a heart attack."

"Roxy, you're too much," Johnny said between laughs.

"Sure made those little farts holiday for them, didn't I?"

*

When the final canoe disappeared around a bend, it grew quiet. The two fishermen had also moved on. Roxy and Animal went back to horsing about in the water and wandered downstream. Only their faint laughter, the call of an occasional bird, and the gentle sounds of a slowly flowing river disturbed the silence. Johnny led Becky upstream into deeper water which felt like cool silk against his flesh. Becky soon had to place her arms around his neck to stay afloat. They stopped in the shade of some large trees and kissed. Then she reversed her arms and turned her back to him.

He watched her body slowly float to the surface. It was like watching Venus emerge from the depths. Her breasts broke through, nipples hard and erect, followed by her tanned body. No jewelry in her navel. Then her hips materialized, between them a narrow, wet thatch of curly dark hair. Finally her legs drifted up, kicking lazily with the current. She rested against his chest, her outstretched body scarcely awash. She tilted her head back and sighed. He gazed into green eyes pivoted toward her forehead to meet his. She smiled and said, "God, this is heavenly." He bent forward and kissed her again.

Becky rolled back over, reversed her arms once more and let her body sink against his. Her smile turned mischievous when she felt him poke hard into her abdomen. "I thought you said you needed to clear your head?"

"Something's come up."

"Uhmm... that could be embarrassing when you get out."

"Stay here forever, I guess."

They kissed, long and hard. Their tongues found each other, bodies pressed tight. Blood surged through his veins and his breath came hot and heavy.

Becky broke the kiss and whispered in his ear, "I think I can help you with this problem." She rose up, wrapped her legs around his waist and returned her lips to his, as his hands slid down her back.

TWENTY-THREE

A while later they waded back to where they'd entered the river. Johnny called and waved for Animal and Roxy to rejoin them. His internal radar buzzed. No doubt Roxy's show hadn't gone unreported for long. "Okay," he said when they rejoined them. "Imagine that old bitch put in at the campground and called the law. Need to get dressed and roll before some pig shows up wanting to arrest us for trespassing and indecent exposure."

"And assault with a deadly weapon," Animal said.

"What? What deadly weapon?"

"Foxy Roxy's body."

Roxy stuck out her tongue at Animal but laughed along with them. Even Becky couldn't completely stifle a giggle.

With the sun approaching its zenith, they rode back through the campground. He didn't see the old bat but did spot some kids who looked like they'd been on the float. Several excited youths, in wet swimwear and talking to campers, pointed their way. A clutch of male thirty and forty-somethings also eyed them and nudged one another, their testosterone flowing. The men stood in a group drinking beer and smoking. One tossed down a half-smoked butt and ground it under his foot. The guy turned, said something to the others and they swaggered toward the road, fanning out to block the bikes' path.

He couldn't hear what had been said over the roar of his engine but didn't need to be a lip reader to catch the drift. *There's only two of them and a dozen of us. What say we teach these punks some manners?* He needed to put a stop to this right now.

He glanced over his shoulder and yelled at Becky, "Grab hold tight and hang on." He felt her tighten her grasp and bury her cheek against his shoulder.

Okay assholes, you want to dance, let's fucking dance. With that he wrenched his throttle open and with a cacophony of unearthly sound, stood his Harley on its tail. Iron monstrosity, its steel maw gaping, he ran with his front wheel above his head for better than forty yards, right through the would-be vigilantes' midst, sending them scrambling and diving to get out of the way. Behind him, Animal did the same and pulled alongside as they set the bikes back down. With a deafening blast of man-made thunder, they roared out of the campground. Roxy thrust both fists into the air ala Rocky Balboa and yelled for the sheer joy of it. She pivoted and flipped off the campers in their wake.

The message was clear—don't fuck with men who can handle a half ton of heavy metal insanity as though it was a child's toy.

Halfway back to the ranch, they pulled off at a small grocery with a pair of weather-beaten gas pumps on a single concrete island to fuel up. Becky slipped off the side. "Thank God," she said to Roxy as they hurried to the ladies room. "I nearly peed my pants when Johnny cut that dido."

"Hey, you always want to make a big exit. It helps keep the squares in line. Sure scattered that bunch of dipshits."

Refueled and relieved, Johnny led them back onto the highway. Traffic had pretty much died out and they had the road mostly to themselves. He felt good. The ride had restored his sense of balance. He still had no idea what he was going to do about Satans Kin but was confident he could handle anything they threw his way. He'd set that damn Doctor straight too.

Becky was going to be a more complicated challenge. He'd find the solution though—he had no intentions of letting her get away. He was the president of the Road Raptors Motorcycle Club. He'd put Satans Kin and Doctor in their respective places and win the heart of the old lady of his dreams. Life couldn't get any better than that.

Watching Roxy screw with the church lady and her flock had been an added bonus.

*

The camp was all astir when they rode in. The club's bikes were lined up, ready to roll and had been joined by scores of bikes from other clubs. Many fired up their engines when they saw them roll in. Wild stood at the front of the column and waved Johnny over.

"What's up?" Johnny said.

"County sheriff's got Dirty Dan locked up for assault. Dan was in a bar when some locals started dissing the colors. And get this shit—they's talking a hundred grand for bail."

"Bullshit!"

"Yeah. Anyway we're loading up to go set them straight. I was going to call you soon as we got somewhere I could get service."

He nodded approval. "Got the whole club together?"

"Everyone but Magoo."

"Where'd he get off to, ride out?"

"Naw, his bike's here, but no one can find him."

"Check the beer stash?"

"I did. Prospect says he was there earlier but left with a full case of beer."

"Shit." He rubbed the back of his neck and glanced around.

"Do we really need him? We got half the other clubs ridin' with us."

He looked back at Wild and switched his hand to his chin. Magoo was perfect for what they had to do, a walking threat all on his own. But they needed to roll before the sheriff could gather reinforcements. "Okay, ride without him."

He turned to Rebecca. "Hop off, have to take care of this. Shouldn't take long. Wait here with the rest of our ladies."

Rebecca climbed off and with Roxy, watched the combined clubs move out. "What's going on?"

"They're gonna get Dirty Dan out of the can," Roxy said.

"They're going to break him out?"

Roxy shook her head. "Shouldn't come to that. They mean to pressure the pigs into releasing Dan or lowering the bail to a sensible amount. No town wants to be invaded by a hundred plus pissed-off bikers."

"They're trying to intimidate the sheriff?"

"Yeah, that's the word, intimidate him and the town. Some of their businesses make a lot of money off the clubs and won't want to see us driven off. Or their shops damaged in a riot. Judge lower the bail to something reasonable, Johnny'll call our bail bondsman and have the money wired."

"And if they won't reduce the bail?"

"Then he'll have to take other measures. But he won't return without Dirty Dan."

TWENTY-FOUR

The afternoon heat was oppressive. The temperature at the campsite pushed triple digits and there wasn't a trace of a breeze. Dust hung heavy in the still air from the departure of so many bikes at once. Rebecca removed her leathers but was still about to melt. She could feel sweat running down each and every crack and crevice of her body. Many of the women had stripped down to their underwear or less to get relief. She thought about joining them but didn't want to sit around sweltering and twiddling her thumbs waiting for Johnny to get back. He could be gone for hours. Plus the camp stank. The stench from too many trashed bikers and biker babes relieving themselves wherever they happened to be when the urge took them permeated every breath. "Want to go for a walk?" she said to Roxy.

"Sure, where to?"

"I don't know. Somewhere where the air is fresher."

"Okay. We'll go over by the lake. Ought to be cooler there too."

"What about Satans Kin? Won't that take us by their camp?"

"We'll give those pricks a wide berth. Hey, Flo, we're going for a walk."

Flo sat slumped against a large, blue cooler, a wet rag over her face. Knees bent with her bare feet flat on the ground, clad only in red bikini panties and a dirty, white tee, sweat beaded on her arms and thighs. Most of her left leg was covered in a tattoo similar to the one on her right arm. The tat wound around her leg and across the top of her foot. She tugged the rag off to see who'd called to her. "Don't get lost," she said and draped the rag back over her face.

*

Sheva trailed after the pair. She really hadn't expected a semi to kill them. Johnny was too good a rider. Besides, she didn't want Johnny killed, just his little whore. And his whore's friend too. She'd kill them both herself if she could figure out a way to do it without getting caught. But not getting caught was the problem. That damn Wild told her if anything happened to the slut, he'd hold her responsible.

The sour odor of sweat enveloped her in a foul miasma, her black tee a steamy compress, her legs slick under her leather pants. She hadn't slept in two days. A dull throb continued to pound where the rotten cunt had sucker-punched her with the cast. The bitch would pay in blood for that. An image from the movie *Hostel 2* flashed through her mind where one woman had bathed in the blood of another. That would be perfect. But how the hell did you set up something like that? She was having trouble concentrating. She blamed her mental fog on that lucky punch rather than the uppers and blow she'd been ingesting to keep going.

She realized she was stalking them. That wouldn't do. Someone might see her and tell that asshole Wild. Or she might get so enraged tailing their saucy asses she'd attack them anyway and to hell with the consequences. She often found herself facing the results of actions she hadn't intended. She turned aside and wandered toward the creek. She needed to get her head together and think this through. There had to be something she could do.

Tears tracked down her cheeks and she swiped at them with both hands. Why did that little bitch have to show up? Her and Johnny had been doing so good. She knew he was getting ready to make her his old lady. Then he ran into that little whore.

"What does she have that I don't?" she cried aloud and wiped away more tears. "I'm twice the woman she is." After her last breast augmentation, she now measured an eye-popping 44 double-E. A trailer trash Barbie she'd overheard her plastic surgeon call her. She'd thrown her cell phone at him, gashing his forehead. The club had to bail her out on that one by convincing the prick it was in his best interests not to press charges.

Becky couldn't be any more than a C cup and stood over a foot shorter than Johnny. They looked ridiculous standing next to each other. Most of the club had started calling Becky his old lady, even though he'd never said anything about it. What did that bitch know about being an old lady? There was more to being an old lady than just riding on Johnny's bike and sucking his cock. An old lady took care of all her man's needs. At a recent party, Johnny had never been without a plate of food or a fresh beer, she'd seen to that. When he got up to go somewhere she watched his drink and took it to him if he was gone too long. She was happy to do this.

She could take care of Johnny in other ways too. Few bikers held steady jobs. Most got by as part-time bike mechanics or laborers and depended on their old ladies to help out. She didn't mind turning some tricks, was good at it. And it wasn't like other women didn't do the same damn things. Like that snooty bitch on that cable reality show, who was putting herself through law school by peddling her ass at night. The one who used all those big, fancy words only a fucking college teacher could understand. Nothing but a whore. They were all whores. Housewives were the worst, acting all high and mighty because they only fucked one man, maybe.

With the club's ridiculous ban on dealing, which she didn't understand at all, ways to make money through the club was limited. Ripping off and parting out bikes and jacking cars didn't bring in much money—was barely worth the jail time a biker would get if caught. Dealing in guns was more profitable, but guns in bulk, especially automatic weapons, were hard to come by and required a lot of front money. Also you ran the risk of selling to an undercover ATF agent or informer. The bastards were everywhere. She wasn't sure how Johnny made his money, but once her career got rolling that wouldn't be a problem.

That thought brought her to a stop. Was that what Johnny saw in the little whore, that she was an actress? More tears flowed and snot dripped from her nose. She wiped it away with the back of a hand. Becky wasn't no actress. Becky had never been in any movies, but she had—several. In her last movie, *Busty Babes in Heat Part IV,* she'd been listed as the first co-star. It was only a matter of time until Hollywood noticed her and her acting career took off. Then she could take real good care of Johnny.

But first she had to take care of his little whore.

TWENTY-FIVE

"Hey, bay-bee," a Satans Kin biker yelled. "Where you goin', huh?"

Rebecca and Roxy quickened their pace to get past the camp that was strung out for about forty yards in front of the lake, just past the ranch. Tendrils of smoke drifted from a smoldering campfire. Sleeping bags, blankets and towels had been strung over tree limbs to provide some shade. Trash, empty bottles, beer cans and wasted club members littered the ground. Motorcycles were parked everywhere, some being worked on. A large panel truck sat off to one side. The camp smelled like a backed-up sewer.

"Why don't you come over and have a seat? Here, I clear a place for you to sit." He ran his forearm across his mouth then wiped his lips and chin with both hands and laughed nastily.

"Ignore him." Roxy said.

"You think he'll follow us?"

"Not with Ducky wanting to make peace. He won't want any of his people screwing with Johnny's old lady."

"But does he know I'm Johnny's old lady?"

"Everyone knows you're Johnny's old lady."

"Hey, don't run off beautiful. C'mon over, you no regret it."

They continued on.

"What's the matter, you on the rag? No problem, I need to earn my red wings anyways."

That disgusting comment caused her to turn her head and glower at him. "Whoa, that got you attention." He laughed again and wagged his tongue at her. Several other bikers joined him and wagged their tongues too.

"Don't look at them. Ignore them," Roxy said again.

She started to look away but as she did, her gaze fell on the white-haired biker she'd noticed earlier. He was younger than she'd thought. He wasn't wagging his tongue or leering or doing anything other than watching them. His unblinking stare gave her the creeps. "Who is that white-haired biker?"

"Juggler," Roxy said without looking at him. "Real bad news. Stay as far away from him as you can."

She felt a chill despite the heat and hurried on.

They made their way to the far side of the lake, putting the water between them and the Satans Kin's camp. The water level was way down and the lake was surrounded by a barren area ranging from ten to twenty yards deep or more. The sun baked clay was fractured with a spider web of inch-wide fissures. They sat on a log, still in sight of the ranch house and she could see Doctor resting on the porch sofa again. A light breeze blew off the lake and it was a little cooler here—fresher at least. Even the sun found a stray, high cloud to duck behind for a spell.

"You know what he meant by red wings?" Roxy said.

"Yes. I overheard Dirty Dan and some other bikers I was waiting on once discussing them. I thought they were making it up to gross me out. Well, that asshole's out of luck. My period's not due for another ten days."

Roxy laughed.

"Johnny doesn't have any wings on his colors, does he?"

Roxy shook her head. "Not everyone's into that. It has to be done in front of two witnesses to count."

"Oh sick."

"Not that big a deal," Roxy said and shrugged.

Rebecca stretched out her legs and yawned.

"Tired?"

"A little."

They watched the lake—the surface calm. A hundred yards away some geese splashed about. "What's with those tattoos on Flo? She's got them on one arm and leg but not the others."

"That's all one tat. It's a dragon, covers most of her back with its head on her right shoulder blade. The tongue runs over her shoulder. One front leg runs down her right arm while the other reaches around and grasps her left tit. The left hind leg runs across her ass and down her thigh with the tail wrapping around her leg and ending on her foot. The other leg wraps around her right hip with the claws right on her twat. Had to have her pube hair lasered off for it."

"What? Why would she get a tattoo like that?"

"Got it when she was a pole dancer, said she saw some actress in a Leonardo DiCaprio movie with a dragon tat. Flo's got the hots for DiCaprio. Sometimes we call her the dragon lady if she's in a really bitchy mood."

"To her face?"

"Ah… not a good idea. Flo's got a hell of a temper. You don't have any tats?"

She shook her head. "I was afraid they might cost me a chance at a TV or movie role."

"Can't they digitize them out or somethin'?"

"If you're a star, maybe."

Across the lake, two of the larger geese got into a fight. *Probably ganders, fighting over the females. Isn't that just like males?* "How long you been riding with the club?"

"Almost a year." Roxy stretched out her legs and wiggled her feet. "Got busted for prostitution and did ninety days in the county jail. One of my last johns was a Road Raptor. He's not with the club anymore, but after my release, I started hanging around the Black List and going to parties at the clubhouse. One day, my pimp came looking for me. Johnny, Wild, Animal and some others beat the holy shit out of him. Told him if he ever bothered me again, they'd cut his balls off and make him eat them. Last I saw of that asshole."

"I guess so," Rebecca said, feeling a bit nauseous.

Roxy looked her in the eyes and grinned. "That's how I knew I'd been accepted. The club's like family and looks out for their own. Better than my real family ever did."

"Uh-huh. How long has Johnny been president?"

"Three… almost four years, I think. He was one of the chapter founders. Met the Buzzard while in the big Q."

"The big Q?"

"San Quentin."

"Johnny was in prison?"

"Yeah, Grand theft auto, assault and armed criminal action," Roxy said as though reciting a lesson. "Those charges were mostly bullshit. He was jacking a car off a parking lot when some would-be Rambo type spotted him, pulled a gun and tried to make a citizen's arrest or some such shit. I mean it wasn't even the guy's car. Anyway, Johnny takes the guy's piece away from him and smacks him in the face with it a couple of times to teach him to mind his own business. Then instead of ditching the piece, he still had it on him when the pigs nabbed him outside a convenience store. So they tacked on armed criminal action claiming he aimed to rob the store. Did five years in the Q."

She blinked and shook her head.

"Like I said, that's where he met Buzzard, although everyone called him Buzz for short. Buzz'd been Sergeant at Arms for the original chapter in Tacoma. They were cellmates and released within a few months of each other. The Buzz didn't like the asshole running Tacoma who he felt had sold him out. So he formed the LA Chapter with Johnny as his VP. When the Buzz was murdered, the club elected Johnny president."

"Murdered?"

"That's what everyone says. Pigs called it an accident despite the extra skid marks on the highway. Forced off the road and into a tree by a phantom driver, pig speak for we don't give a shit about a biker. What the fuck."

One of the ganders drove the other away. She could hear its angry squawks as it flew over. "Has Johnny done any other time?"

"Been arrested a few times, assault and other bullshit charges. That kind of shit happens when you're a biker. Pigs always trying to pin something on you. He's never done any other time that I know of. All those charges were dropped or thrown out."

She wasn't sure how she felt about this—didn't sound like the Johnny she knew at all.

Across the lake, the alpha gander mounted one of the females.

*

Sheva continued on, stumbling over the rough ground and picking her way through the brush, not sure where she was or where she was going. As long as she stuck to the creek she figured she couldn't get lost. All she needed to do was turn around and follow it back to camp. The heat was becoming unbearable and her back ached. She wished she had some more blow. Maybe it was time to head back. Surely someone in camp had some extra she could score. It wasn't considered dealing when someone sold a hit to a fellow club member while on a run. At least it wasn't as long as they didn't mark it up, which most of them did. Since she was out of money she'd need to barter something for the coke. How do you mark up a blow-job? Two times instead of one?

She still hadn't decided how to deal with Johnny's little whore. Maybe the drugs would help. That scene from *Hostel 2* kept playing in her head. Perhaps she could hang the fucking slut upside-down from a tree limb? No, that would never happen. There were too many people around who'd interfere. Besides, she didn't have a scythe to carve the bitch up with. Still, it was nice to daydream about. The whore's hot blood splattering all over her nude body while the naked cunt screamed her head off and begged for mercy. She got wet thinking about it.

Deep in these pleasant thoughts, and concentrating on where she stepped, she happened to look up and slowed to a stop. Seated on a fallen log a few feet away, amidst a scatter of mostly empty beer cans, sat Magoo. *What's this big goon doing out here? Why didn't he ride out with the club? Oh yeah, Wild couldn't find him.*

Even though Magoo faced straight at her, he gave no indication of having seen her. She altered her course to go around him, but as she did, he spoke in a voice so low and sad she almost missed it.

"It ain't fair," he said.

TWENTY-SIX

Johnny was good and pissed. He had an almost overwhelming urge to torch the town. Burn the goddamned place to the ground. But any pleasure he'd receive from that would be short-lived and scant comfort over the next thirty plus years he'd spend behind bars. Still... he shook his head. One thing for sure, after this run, they were through with Doctor and his damn ranch. They'd find a new location for next year's Memorial Day Run.

It was a shakedown. He'd suspected as much when they'd arrived to find the sheriff hadn't called any surrounding towns or the state police for backup. Except for a couple of bars, the downtown was deserted. The pigs hadn't even impounded Dirty Dan's bike. He told Wild to take some brothers and locate the motorcycle before someone ripped it off. Then he followed the sheriff into his back office for a private talk.

The lawman sat in a swivel chair and leaned back, the chair squeaking in protest. He plopped his feet onto the desk, crossed his ankles and laced his fingers together over his belly and gave him a long, hard stare.

Okay asshole, I get the message, you're not scared of us. A pointed letter opener lay on the desk. Johnny wondered what the pig's reaction would be if he suddenly snatched it up and buried it in the fat fuck's throat. Instead he pulled up a wobbly, wooden chair, the only option, and sat across from him.

"That boy of yours, in a lot of trouble," the sheriff said at last, speaking slowly and pronouncing boy like some southern cracker.

He didn't respond. No point in doing so until this bastard finished his spiel. And the less he said the better as he was sure the sheriff had a tape-recorder going somewhere—camera too. He glanced around. The room was small, cramped and smelled of stale sweat and rot. It was hot. The window AC unit, despite sounding like a taxiing airliner, wasn't putting out much but lukewarm steam. Water dripped from one corner of the useless appliance into a red, plastic bucket. An oscillating fan on a counter stirred the humid air and rustled papers stuck on a bulletin board.

"Judge takes a dim view of law-abiding citizens being attacked. Says your boy is looking at ten years hard time minimum." John Law paused to let that sink in and when he didn't respond, said, "Means it too. Judge is one ornery son of a bitch," and snorted out a laugh. "I should know. That prick is my brother-in-law." The sheriff paused again and cocked an eyebrow. When he still made no response, the man said, "Haven't gotten around to running a record check on your boy yet. Wonder what I'd find if'n I do?"

He wanted to yell at the asshole to cut the shit and the cornpone act and tell him how much, but managed to remain quiet and shrug.

The sheriff picked up some important-looking, legal-size papers and studied them for nearly a minute before tossing them on the desk, just out of Johnny's reach and half-covered them with a legal pad. "Look, I know your boy was just having a good time and got a little carried away. You bikers all too touchy 'bout your colors. And I know how dumb some of those loudmouths in the bar can get, especially the two your boy assaulted. Shame to see him go to prison for just defending your club's honor. Maybe I can convince them to settle out of court, if'n your willing to be reasonable."

"How reasonable?"

"Ten grand, same as you'd pay for the bail, only this way the charges get dropped and there's no trial."

"Bullshit, rather pay the ten grand bail and take our chances in court. We win, we get the money back."

"Your lawyer work for free?"

"Rather pay that asshole than you."

The sheriff's face darkened. "You gotta smart mouth. Think I was born yesterday? We both know your boy won't show. You bikers look at bail as a get out of jail free card."

"Ten's too much. One and everything gets dropped."

"Guess I better have that record check run," the sheriff said, stood and hitched up his pants. "See where else your boy is wanted."

He shrugged again and the sheriff left the room.

He sat back, lit a cigarette and crossed his legs. He wasn't about to touch those papers the pig had left so invitingly close. Let the prick nail him for smoking in a public building if he wanted—a misdemeanor at best. The sheriff would eventually grow tired of watching and come back in. The bastard also wasn't turning Dan over to anyone else either. No payday in that. Oh, if the asshole found something he'd threaten. But as far as he knew, except for some traffic tickets, Dan was clean.

He glanced at his watch, faked a yawn, laced his fingers behind his head and did his best to look bored. *Well shit!* Looked like he was in for a long, expensive afternoon of negotiations and bullshit theatrics. Might make him late for his meet with Ducky.

*

"What ain't fair?" Sheva said and staggered to a halt. It was an automatic response on her part, triggered by innate curiosity, as she truly didn't give a damn what Magoo thought about anything, but the words were out her mouth before she realized she'd spoken them. She waited for an answer.

"Johnny," Magoo finally muttered.

"Johnny?"

Magoo blinked several times, sat up straighter and looked at her through blood-shot eyes. "Not fair he gets all the hot bitches. First you, now Becky."

She opened her mouth to curse him for comparing her to that slut when the impact of his words slammed into her brain. She snapped her mouth shut before anything else escaped and gaped at him, hardly believing what she'd just heard. *Is this goon pining for that little whore?*

His head sagged onto his chest. "I seen her first... real friend wouldn't cut in." He crushed the empty beer can he held and tossed it away.

She licked her chapped lips and looked around. They were alone. Everyone else must be back at the camp trying to stay cool. It felt like an oven under these trees despite the sparse shade they provided. Even the bugs were quiet, nothing buzzing around or chirping like they had all night. She picked up a plastic ring holder that still held an unopened beer, tugged the can out and popped the tab.

Magoo watched her closely, his brow wrinkled, face bathed in sweat.

She approached him cautiously and sat on another rotting log near him. "You're right," she said as sympathetically as she could and handed him the beer. "A real friend wouldn't."

He glared hard at her and she was afraid she'd made a mistake, but then he took the beer from her. After a long swallow, he wiped his lips with the back of a hand. "Fuckin' right he wouldn't."

She let out the breath she'd been holding. "Shame, too," she said, picking her words carefully. "Becky don't even like Johnny."

"What the hell you talkin' 'bout?"

"I overheard some of the other old ladies," she lied. "They say Becky just wanted to ride with the club and only rode with Johnny 'cause he's the one who asked her. One of them used to waitress with her. Says Becky likes to party and get high, but's afraid to while with Johnny." She shrugged. "You know how he feels 'bout drugs." She shook her head. "Too bad you didn't ask her first."

Magoo wiped at his face and stared at the ground. "Now she's Johnny's old lady."

"He's never said she is. Why don't you talk to her? Tell her how you feel 'bout her."

He slowly shook his head, "No, she's ridin' with Johnny."

"Johnny's not here."

"Where'd he go?"

"He and the club rode out to get Dirty Dan outta jail. The county sheriff locked Dan up for—"

"They rode without me?" Magoo jerked his head up and scowled.

"They couldn't..." She paused as an idea burst into life. But to make it work she'd have to play it right. This guy was too unstable and might beat her half to death if he didn't believe her. "I... I shouldn't tell you—for the good of the club."

"Shouldn't tell me what?"

She bit her lip, tried to look worried and glanced around as though looking for a way out. An Academy Award performance, she was sure.

"What shouldn't you tell me?" He grabbed her by an arm and she winced at his grip. "Tell me, goddamn it!"

"I… I heard Johnny tell Wild not to look for you. That he didn't need you and he didn't want you riding with them."

"What the fuck!" he yelled, turned her loose, shot to his feet and loomed over her. "Why'd he say that?"

"I don't know. I just heard him say it."

"Son of a bitch!" He threw down his half-empty beer can and kicked at a pile of empty cans, scattering them.

"I'm sorry, I shouldn't have told you," she said meekly, got to her feet and placed a hand on his shoulder. "But I hate the way Johnny treats you." She added a sob for effect. "You're supposed to be his best friend. But ever since he became president, he's treated you like shit. You owe him nothing. And you don't need his permission to talk to Becky. I saw her and Roxy over by the lake. Maybe you can take her for a ride somewhere. Just the two of you and you can tell her how you feel. Just don't say I told you to. Me and her got off on the wrong foot."

He spun away, turned and locked eyes with her. His had taken on an insane glow, his face dark-red. He kept clenching and unclenching his hands while he shook with barely controlled rage. She got ready to flee for her life if he started her way. To her immense relief, he turned and stormed off through the brush.

She exhaled again and watched him go, unsure of what she'd set in motion. Whatever she'd unleashed, she needed to distance herself from it as fast as she could. More blow now forgotten, she needed to get back to camp. When this went down she needed to have a good alibi established, with witnesses. Flo, she was the key. Make sure Flo knew she was nowhere near the explosion.

And given Johnny and Magoo's tempers, an explosion it would be—physical and violent. The club wouldn't like seeing two club founders falling out over some bitch. Women didn't count for shit when it came to club brothers. Something like this could tear the club apart. Wild would be forced to act. At the very least, Johnny would have to send Becky away. That wouldn't be as satisfying as bathing in the whore's blood, but it'd do. And that was the very least that could happen. The most that could happen? She had no idea. Maybe she'd get lucky and find out.

TWENTY-SEVEN

Chico was ready to kill Ducky's mole—Elwood. The guy was a tweaker and driving him nuts. At least the shit for brains had enough sense not to ride out with his club when they'd gone along to help spring the Road Raptor from jail. Or maybe he'd been flying so high he hadn't realized they were leaving. Chico couldn't believe Ducky trusted his life to this junkie's aim. Didn't he know the guy was a meth-head?

Elwood couldn't stand still, kept shifting from foot to foot, glancing around and trembling. The guy's hands were covered with scabs that he kept picking at and he couldn't look Chico in the eyes. He was so soaked with sweat he looked like he'd just climbed out of the fucking lake—smelled like it too.

Chico wouldn't want to be within a half-mile of the ranch house when this cat burst in and opened fire. What was that movie where some junkie barged in on the Saturday Night Fever guy and some black dude, emptied an automatic at them from four feet away, and missed both of them? No man, they could have their damn patch back before he'd be sitting in Doctor's parlor come four o'clock.

"Okay mano, one more time, you know what to do?"

"Yeah man, yeah. Jeez, we've been over it like a million times. I got it man. I got it. Jeez."

"And no more crank until this is over."

"Yeah, yeah, yeah." Elwood wiped snot from his nose with the back of a hand.

"I don't need to tell you what Juggler do to you, you fuck this up, right?"

"Right man, Juggler. Yeah I got it. I'm cool, I'm cool."

Chico shook his head. What the hell. He'd delivered the message. The rest was up to this strung-out puke. Maybe he'd pull it off, who knows? "Okay, I tell Juggler you ready."

"Yeah, tell Juggler I'm ready. Tell him I'll grease those cocksuckers good. Just like Iraq." With that Elwood finally looked him in the face and laughed like a madman.

Chico turned and walked away. He had to get clear of this prick before he strangled him. He hoped the fuckup did pull it off. With Johnny iced, maybe that hot little bitch of his would be more interested in that seat he'd offered her earlier. After all, she'd need a ride home.

*

Rebecca peeled her sweaty tee off and tied it around her waist, leaving her clad in jeans and a white bra. The jeans would have to go when they got back to their camp. "I'll work on my tan," she said.

"Flo's probably got suntan lotion," Roxy said, taking her seriously. "She usually thinks of everything."

She gave Roxy a thin smile in response. They were nearing camp but her mind was still back at the lake, trying to digest what she'd learned about Johnny's criminal past. It seemed so out of character to her. Subconsciously she slipped her phone out of a back pocket to check for messages—something she did dozens of times a day—forgetting there was no service here. She glanced at the phone. She had a text message. It must have come in while they were on their morning ride and she hadn't heard the alert over the sound of the bike. There was no name, only a phone number she didn't recognize. She opened the text. "Oh, my God," she said and halted.

"What?" Roxy said.

"The Afterglow Theater is casting *Macbeth* with open auditions later this week."

"That's Shakespeare ain't it?"

"Yes."

"You gonna try for a part?"

"You bet I am. Wonder who sent this?" She turned her phone over as if that would tell her anything and shook her head.

"Does it matter?"

"Not really." She slipped the phone into a rear pocket. "I'll need to get there early. There'll be a lot of competition. Oh wow, if I could add a performance at the Afterglow to my resume… hell, if nothing else, maybe I can snag a role as one of the witches."

"Get to ride a broom?"

"No silly." She gave Roxy a playful shove. "The Afterglow is pretty artsy. With my luck they'll want the witches to perform in the nude. I've seen *Macbeth* done that way."

"And you'd let that stop you?"

She thought about it for a moment and shook her head. "No, it'd be a night scene and the stage lights will be dimmed."

"Maybe they'll spray paint you green."

"I—"

"Becky, wait up," came a shout from behind.

She turned to find Magoo striding toward them, looking sweatier and more disheveled than ever. He wasn't wearing a shirt under his cut, his hair and beard a tangled, greasy mess. Her flesh grew even hotter. "What the hell?" she whispered. "What's he want?"

"What the hell do you want?" Roxy said as he stopped a couple of feet away, swaying slightly. He smelled like a loaded beer truck that had rolled several times.

"Wanna talk to Becky?"

"Well, Becky don't wanna talk to you."

Rebecca caught Roxy's arm and squeezed it. "It's okay. What do you want, Magoo?"

"Go for a ride?"

"What?" Roxy said with a bark of laughter.

She squeezed Roxy's arm again to quiet her. "Magoo, I need to get back to camp," she said, doing her best to make her voice sound reasonable. "Johnny should be back soon."

Roxy took a step closer. "Why do you think she'd go for a ride with you?"

"Maybe you like me," he said, directing his answer to Rebecca.

She was too surprised to respond while Roxy broke into a fit of laughter.

"Get outta here," Roxy finally said and shoved at his chest with a hand.

His right fist shot out and buried itself in Roxy's side, bending her double. She let out a loud yelp and collapsed in a heap.

"You son of a bitch!" Rebecca screamed and hit him in the face as hard as she could with her cast. For all the good it did, she might as well have punched a statue. The only effects her blow had was to send a bolt of electric agony shooting up her arm and to trigger a reflex action in Magoo. He backhanded her across the mouth, knocking her to the ground.

She landed flat on her stomach and rolled over onto her back. Her heart pounded in her chest and she felt dizzy. Blood trickled down her chin from her split lower lip. Next to her, Roxy doubled up into a fetal position, her face contorted in pain. Magoo towered over them, the sun casting a shadow over his features.

Magoo dug in his mouth with a finger and spit out a gob of blood. "Stupid cunt. Jus' wanted to talk." He stepped forward and reached down a hand to help her up.

"Get away from me!" she screamed and crab-crawled backwards.

Roxy let loose with a horrible screech of pain.

"Goddamn it," Magoo said, frowned and glanced around. "Go somewheres we'll be alone."

She rolled back over and scrambled to her feet, but he snagged her arm just above her cast. "No! Turn me loose!" She clawed and dug at his vice-like grip while he effortlessly pulled her toward his bike.

She tried to dig in her heels but skidded in the dirt and nearly lost her balance. If she fell, he'd drag her. She looked around in desperation. Several people watched them but none made a move to intervene. A short distance away, several women from the club stood at the edge of their campground, appearing frozen in place. "Help me!" she cried, as Magoo continued to pull her toward his bike.

She saw Flo stagger to her feet, rub her forehead and yawn. Then Flo's eyes went wide and she paused in mid yawn. "Magoo… what the hell are you doing?"

He ignored Flo's call and climbed on his bike.

"Help me!" Rebecca yelled again, made eye contact with Flo and tried once more to pull free.

"Magoo! Turn her loose!"

Instead, he started the bike, seized Rebecca by the back of her neck and slung her over the fuel tank.

She landed hard, a bolt of pain shot through her torso, the gas cap dug into her stomach. The phone slipped from her rear pocket and tumbled to the ground just out of reach. Her world turned-upside down she tried to get her breath. She managed to raise her head and saw Flo snatch up a stick of firewood, and brandishing it like a club, run toward them. Several other women followed behind her, their yells drowned by the ungodly din of the Harley's engine. Then everything was lost in an explosion of dirt as the rear tire dug in and became a spinning blur.

*

Flo flung the piece of wood at Magoo's back but it fell several feet short and tumbled along in his wake. She slowed to a stop. "What the…" She'd been sound asleep when the yelling awoke her. She hoped this was just a bad dream. A cloth caught her attention and she picked it up—Becky's T-shirt. "Well… hell."

"Johnny ain't gonna like this," one of the women who joined her said.

Flo stared at her, too dumbfounded to respond to that inane statement.

"Here's her cell phone," Brandi said and picked it up.

"Oh, shit… Roxy," someone else said and pointed past Flo.

Roxy staggered toward them, clutching her side. She let out a shriek of pain and collapsed.

Flo dropped the tee, ran over and knelt beside her. "Roxy, what the hell is going on?"

"Magoo hit me."

She pulled up Roxy's shirt. Roxy's side was purple and swelling. She poked it gently which resulted in a scream. A thin trickle of dark blood ran out the corner of Roxy's mouth and down her chin. "Oh, shit."

She tugged a set of keys from her pocket and tossed them to Brandi. "Bring the Silverado over. We'll take her to the ranch house."

"But Doc's not a people doctor," Brandi said.

"I know that lard-ass is a horse doctor but he's all we got. Move it."

She turned back to Roxy and smoothed the hair off her forehead. Her brow was hot. "Hang in there baby. We'll get you help."

"How's she doing?" Sheva hovered over them, a concerned look on her face.

"I don't know. We'll get her to Doc."

"Good." *I hope she dies.* Sheva had almost cum on the spot when she'd seen Magoo sling that whore over his gas tank and roar off. It'd been all she could do not to run around giving high fives.

"Becky's been nothing but trouble since she got here," one of Sheva's friends who stood next to her said.

Flo gave her a withering look. "Trouble's not the word for what's going to happen when Johnny gets back. He'll go berserk."

TWENTY-EIGHT

It cost the club thirty-two hundred to get the charges dropped on Dirty Dan. Johnny figured the two "victims" wouldn't see more than a Franklin a piece of that money, with the sheriff and his brother-in-law splitting the rest.

He left the courthouse where he picked up the order dismissing the charges. He read through the document—he'd insisted in getting it in writing—and it looked okay. He was getting good at deciphering legal double-talk.

Tiny, the club treasurer met him coming out the door and handed him an envelope. "Thirty-two Ben Franklins," he said. "This run's getting expensive."

Johnny stuffed the envelope along with the court order inside his cut, shook out a cigarette and lit it. He sucked the smoke deep into his lungs and then exhaled. "Where we gassed up yesterday, there's overnight trucker parking."

"Just off the interstate."

"Tell Animal to take some mamas over there tonight and put 'em to work. They're not doing nothing but sitting around on their asses. Have him take Dirty Dan and the prospect Ronnie with him.

And find the other club presidents. Tell 'em we're good and they can split if they want. Tell 'em thanks."

Across the street a red light flashed, a warning siren sounded and a garage door went up on the fire station. A red, box-like ambulance pulled out. With lights flashing and siren warbling, it hung a right onto the street and wailed off, accelerating rapidly.

"Better not be headed to the ranch," Tiny said.

Johnny left him and walked back to the jail. Wild and a handful of brothers stood in the street in front of the pig station, smoking and drinking beer. They had Dirty Dan's ride with them. The rest of the club lounged on their bikes parked along the curb. Empty longnecks were scattered around a *No Littering* sign.

"Where'd you find it?"

"Bunch'a wetbacks were loading it on a pickup. They scattered on foot when they saw us." Wild said.

"They's gonna stay on foot," Animal said. "Least ways till they get four new tires, a windshield, lights all around, a radiator, plug wires, battery and battery cables. Would'a cut up the upholstery but it was already in shreds."

"And they better change the oil," Wild said. "Prospect here," he gave the young biker Ronnie a shove, "ripped off a sugar jar and emptied it down the oil fill."

"Oil fill, huh?"

"Yeah," Ronnie said. "Only a punk puts sugar in the gas tank. That don't do nothin'. Flush the tank, change the filters and you're good to go. But next time Jose fires up this motherfucker, it's gonna blow a hole right through the engine block."

Johnny chuckled and entered the jail. The last thing the club needed was for Dirty Dan to smart off to the sheriff and get tossed back into the can. He handed the bastard the court order and waited while the ass-wipe took his time reading it. Finally, the sheriff nodded to one of his men and Dan was brought in by a pair of deputies, his hands cuffed in front of him. Dan's thin face was badly battered and he walked like he was hurting. Still, he managed a grin when he saw Johnny.

"That necessary?" Johnny said.

The sheriff glanced at him then at Dan. "We never touched him." He held out his hand, palm up.

Johnny gave him a dirty look but decided not to press it. He slapped the envelope onto the sheriff's paw, watched him open it and count the money.

The sheriff grunted and locked the money in a desk drawer.

When he started to place the court order in a tray, Johnny snatched it out of his hand. "I'll hang on to this."

"Right. Take your man and go."

One of the deputies removed the cuffs, grasped Dan by an arm and shoved him in Johnny's direction. Dan jerked his arm away and stretched it over his head a couple of times. He grimaced but said nothing.

In the hallway, Johnny said, "Pigs do that to you?"

"Naw. Two pukes I decked, some of their buds jumped me. Bunch of pussies. Don't even know how to rat pack someone. All tried to stomp me at once. Ended up kicking each other more than they did me."

Johnny didn't bother to tell him it'd been a set up—wouldn't have made any difference anyway. Dan defended the colors, and that's what mattered.

The club let out a cheer when Johnny led Dan outside. Dan clasped his hands over his head, shook them and managed another grin. "Good, you found my bike," he said. "Was afraid some greaser would rip it off."

"Some tried."

The club fired up their bikes while Johnny and Dan mounted theirs. Johnny felt tired again and still had that meet with Ducky awaiting him. He'd need to keep his wits about him, dealing with that piece of shit. He hoped that didn't take long or get out of hand. He wanted to get back to Becky and spend time with her.

*

The ground blasted past Rebecca's face. She stopped struggling and tried to keep her balance as they bounded over the rough trail. Draped over the gas tank there was nothing for her to grab hold of. She was afraid she was going to slip off one side or the other and end up under the Harley's rear wheel. Her body hour-glassed, her head dangled scarcely off the earth. Dust and grit from the front tire peppered her face, filled her mouth and nostrils. She could hardly breathe. Blood rushed to her head, her senses pummeled by the deafening roar of the engine only inches away.

They hit a bump, tossing her into the air. She slammed back down, knocking the air from her lungs. She knew she was going to die. She was going off head first. She kicked with her legs, legs that felt encased in concrete, to try and regain her balance. All her struggles did was to propel her forward. She flailed with her arms, felt a fingernail tear loose when she brushed the ground, her scream of terror whipped away by the wind along with her tears. At the last instant, Magoo grabbed her by her rear waistband and yanked her back onto the fuel tank. Her bladder let go, drenching her jeans with hot urine.

After she nearly slipped off a second time, Magoo slid the motorcycle to a stop. He tugged her off the fuel tank and onto her feet by the idling bike. "Get on," he said.

"Please don't hurt me," she begged. Her legs shook so hard she could barely stand. The rear and inside of her jeans were saturated. Urine continued to trickle down her thighs and calves

"Get on."

"Please let me go."

He grabbed her arm. "I said get on, damn it!"

She started to climb on behind him but he jerked her forward. "In front."

She managed to half climb, half be hauled, onto the front edge of his seat. He squeezed in tight against her. His huge arms imprisoned her as he grasped the ape-hangers. Both of his arms were completely sleeved out in tattoos. The stench of his beer-soaked sweat engulfed her, his hot breath steamed against the side of her face. She could taste the anger that radiated off him in waves. He gunned the throttle and they took off at a breakneck pace, bouncing over the rough lane. When he joined the other dirt road he increased his speed even more.

Without a windshield, she caught the full brunt of the hot air they raced through. The sun beat down mercilessly, scorched her exposed flesh and she felt like she was going to vomit. She shouldn't have taken her T-shirt off. She had no idea what had become of it. The shirt was no longer tied around her waist. Not only was she scared half out of her wits but completely humiliated for having wet her pants. Magoo either hadn't noticed or didn't care. She prayed they'd meet Johnny and the rest of the club returning from the town so he could rescue her. But they reached the blacktop without encountering anyone.

Magoo paused on the shoulder of the highway, letting his bike idle. This road was deserted too. He sat there as if in deep thought, gazing off into the barren landscape. Did he have any idea where he was taking her? And what did he intend to do after they got there? He was crazy and drunk, capable of anything. Roxy shouldn't have laughed at him.

In the distance she could hear a siren coming from the direction of town. It was drawing closer. Maybe if she moved fast enough she could duck under an arm and be off the bike before he could stop her. With normal handlebars she'd have no chance but with the ape-hangers... she took a deep breath and made ready to make her move as soon as the emergency vehicle came into sight. *There are the lights—*

Magoo spun the Harley to the right onto the blacktop and opened the throttle wide. She rocked back against his body. Any chance to escape was gone. To jump off at this speed would be suicide. She'd have to hope for another opportunity.

Where was Johnny?

TWENTY-NINE

Johnny pulled to a stop at the crest of the last rise to again look down on the ranch. He always wanted to know what he was leading the club into. Once more he didn't like what he saw. The ambulance had come to the ranch and was parked in front of Doctor's ramshackle building, lights flashing, a mob of people gathered around it. Worse, both of the club's pickups were there with the Silverado Flo drove right beside the emergency vehicle. *Shit! Goddamn it!* He was surprised to see no pigs. No doubt a small army of them would soon descend on the site.

He sped down the slope but had to slow to a crawl as he neared the ranch house. He dismounted, figuring he could make better time on foot. With Wild right behind him, he forced his way through the throng. Most of the women gathered nearest the ambulance were from his club and scattered as he approached. His blood pressure soared, this was getting worse by the minute.

Flo spotted him and hustled over. She looked upset.

He grabbed her by an arm and jerked her close, barely resisting the urge to shake her. "Who the fuck called for a damn ambulance? You?"

Flo shook her head frantically. "No... it was Doc. It's okay, he says the fire chief owes him some favors. Called him on a private line. There won't be no pigs. They're going to pass it off as appendicitis or something."

Johnny let out a hot breath. That explained the lack of cops. *Might work*. He turned Flo loose. "Who's hurt?"

"Foxy Roxy, they think her spleen is ruptured and need to get her to the hospital."

"What happened?"

"Magoo hit her."

"Why the hell he do that?" Wild said. "She smart off to him?"

"I don't know."

Johnny looked around for Becky. He didn't see her anywhere. The EMT crew had Roxy strapped to a stretcher and were lifting her into the ambulance. He was surprised Becky wasn't there. "Where's Becky?"

Flo didn't answer.

He looked around some more then directly at Flo. Now Flo looked scared. In fact she looked terrified. She wouldn't meet his eyes and her lower lip trembled. He grabbed her arm and jerked her close again, getting right in her face. "Where the hell is Becky?"

"Well... that's our other problem," she said, her voice about to break, still not meeting his eyes. "Magoo took her."

"Took her? Whatta you mean, took her?"

"He took her—kidnapped her. Threw her over the front of his bike and lit out with her kicking and screaming."

"Why'd he do that?" Wild said.

"I don't know." Flo dissolved into tears and finally looked at Johnny. "I tried to stop him. But... but I... I couldn't reach them in time. I'm sorry, Johnny. I tried. Magoo's gone crazy."

He released her with a little shove and stared at her. He felt a terrible emptiness in the pit of his stomach and his flesh turned cold. Disbelief slowly morphed into anger and then exploded into murderous rage.

"I'll kill that son of a bitch!"

*

"Oh, shit," Wild said and watched Johnny stride to the F150, where he flung open the door and felt under the seat. Johnny withdrew the Smith & Wesson .357 Magnum hidden there, checked the load, snapped the cylinder shut and stuffed the gun into his waistband behind his back.

He wanted to intervene but knew better than to try. There'd be no reasoning with Johnny until he calmed down—if he calmed down. Hopefully he'd cool off by the time they found Magoo and Becky. But if Magoo hurt her, or worse, he'd better keep going until he reached Brazil. Even that might not be far enough.

Johnny walked back to Flo. "Where'd he go?" he said, his voice like dry ice.

"I don't know." Flo licked her lips and glanced around. "I checked with the other clubs that just returned but they didn't see him. Neither did the ambulance crew. They couldn't have missed him by much."

"He didn't go to town or we'd seen him," Wild said. "Must'a gone the other way."

Without another word, Johnny turned and started for his bike.

Wild hurried after him. "Johnny, what are you going to do?"

"Gonna get my woman back and kill Magoo."

He grabbed Johnny by an arm and jerked him to a stop, turning him half around. "That's not how we handle things in the club, you know that. Magoo's a brother. He gets a chance to explain himself."

Johnny shucked his arm loose and got in Wild's face. "Fuck that. This is between me and him."

"The club won't like it."

"The club can stay the hell out of it. You too."

Before he could say anything else they were interrupted by Doctor who had to call three times to get Johnny's attention.

"What?" Johnny snapped and spun toward the man who waddled their way.

Doctor huffed over and stopped, out of breath and looking like a candidate for a massive heart attack. "You and Wild have a meeting with Duc—"

"The meet's off."

"You can't do that," Doctor said, still trying to catch his breath. "I spent a lot of time and effort setting this up. Ducky will—"

"To hell with Ducky and to hell with you." Johnny turned his back on him and strode away.

"Wild, you gotta talk some sense into him. This is much more important than some stupid twat. The two of you can't afford to miss this meeting. Think what's best for your club."

"You heard him, the meets off."

"But—"

"And you can tell Ducky and Tramp to go to hell for me too." He hustled after Johnny, leaving Doctor standing by himself.

Several brothers had wandered over to find out what was going on. They quickly scrambled back to their bikes and filled in the others while they mounted up.

Johnny climbed on his bike, fired it up and roared out.

Wild mounted his, waved for the club to follow and raced after his president who was pushing hard. He flew up the slope and down the hard-packed trail concentrating on keeping control of his heavy street bike. Where the trail joined the dirt road, he chanced a glance over his shoulder. The club was strung out in a line behind him as far as he could see.

He pulled onto the dirt road and gunned the throttle then slammed on the brakes and skidded to a stop nearly running into Johnny, who had also slid to a stop.

Heading toward them were a pair of bikes that Johnny flagged down. The bikers were both Hangmen MC. "You come from town?" Johnny said.

"No man, the other way."

"You pass a biker with a woman slung over his gas tank?"

The Hangmen looked at each other then back at Johnny. "No," one of them said. After a brief pause, he added, "Did pass a biker with ape-hangers. Had a bitch seated in front of him—dark hair, in a bra and jeans."

"That's them," Wild said. "Gotta be. Only Magoo rides with them damn ape-hangers."

"Where?" Johnny said.

"Four… maybe five miles down the highway."

Johnny rode off without another word.

"Thanks brother," Wild yelled and followed after Johnny again.

The brief stop had allowed some of the club to catch up.

When Johnny reached the highway, he didn't slow down, instead raced out cutting off a car that slammed on its brakes, slewed sideways into the other lane and got clipped by an oncoming pickup that couldn't dodge him. The truck made no move to stop but kicked it in the ass and kept going.

"Oh shit," Wild said and paused on the shoulder as the rest of the club spilled onto the highway on both sides of the damaged car. *Damn it!* Only one person was in the car. The driver looked okay. The car was an older model Oldsmobile that had seen better days. He motioned Tiny to a stop. "Take care of this. We don't want the pigs involved."

Tiny dismounted, walked over and rapped on the driver's door window.

Wild rode on. Tiny could be very persuasive. He'd convince the driver it was in his best interests to accept a quick cash settlement and not involve the law. He shook his head. If Johnny didn't let up, someone was going to get hurt or killed.

But he knew Johnny wasn't about to let up. He'd been betrayed by a life-long friend and brother. He couldn't allow Magoo to get away with it. Why the hell had Magoo carried off Becky?

THIRTY

Juggler didn't like the vibes coming from the ranch house. Who in hell called an ambulance? And why hadn't any pigs shown? It was a golden opportunity for them to swarm in, in force.

Ducky was still perched on his tree stump throne but got to his feet as Tramp approached. "Time to go?"

"Sit your ass back down. Johnny called off the meet."

"Because of all that racket we've been hearing?"

Tramp nodded. "According to that fat-ass vet, Magoo snatched Johnny's new bitch. Slung her over his gas tank and rode out with her dangling off each side. Johnny and his club rode out to get her back."

"No Shit?" Ducky threw back his head and roared with laughter. He laughed long and hard, bending over and slapping his knee several times. He turned a complete circle in his hilarity, nearly stumbling over his seat. "Magoo kidnapped Johnny's bitch! I bet Johnny's going ape shit."

"I don't see what's so damn funny. Blows our plan all to shit."

Ducky quit laughing and frowned. "Yeah... it does." He rubbed the back of his neck and shook his head once. "Fucking Johnny, always had a soft spot for bitches. Well, damn."

"Want I should try and reset the meet?"

Ducky shrugged and glanced around.

Juggler had heard enough. He needed to take control before this pair of morons screwed up everything. "How 'bout I take a crew, find Johnny and Wild and kill 'em both?"

"That'd work," Ducky said and motioned at the Uzi lying next to his tree stump. "I'll hang onto this one, but you can take the other five."

"I thought the plan was to pin this on the Storm Troopers," Tramp said.

"I'll take our mole with me. We don't need him anymore. I'll leave his carcass and one of the Uzis near their bodies."

Ducky nodded.

"What if someone sees you ridin' around out there?" Tramp said.

"What if someone does?" Ducky broke in. "Juggler can say they're helping Johnny look for his bitch. After all, that's the kind of caring guys we are."

Tramp snorted, shook his head and glared at Juggler. "So's you're just going to ride around and hope you stumble over them somehows?"

"No. I think I know where Magoo went."

Ducky studied him for several moments, then his eyes widened. "You think he went to that old shit-dump shack we found, don't you?"

He nodded. "Even if he didn't, it's one of the places Johnny will look."

"Johnny has a big head start on you," Tramp said.

He kept his face impassive and his voice as devoid of emotion as he could, instead of telling this idiot to shut the hell up. "Riding Harleys, Johnny'll have to stick to the roads. I'll cut cross country."

When Tramp didn't respond, he turned to Ducky. "I'll need the dirt bikes outta the truck."

"Take em."

He turned and walked away before either one of them could come up with any bright ideas of their own, like maybe wanting to meet their mole. Either Ducky or Tramp get a look at that tweaker, and they'd use both Elwood and him for target practice.

*

Flo watched the EMT crew remove Roxy from the ambulance and load her onto the MedEvac chopper that had put down near the ranch house. The paramedic had decided Roxy was too badly injured to chance the long ambulance ride to the hospital. Flo said a silent prayer as the bird lifted off in a whirlwind of dust and whining machinery. If Roxy died and Johnny didn't kill Magoo, she would.

God damn that miserable son of a bitch. Roxy had never harmed a soul in her life. All she ever wanted was just to belong. The Road Raptors were her family even though many of them treated her badly. She never complained and always remained cheerful. Now when she'd found a friend in Becky, this had to happen. But then Becky wasn't here anymore either, was she?

The paramedic, who looked all of seventeen, walked over carrying a clipboard. He stopped a couple of feet away and studied her, his lips forming a scowl. "I suppose you tripped and fell too?"

"Ran into a bear. You should see him."

The man's scowl deepened and he shook his head.

"How's Roxy doing?"

"I have her stabilized, but she needs to go into surgery. I called the hospital and alerted them of her condition so they'll be ready for her on arrival." He glanced at his clipboard, ink pen at the ready.

"Do you know if there is anyone we should contact, husband, any relatives and alert them to her injuries?"

"She has a couple of sisters. The younger one lives near Frisco. God alone knows where the other is." The last time she'd seen Roxy's older sister, the woman appeared hell-bent on killing herself with drugs.

"Someone should let them know."

"I'll do what I can."

The paramedic nodded his head, made a notation and stuck the clipboard under his left arm. "I'm going to notify the authorities," he said and glanced around. "I can't understand why a sheriff's deputy hasn't shown up."

"Notify them about what? It was an accident. She slipped and fell."

"Yeah, right, and landed on someone's fist I suppose? Or was it their boot? I've seen enough abuse in my life to recognize it and by law I have to report it."

"You might want to check with your boss first, sonny."

He gave her a look that told her just exactly what he thought of his boss, turned and walked away.

Damn. Fucking do-gooder. Johnny's gonna love this. She thought about trying to threaten or sex the paramedic into keeping his mouth shut but didn't do either. She'd be wasting her time. There was something hard in paramedic's eyes, determined. He wasn't near as young as he looked. Besides, if his boss couldn't control him, all she'd do is make matters worse by getting involved. *Damn, damn, damn.*

*

A trio of Satans Kin bikers unloaded a half dozen dirt bikes from the back of a panel truck while Juggler watched. He'd sent Chico to fetch Elwood. He snorted and folded his arms across his chest. Ducky had screwed up calling Elwood a mole. The proper term was assassin. Ducky screwed up everything, ignorant bastard.

He wanted to get this bullshit with the Road Raptors over with so he could get back to the important business. It'd been a good plan. He'd provided Elwood with a pair of 9mm Browning Hi-Powers with thirteen round loads. No doubt that meth-head wouldn't have stopped shooting until he'd emptied both guns. With luck, Elwood would have killed everyone in the room, including Ducky, Tramp and that fat fuck of a vet. He'd neglected to tell Elwood the part of the plan that called for him to intentionally miss them, didn't want to confuse him any. Now that plan was out and Elwood had become a liability that needed to be taken care of.

"We'll need to gas these up," one of the unloaders said and wiped sweat from his brow with a forearm.

"Do it, and check the oil and tires. I don't want any of them crapping out on us." He leaned back against a door of a black Dodge Quad Cab, gnawed on a toothpick, and planned his next moves.

THIRTY-ONE

The road disappeared under the tires of Johnny's speeding bike, his rage growing with each passing mile. Why hadn't they caught up to them yet? He could feel the blood pounding through his veins. His head felt like it was literally going to burst open. If Magoo had hurt Becky, he'd rip him apart with his bare hands. Where the hell were they?

Wild pulled alongside and signaled him to stop. He couldn't stop. He hadn't caught them yet. Maybe Wild knew where they were. He locked up his brakes and Wild shot past him before skidding to a stop. He pulled alongside.

"Johnny, where are you going?"

The question was so pointless—he couldn't do anything but answer it. "I'm going after Magoo and Becky."

"Do you know where they went?"

He started to answer but his voice caught in his throat. He should know where they went. The answer should be obvious. He could feel it clawing at the back of his mind. But it couldn't fight its way through all the fury.

"Johnny, we've come several miles past where the Hangmen said they saw them. They could be anywhere. Hell, they could have turned off. We've passed a couple of side roads. We need to stop and think this through."

Wild was right. He hated Wild for being right, wanted to kill Wild for being right.

"We got the whole club with us. We need to split into twos and threes so we can cover more ground." Wild pulled out his cell phone and looked at it. "Shit." He looked around and pointed up the road. "Let's ride to the top of the next ridge. We should be able to get a signal there. We'll let the club catch up, split into teams and find them."

Johnny nodded once.

The road ran up the ridge and through a cut that looked like a jagged red scar. At the top was a dirt and gravel turn-out with a couple of trash barrels set in front of short, wooden posts connected by a single strand of steel cable, marking the far boundary. Soft drink bottles and beer cans were scattered about. Broken glass reflected bright sunlight like bits of discarded jewelry. He pulled off with Wild right behind him, his tires crunching to a stop. The rest of the club straggled in.

Wild dismounted and looked at his phone. "Good, we've got a sig—"

Johnny didn't hear the rest, brushed past his VP and ran out into the road. Several bikes were approaching from the other direction. Dressed head to foot in leather, with fishbowl helmets, they weren't real bikers—civilians, out for a ride. To confirm it they rode a quintet of rice-burners. Two of them were bitch packing smaller kids.

The citizens didn't want to stop but he left them no choice. He got right in front of the lead Kawasaki and grabbed the handlebars on each side of the fairing while it slowed to a halt, carrying him backwards several feet, but he kept his balance.

"We don't want no trouble," said the rider, his face concealed behind the dark-tinted shield of his helmet. A young girl clung tightly to him from behind, all wide eyes behind her clear face shield.

"Did you pass a biker with a woman on the front?" Johnny said.

"Harold, what do they want?" a woman on a second Kawasaki that rolled to a stop behind the lead bike called out, one spike-heeled boot on the pavement.

"You'd better leave us alone," the teenage rider of the third bike, a Yamaha, said. "I'm in pre-law," he added, failing to impress anyone.

"Junior, be quiet."

"Yeah, junior," Animal said. "Listen to Mommy."

Wild stepped next to Johnny. "Did you pass a biker with a woman riding in front of him? Brunette in bra and jeans, has a cast on one hand."

"We don't want no trouble," Harold said again.

"Did you see them?" Johnny said.

"I'm calling the police," Junior said, removed his helmet and pulled out his cell phone.

Animal snatched the phone from his hand, threw it to the pavement and stomped on it.

"Hey!"

"Did you see them?" Johnny said for the third time.

"We don't want any—"

"Fuck you!" Johnny yelled, turned loose of the handlebars, stepped around the windshield and seized Harold by the front of his custom-made, leather jacket. He jerked the man half off his bike, his daughter still clinging to his back. "Did you fucking see them?"

"We didn't see anybody," his wife said. "Please let us go."

Wild walked over to her. "One of our women has been kidnapped. She's riding in front of the kidnapper on a customized, red, classic Harley-Davidson Panhead with ape-hangers. All we want to know is if you've seen them."

"Ape-hangers?"

"Tall handlebars."

The woman licked her lips and shook her head. Her face shield only covered the upper half of her face unlike Harold's Darth Vader. "I didn't see anyone like that. Did any of you?" she said and turned to face the other riders.

They shook their heads.

"Are you sure? We're not going to hurt you. All we want is to get her back."

The woman looked at the others again, and once more they shook their heads.

"What about you Harold?" Wild said and stepped back to him.

"No... no, I didn't see them."

"How long you been on this road?"

"What?"

"Where'd you come from, numb nuts?" Johnny yelled, splattering the man's face shield with spittle and jerked him closer.

"Cantrell," his wife cried. "Please, let us go."

"That's thirty miles up the road," Wild said. "No way Magoo got there before they left. He must have turned off."

Johnny stared at him for a moment then back at Harold. "You always let your cunt do your talking for you, shithead?" He gave Harold a shove back onto his bike.

"Please, can we go?" his wife said.

"Yeah, get the hell outta here."

"Somebody owes me for a phone," Junior said, trying his best to sound tough.

"You don't get the fuck outta here, I'm gonna owe you for a head," Animal said.

Junior's eyes got big, and he pulled his helmet back on and snapped the chin strap.

"All right, gather around," Wild hollered, ignoring the departing family. "We're going to split into groups and find Magoo. Animal, take some brothers and check out those roads we passed."

*

They crossed over the river. Rebecca's shoulders and chest burned from the sun's ultraviolet wrath. Her lips were chapped and swollen, the lower thrice its normal size. Blood had dried on her chin. Her face felt like it had been sandpapered, her eyes splashed with acid. Through a blur of tears she spotted a sign for the turnoff to the state campground, only two miles ahead. Her heart beat faster in anticipation that Magoo would take the turnoff. If only he would, they'd soon be immersed in a sea of campers. He'd be forced to slow down. Then she'd chance diving off the side of the bike and screaming for help. If Magoo caught her and held her on, she'd throw her weight against one of the handlebars and dump the bike. She was willing to risk a low speed impact and possible injury to escape. Anything, anything to get out of this lunatic's clutches.

They'd followed the route Johnny had taken earlier this morning. Traffic was sparse to non-existent. Still, they passed the occasional car or truck headed the other way, even a few bikers. She tried to signal them for help, but her frantic waving was mistaken for a greeting or ignored altogether. All her efforts garnered were a few return waves and a thump on the side of her head from Magoo with an order to knock it off. Yelling was pointless. If they passed a cop she'd flip him off. That ought to get a response. But they didn't encounter any.

The best she could hope for was that someone would remember seeing her and tell Johnny when he came looking for her. He was looking for her, wasn't he? Surely he must be finished in town by now and know what happened. Then again, maybe the sheriff locked him up too.

No, she couldn't afford to think that way. Johnny was coming for her. He had to be coming. He wouldn't leave her to the mercy of this goon to be raped and... God knows what else. Maybe he was right behind them. She had to keep her hopes up and be ready to make an escape when the opportunity arose. Johnny would come. She just had to hang on until he got here.

Another signpost flashed by. The turnoff to the campground was only a quarter-mile ahead.

They came out of a turn, scattering several birds that were picking at a road-kill. One scavenger, reluctant to surrender its feast, barely avoided going under the bike's front tire. She could see the turnoff at the end of the straightaway, drawing ever closer. There were no vehicles about, no hikers, only a sign, *State Campground* with an arrow to the right. She tried to control her breathing while time slowed to a crawl. *Oh dear God, please let him turn down there.* She could hear her father's voice in her head. *Why should God answer the prayer of a whore?*

They drew closer. Remarkably she could hear the angry squawks of the birds they'd scattered over the roar of the engine. Magoo gave no indication he intended to turn. They were nearly on top of the intersection. *No! He's going on by!*

Then the bike's speed decreased rapidly.

THIRTY-TWO

With both feet firmly on the pegs and his rear rarely touching the seat, Juggler led his crew across the rough, desolate terrain. The sun's blinding glare reflected off the sun-baked, yellow earth. The trio he'd chosen were all experienced off-road bikers and Chico could hold his own. But Elwood was hopeless. They constantly had to pause so the asshole could catch up. He thought about killing the tweaker and leaving him for the buzzards. But what would he do with the extra bike? He didn't want the dirt bike traced back to the club. Ducky'd had the serial numbers filed off but the pigs had ways of raising them. No, he'd have to wait until he had a place where he could stash the bike for pickup later. Besides, he needed to leave Elwood's dead ass near Johnny's.

Or did he?

There were certain advantages to letting the other clubs know just exactly who was behind the killings.

The days of the independent outlaw clubs were all but over. A fact Ducky refused to accept. To survive, let alone prosper, Satans Kin needed to align itself with one of the major outlaw clubs. The major clubs controlled the outlaw scene, not just in America, but worldwide. There were two ways to align themselves with a major club. One was as an ally—the other was to become an associate club.

In college, he'd taken several history courses. He'd also read *1984,* twice. Allies could be sold out, abandoned, or crushed, depending if the needs of the stronger party changed. Better to become an associate club with the goal of patching over. He'd already put out feelers to the Sin Eaters MC. They were interested, but not as long as Ducky ran the Satans Kin.

That was just as well as Ducky would never go along with the idea. Ducky preferred to play the major clubs against each other while providing a conduit for their drug trade through associate clubs, a policy that was bound to lead to disaster.

Ducky had delusions of one day joining the major clubs as an equal member. Did he think this was Division One football where you could join a conference? The major clubs all had dozens of chapters throughout North America, Europe, Australia, even the Far East. They also hated each other. In Europe, they'd gone so far as to fire stolen grenade launchers at each other during a war last century. That was some serious shit. The only thing these clubs agreed on was crushing any upstart, independent clubs that got in their way. And while there were some clubs who managed to maintain their freedom, they'd still had to reach some sort of understanding with at least one of the big boys.

No, it was better to be an associate club and work toward eventual membership than to be an ally. And nothing impressed the major clubs more than ability to take care of business.

He slid sideways to a stop in a spray of dirt. He wanted to check his GPS and give fucking Elwood another chance to catch up. They'd only be able to go so far cross-country. Eventually they'd have to get back on the highway to cross the river. No doubt there were fords which would shorten the trip considerably.

But he didn't know their locations and didn't have time to hunt for them.

The other four Satans Kin bikers pulled to a stop around him and broke out their water bottles. Each had an Uzi slung across their backs. That could be a problem when they rejoined the highway. The stretch of road he was aiming for wasn't that well traveled. They'd just have to chance it. He'd have his crew shift the weapons under their right armpits and hope they didn't run up on a cop. If they did and he spotted him in time, he'd lead his men back off road. If it was too late for that… he'd kill the pig.

Elwood rocked in, fighting the handlebars and streaming sweat. "Jeez, Juggler, we like in some kinda' fuckin' race or somethin'?"

He ignored him, took a sip of water and looked away, west, toward the distant woods that grew along the river.

"Holy shit, man. Is this like some sorta' Moto-cross race? Can't you dudes like slow down? Jeez."

Again he ignored him, screwed the cap back on his water bottle and continued to look away.

"Anybody got any extra water?" Elwood said, straddling his bike and still grasping the handlebars.

"What you do," Chico said, "drink all yours?"

"No man, musta' lost it somewhere, bouncin' all over Hell's backyard." He looked at the ground on both sides of his bike and shrugged. "Somebody give me some."

"No," Juggler said.

"Jeez, don't be a dick."

He stared at Elwood for a long moment, his body going tense. He forced the anger that threatened to erupt into some deep recess of his soul, to be revisited later. Then he spun his bike around and sped off.

Fernando climbed off his bike and walked over to the gate. A galvanized farm gate, four and a half feet tall, stretched across the entire one lane, dirt road. A rusty chain coiled around one end and an adjoining steel fencepost, held in place by a large padlock. The fence ran off to each side, uninterrupted for as far as he could see. A pair of faded signs decorated the gate—*No Trespassing* and *No Hunting. Hunt what, rattlers?* He seized the padlock and jerked it twice. It didn't open. "Hell, man, this is a dead-end. No way Magoo came down here. He'd need a key." He looked closer at the lock and released it with a flip of his hand. "Damn thing's rusty. Bet it ain't been opened in months." He walked back to his bike.

Dirty Dan took a drink from a plastic bottle then squirted some water onto his face. He wiped it around, grunted, grimaced and slumped on his seat. "Think those assholes musta' cracked some of my ribs." He sat quietly for several moments. "This sucks," he said at last. "Why the hell would Magoo carry off Johnny's bitch?"

Fernando answered with a shrug of his shoulders and climbed back on his bike.

"Don't make no sense," Dirty Dan continued and shook his head. "Now Johnny's ready to kill his ass on sight. That ain't right. Magoo's a brother. He should get a chance to explain hisself."

"Gonna be a tough one to explain away, Bro." Fernando pulled a water bottle out of a leather satchel he hung on one side of the rear fender.

"I mean what the hell. Maybe the bitch led him on or somethin'. It ain't right."

Fernando shrugged again and took a drink. He swallowed some, swished the rest around in his mouth and spit it out on the ground. He screwed the cap back on and shoved the bottle back into the bag. He was originally from Argentina. His parents moved to the States when he was two and he sounded no different than any other Road Raptor although he did bear an uncanny resemblance to Che Gueverra, especially when he wore his beret. The look was intentional. He'd heard Che had written a book called *The Motorcycle Diaries* so he figured Che must have been a pretty cool dude—for a commie. "Johnny's the pres. What he says goes."

"No it don't. On somethin' like this the whole club gets to vote. But not until Maggo has had his say."

They sat quietly for awhile and digested this. At length, Dirty Dan turned to the third member of their trio. "What's with you? Normally you're runnin' your hole nonstop. You sick?"

"What? Oh… no. I was thinking," Clean said.

"Well whatta you think 'bout this?"

"Huh? Oh, yeah. Yeah, Magoo should get his say."

"Damn right he should."

"If'n Johnny doesn't shoot him first," Fernando said. "So what we do now?"

"Head back, I guess," Dirty Dan said. "See if someone else found him."

They restarted their bikes, turned around and thundered off. Dirty Dan took the lead with Clean bringing up the rear.

Clean seriously considered pointing his bike south when they rejoined the highway and running for it. Ducky's plan had gone all to hell thanks to Magoo. No doubt the Satans Kin's president had an alternate plan, probably involving that pock-marked, Sgt at Arms freak, but he had no idea what it was or how he fit into it. Ducky had given him the number of a throw-away cell phone and he desperately wanted to call him. But he couldn't with the other club members close by, even if he could get service which was doubtful. Surely Ducky still needed him to take control of the Road Raptors once they'd disposed of Johnny and Wild. Only now his ability to take control of the club was seriously in doubt. Damn Magoo anyway. He'd been counting on Magoo's support to succeed Johnny.

He'd spent a lot of time and money, palling up to Magoo, picking up food tabs, buying him drinks and drugs. With Magoo's support, he was sure he could get elected president. He'd make Magoo his VP. Or if that big oaf got ambitious, he was willing to reverse the roles. Johnny listened closely to Wild. There were some advantages to being the vice as most club members went there first with any problems or concerns. Now that was in jeopardy, all because of some stupid twat. Serve the bitch right if after Magoo got done raping her, he'd wring her neck. Only that would wreck things for sure. It'd be better if they got the bitch back in one piece and unmolested. Dirty Dan and Fernando already had their doubts about her. Maybe he could find a way to turn that to his advantage. If handled right, it could gain him more support with the other brothers.

They reached the highway and the two bikes in front hung a left. He hesitated for only an instant and then followed them. It was too soon to cut and run. He'd play this hand out a bit further and see if his luck improved.

The pressure against his spine from the snub-nosed .38 revolver he'd tucked into the back waistband of his jeans felt reassuring.

THIRTY-THREE

Rebecca was almost ready to throw herself off Magoo's bike and end it. Magoo had slowed to a complete stop in the intersection at the state campground turnoff. He'd looked down the road as if considering it, and then gone on. She found that devastating, worse than if he'd blown on past. Was this God's answer to her prayers? If so, he truly was the God of her father.

They ran a couple more miles before turning onto another blacktop. This road only went to the right also, which might explain Magoo's hesitation at the campground turnoff. After several additional miles he swung left onto an even narrower blacktop without a centerline.

She did a double-take at the road sign. *Desolation Lane* it read. Despite her anxiety, she couldn't help but wonder who would hang such a name on a road.

Five or six miles further, Magoo turned off on an unmarked, narrow dirt road. He ran down it for a ways and then came to a stop in front of a dilapidated, clapboard building. The deserted building's roof sagged in the middle and the walls were bleached gray and covered with graffiti. She couldn't make out any of the writing as the front wall was now in shade. The front door was missing as were the windows.

Magoo killed the engine and dropped the kickstand. He straddled the bike and leaned it against the stand, pivoting the front wheel, but didn't dismount. He stared at the shack. After a minute or so he suddenly yelled, "Aw, goddamn it!" He climbed off the bike and hurried over to the building and yelled, "Goddamn them!"

She slid off the bike and staggered after him while he searched around the ground. He found an old rag and went to scrubbing the wall. He paused to look and then went back to work. The cloth snagged on the rough boards and ripped into tatters. Still he kept working the rag back and forth. At first she couldn't see what he was trying to rub off. She stepped to his side. A large, red circle with a diagonal line through it covered some faded, white lettering. Beneath the circle, in red letters that had run like streams of dried blood was *Satans Kin Rules*.

Magoo eventually gave up and threw the rag down. "Motherfuckers!" he bellowed and lumbered away.

She stepped closer and peered at the faded writing. It took her a moment to decipher the partially covered words. *Johnny and Magoo, brothers forever, Road Raptors MC.* She reached out and ran her left hand across the rough, splintered wood. Her heart skipped a beat when she touched Johnny's name. Then she screamed in anguish when Magoo placed a hand on her sunburned shoulder. She spun out from under him and turned to face him, tears of pain blurred her eyes.

He frowned, then his squinted eyes opened wider. He turned and walked over to his bike where he dug in a canvass bag strapped to his rear fender. With a jerk, he tugged out an olive green T-shirt and flung it at her. "Put that on."

She didn't want to accept anything from him, but her upper torso was frying. She caught the shirt and shook it out. The tee was filthy and stiff, stained with oil. On the back, a grinning, white skull with a skeletal hand flashed the bird above the letters *FTW*.

"Stands for fuck the world," he said with a snort.

The front of the shirt read, *Sturgis 2012*. She struggled into it. The shirt stank of grease, gasoline and sweat. Size XXXL, it hung past her knees and one shoulder protruded through the neck hole. She tugged it down in front which helped some. A knot in the bottom would have worked better, but she couldn't manage that one-handed.

"Me and Johnny wrote that." He looked past her and stared at the wall again. "Motherfuckin' Satans Kin." His eyes looked vacant as if he was trying to remember something. "Me and him grew up together."

"If you and Johnny are brothers, why'd you kidnap me?"

He looked at her. His eyes narrowed and his forehead furrowed. "I seen you first."

"What?"

"In the bar, I seen you first. You smiled at me."

"I was working. I smile at all the customers. It's part of the job."

He shrugged. "Other waitresses never smile at me."

Dear God, did this big ape think I was flirting with him?

"Johnny shouldn'ta cut in. Brothers don't do that."

She tried to pick her words carefully. "Johnny was just helping me after I hurt my hand. He took me to the hospital, that's all."

He shrugged again.

"You weren't there that night."

"You rode with Johnny on this run."

"He asked me."

"You been ridin' with him for weeks. Fuckin' him too."

She didn't know what to say.

"Not fair Johnny gets all the hot bitches." His voice grew louder and he began to clench and unclench his fists. He rocked back and forth slightly. His eyes took on an insane glow as he stared into the distance. Sweat ran down his mammoth biceps and bare chest.

"Ain't right, some fuckin' bitch come between brothers."

Her flesh turned cold and her legs went weak. A wave of dizziness swept over her and her heart felt ready to explode out of her chest. She couldn't get her breath, couldn't swallow. She looked around for somewhere to flee to. But they were in the middle of nowhere. There were no other buildings in sight. The land was barren, right on the edge of the desert. There were no trees, just some scrub brush. Besides, she doubted she could outrun this lunatic under the best of circumstances. Hitting him with her cast hadn't done any good, just made her hand ache. With her brain threatening to lock down, she opened her mouth to say she knew not what. "I'm thirsty," came out.

He looked at her hard and she couldn't meet his eyes, dropped hers to stare at the ground. "Water bottle in the saddle bag," he finally said.

She walked over to his bike. She wished she knew how to ride it. *Maybe there's a gun in the saddlebag.* She took a deep breath—she knew how to handle firearms. That was one of the few useful things her father had taught her, just in case his church should ever be besieged by Catholics or the Anti-Christ and his minions show up for Sunday Service. Reverend Spade didn't intend to go down without a fight and expected his entire congregation, women and children included, to go down with him.

One of the deacons was an ex-jarhead and taught the members how to handle everything from handguns and shotguns, right up to fully automatic assault rifles. She'd even learned how to make Molotov Cocktails and pipe bombs. She didn't know if she could handle a gun one-handed, especially left-handed. But she was willing to try.

She lifted the flap and reached inside.

"Watch out for needles."

She jerked her hand out and Magoo laughed.

"Jus jokin'. That's what the pigs always ask, 'any needles in the bag?' Motherfuckers."

She stared at him, not sure whether to believe him or not. She couldn't see any marks on his arms to indicate intravenous drug use. But who could tell with all those tattoos? Deciding HIV was less of a threat than dehydration, and moving slowly—she felt in the bag and located the water bottle. She pulled it out by its cap and didn't reach any deeper. She placed the bottle on the inside of her right arm, held it against her body and popped off the cap. She took a long drink. The water was disgustingly tepid and sour, just like how she imagined urine would taste… it couldn't be, could it? No, she shoved that thought out of her head, placed the bottle back between her arm and body to recap it. As she pushed the cap down, the bottle slipped out. She grabbed for it, fumbled and dropped the bottle. It hit the ground with a wet *whap* and rolled away. Water pulsed out onto the ground like blood from a severed limb.

"Shit!" Magoo yelled and rushed over. "You stupid cunt." He shoved her out of the way and reached for the bottle but knocked it further away. The bottle rolled under his bike. He dropped to his hands and knees to retrieve it. When he did, she spotted a rock about the size and shape of a softball lying next to him.

Without thinking, Rebecca snatched up the rock with her left hand, yelled and swung with all her might at the back of his head.

THIRTY-FOUR

The call kept breaking up and Wild had a hard time understanding the caller. Johnny stood right on top of him. Wild turned away and covered his other ear. Johnny moved with him. Wild caught the gist of the call, looked at Johnny and shook his head. Johnny turned and stalked off. "Okay, got it. Head on down the highway. You'll come to a railroad crossing. Check out the first road after that." He disconnected. This wasn't working. They'd been here nearly three-quarters of an hour and that was only the third call they'd gotten. No doubt the brothers were having trouble getting service.

He looked at the western sky, still about three hours to sunset. If they hadn't found Magoo by then… he turned toward Johnny who was wearing a rut in the earth next to his bike. He didn't know how much longer he'd be able to keep Johnny here. He half expected him to climb on his bike and roar off any minute. Johnny wasn't the patient type.

The family they'd encountered earlier was also a concern. Cutting them loose might have been a mistake. No doubt Harold was a spineless wimp, but Johnny made him look real bad in front of his family. Most fathers couldn't swallow that sort of humiliation.

The farther away daddy got, the madder and braver he might get. The jerk-off might work up enough spine to call the highway patrol. The last thing they needed was for the pigs to stick their snouts into club business. But if he'd made the group remain here, he'd had to put some brothers to guarding them which would run the risk of a passing motorist noticing and calling in the cavalry. He shook his head. Hopefully, Harold was so pussy whipped he'd listen to his wife not to get involved.

His phone rang and he answered it only to have the call dropped. "Shit!" He waved Johnny away, hit the call back button and got a canned voice mail message. He dialed Magoo's number but got the same recording he'd been getting that the cell phone customer he was trying to reach had left the service area or turned off his phone. "Shit, damn it!"

The roar of approaching bikes broke into his thoughts. No mistaking the sound—these bikes were Harleys. Animal and the prospect, Ronnie, rolled in, pulled up to him and killed their engines. "Any luck?"

"Naw," Animal said and remained seated on his bike. "Pavement ran out after 'bout a mile off the highway, turned to dirt. No tire tracks. I sent crews to check out the other turnoffs we passed. Anything from them?"

"No."

Animal spit off the side and gazed down the road. "Two... two and a-half miles further on, another highway takes off to the right, runs past a campground. We ran out that way this morning. No idea where it goes after that. If Magoo took that, he could be anywhere."

"You think he could have reached it before passing that family?"

Animal shrugged. "Don't know. Depends how fast Magoo was going and how much ass-dragging they were—"

"Goddamn it! Son of a bitch!"

Wild spun to find Johnny facing them. He'd been listening in. His hands were clenched and his face red. Johnny started toward his bike.

"Johnny! Johnny!" Wild called and ran to intercept him. He caught Johnny just as he reached his bike. "Johnny, what's going on?"

Johnny glared at him, nostrils flared, teeth bared. "I know where he took her." He shook Wild's hand off his shoulder and climbed on his bike.

"Oh shit." Wild turned to Animal who'd dismounted and followed him over. "Switch phones," he said and tossed Animal his phone.

Johnny fired up his bike and blasted out with a spray of gravel and dirt.

Animal fumbled in his pocket, found his phone and pitched it to Wild.

"Stay here and take the incoming calls. Anything I should know, call me. I have to stay with Johnny." He mounted his bike and raced out after Johnny.

But Johnny already had a hundred-yard lead. And Johnny had his throttle wide open.

*

The sound of stone striking skull was lost in Rebecca's bellow of rage. The shout began as a growl deep in her gut and erupted from her mouth. She felt the impact of the blow all the way up her arm to her shoulder, nearly tearing the rock from her grasp. Magoo crumpled forward without a sound and lay still.

Had she killed him? Alternately, she wondered if she should hit him again. He could be playing possum. The weight of the bludgeon in her hand belied that thought. He wasn't faking. To be sure, she eased around his side, never taking her eyes off him, the rock clutched tight at shoulder level. Long, tangled hair obscured his features. Blood seeped through the back of his scalp, matting his greasy locks.

"Magoo," she said and got no reply.

"Magoo," she said again, louder. Still no response.

She held her breath, placed the sole of a shoe against his shoulder, shoved hard and hopped back. Nothing, either she had killed him or knocked him out. She threw back her head and howled like a she-wolf, thrust both arms into the air and danced in a circle, the relief all consuming.

A hot wind blew a swirl of dust about her. She stopped celebrating and looked around. They were all alone. "Okay, so now what?" she said out loud.

She kept well back as she circled around him to the rear of his bike. She placed her stone on the seat and carefully emptied the saddlebag, constantly glancing at the inert figure sprawled beside the Harley, alert for the slightest movement. She didn't find any needles, nor did she find a gun, not even a knife. What kind of outlaw didn't carry a weapon? *A big, nasty one.*

The only useful thing she found was his cell phone, but it showed no service. She slipped it into a rear pocket. Other than that, the bag held a grimy, wadded up plastic grocery bag containing a sleeve of condoms which she thought out of character, several blunts and a half eaten bag of Jack Link's Beef Jerky. She hoped that wasn't an omen—*messin' with Sasquatch*—and couldn't stifle a nervous giggle. There was also a dingy, red ball cap with *Bud's Auto Parts* stenciled on it which she put on. Another T-shirt, even nastier than the one he'd given her, was wrapped around a nearly empty half-pint of *Fireball Cinnamon Whiskey*. She unscrewed the cap and sniffed. Smelled like liquor. She wiped off the lip, took a sip and nearly gagged while trying to spit out what she hadn't swallowed. Now her insides burned as bad as her outside. She recapped the bottle, wiped her prints off with the shirt, and returned it and the other items to the saddlebag.

The water bottle lay on its side beneath the bike. She carried the bottle and her rock back around and sat near Magoo, close enough for a quick lunge should he show any signs of coming back to life. If he was dead it was his own damn fault. She felt no remorse after what he'd done to Roxy and would have done to her. There was just over an inch of water left in the clear, plastic bottle. She drank half, clasped the bottle between her thighs and got it recapped.

The way she saw it she had two options. One was to wait here and hope Johnny showed up, braining Magoo again if he came to. Johnny had to know about this place. His name was on the wall. But what if he didn't show up? What would she do after it got dark? Her other option was to walk out, back to Desolation Lane and catch a ride with someone. It was a paved road. Someone had to use it. Of course with her luck she'd get picked up by the inspiration behind the movie, *The Hills Have Eyes*. Bullshit—she had too active an imagination. She'd promise the driver anything to get out of here. Once back to safety she could renege on the promise if it was too outrageous or disgusting.

To try to ride a six-hundred-plus pound bike she had no idea how to operate, and one-handed at that, wasn't an option. At least it wasn't an option she cared to try. Get pinned under that heavy metal monster and she would be screwed.

She'd walk out.

She studied Magoo's still form. What if he's not dead and comes to? He could come after her. She could make certain he wouldn't come to and now was the time to do it if she was going to.

It made her queasy to think like that, even if he did have it coming. Besides, years of watching *CSI* and other cop shows told her so far everything she'd done was self-defense. To bash out his brains now would be considered murder. Yet she needed to do something.

Magoo wore a heavy, thick leather belt. She could use that to bind his hands behind his back. But she'd have to roll him over, if she even could, to get it unbuckled and that risked possibly reviving him. And didn't his belt have some fancy buckle? She wasn't sure but thought she remembered seeing one. There might not be a loop in the belt to feed it through and pull it tight. Tying a knot in something that big wouldn't be tight or hold for long. Of course she hadn't worn a belt of her own what with her hip-hugging, skinny jeans.

She retrieved the shredded rag he'd used on the walls, wrapped it around his wrists several times and using her one good hand and her teeth, pulled it as tight as she could and knotted it behind his back. The cloth wasn't much of a restraint and probably wouldn't last long if he did come to. Only now did she think to check for a pulse, but she'd just covered his wrists. She started to feel for a pulse in his neck then decided not to. What was the point? She'd done everything she could to disable him. The hell with it, she was wasting time. She picked up the water bottle, tossed the rock as far away as she could, and set off down the dirt road at a trot.

Twenty minutes later, she was all but convinced that she'd made a bad decision. There was no shade along the dirt road and she'd misjudged how far off the black top they'd traveled. Sweat trickled down her face, blurred her vision and dripped off her chin. The upper half of Magoo's souvenir tee was soaked. A dark, deep V reached below her chest. The back clung to her in a clammy embrace. She paused to finish the last of the water and pitched the bottle aside. How much farther to the road?

She checked his phone but there was still no service. Worse, his battery was low. She turned the phone off, returned it to her pocket, took a step and jerked to a stop. Something slithered across the road in front of her concealed in a fan of dust. They were near the desert. Snakes lived in the desert, rattlesnakes and coral snakes. Had that been a snake or a lizard? She hadn't heard any rattles. Whatever it was, it'd gone off the left side of the road. She moved to the right and continued on.

Once past the path of the reptile, she glanced back over her shoulder to see if she could determine what it was. Her toe stuck a rock. She stumbled and landed hard on her hands and knees. A bolt of agony shot up her right arm and wrenched a yelp of pain from her. She was afraid she'd reinjured her hand when she'd first struck Magoo. Now, after taking the brunt of the fall, the hand throbbed madly. She rolled into a sitting position, cupped the cast against her stomach and rocked. The left knee of her jeans had ripped and she felt the burn of skin scraped raw beneath it. Damn it, how could she be so clumsy? She needed to keep going, find some shade if nothing else.

After what seemed like an eternity, she reached the blacktop, wandered into the middle of the road and turned a complete circle. There were no signs of life anywhere. A furnace-like breeze swept dirt across the asphalt. Heat waves shimmied off the roadway in the distance. The horizon danced. The scorched pavement baked through the soles of her shoes. The only sound that of the wind swirling around her body. Desolation Lane—never had a road been more appropriately named.

She started down the highway. The heat was getting to her. Her legs felt heavy and her toes dragged across the surface. The cast had grown tighter and her right hand felt like a massive toothache. The left leg of her jeans stuck to her knee and pulled at her flesh with each step. Where the hell was Johnny? Was he coming for her or not?

A small shadow flashed across the bleached roadway. She stopped, looked up and swayed with the effort nearly losing her balance. Several large birds circled above her. "Shoo," she hollered and waved her arms at them. They ignored her and continued to drift about on the wind currents.

Wonderful. Had she escaped that maniac only to end up a snack for vultures? Was that what her father's God had in mind for her? No, that wasn't going to happen—she wouldn't let it. She took a deep breath and continued on.

The sun was merciless and she had trouble focusing, her thoughts a jumbled mess. Why had she come on this damn run with this motorcycle gang anyway? Had she truly believed she'd meet some agents and land an acting job? No, she'd come along to be with Johnny. In Johnny, she'd found something she hungered for more than a career. When she lay in his arms at night, she felt loved and valued for the first time in her life. She supposed her mother loved her. But her mother was so crushed after decades spent under her father's iron control that any emotions she'd once had, had long since been wrung dry. Her siblings had been subjected to the same overbearing constraints, their only emotion in common—fear of their father's wrath. She doubted her father was capable of love.

How ironic that her lover had the same first name as that tyrant.

If Johnny didn't come for her… they were through.

A low rumble infiltrated her consciousness, moving like a thief, there before she was aware of it, deceived by its familiarity. She paused to listen. It was a motorcycle. *Damn!* Had Magoo revived and gotten loose? She looked around for some cover to hide behind. There wasn't any. The land was desolate. She looked behind her. The road was empty. Yet she could hear the bike plainly, the growl growing in intensity. Then she realized the noise wasn't coming from behind her but from in front.

Down the road a quarter-mile or so, bikes swerved out of a curve, leaning heavily then jerked upright. They were coming on fast. The lead bike's front tire lifted off the roadway as the rider gunned the throttle.

It's about time. She ran toward them, waved her arms over her head and laughed in relief. It was Johnny. It had to be Johnny. He had come for her.

The riders spotted her, slowed rapidly and rolled to a stop a dozen feet away. They pulled side by side, completely blocking the road.

She slowed to a stop. Her smile melted away and her stomach turned to acid. If she'd had anything in her bladder, she might have wet herself again. She didn't know the names of any of these bikers, save one. She'd seen their leader before.

"Well, look what we found," Juggler said.

THIRTY-FIVE

Fear propelled Johnny forward. Fear he'd arrive too late. Fear she'd been harmed or would be before he could reach her. Fear she'd never have anything to do with him again. But it was anger that caused him to take insane chances, caused him to blow by traffic without slowing, drove him to pass on blind curves and below the crests of hills. It was anger that threw his bike into sharp curves at breakneck speeds. A pothole, loose gravel, even a discarded burger wrapper could lead to an instant loss of control and obliteration against a guardrail, shoulder, ditch. It was anger at his inability to go faster. It was anger at betrayal by a lifelong friend. Most of all it was anger at himself.

Several years before, he and Magoo had gone riding, just the two of them. The Buzzard had still been president and they were on another Memorial Day Run. They'd gotten bored hanging around the ranch and decided to clear their heads from the previous night's blowout. No better cure in the world for a hangover than to ride. Just let the bikes take you where they would.

They rode out past the state campground then turned onto another road. It was Magoo who spotted the road sign—Desolation Lane. How could you not turn down a road with such a name?

Why they left it for a dirt trail he couldn't remember. They found an abandoned cabin and stopped.

It was the perfect afternoon. The Road Raptors had won their turf wars and were finally at peace with the other clubs. The bullshit murder charges against him had been thrown out for a lack of evidence. The prosecutor's main witness had decided to relocate to another part of the country for his health. They could relax. Magoo had a bottle of Tequila and they shared it, seated in the dirt, backs against the wall. Magoo had been unusually talkative and fascinated by the old shack and its location. It was quiet. It was private. Magoo had been ready to move in despite the building's dilapidated condition. They'd written their names on the wall, brother's forever. Magoo had talked about it several times since.

He knew that was where Magoo had taken Becky. Magoo had little if any imagination. He knew in his soul that was where they'd gone. Why hadn't he thought of it sooner? He never had trouble thinking straight, no matter how stressful the situation. But this time he failed. If Magoo had harmed Becky, he'd kill him. It'd mean the end of his days as a Road Raptor. Only the club as a whole could pass judgment on a brother, regardless of his sin. That was their most ironclad rule and he'd violate in an instant if any harm had come to her. He'd be stripped of his presidency, his patch and probably stomped for good measure. He didn't care, not anymore. The only thing that mattered now was rescuing Becky.

*

Rebecca stared at the bikers who stared back. What were they doing out here? They were Satans Kin, although she was pretty sure she'd seen the biker parked next to the pack's leader in another camp, but she couldn't recall which one. She'd need to get a look at the back of his cut. That man ran a hand over his grizzled chin and leered at her. There was little doubt what was on his mind.

She felt her limbs tingle and had an overwhelming urge to turn and run but resisted it. She didn't consider herself particularly brave but knew better than to show fear to this crew. Well, she did call herself an actress. She shook her hair back, held her chin high and hoped this role didn't get her raped and murdered. She never was much good at improv.

The white-haired leader leaned forward, rested his arms on his handlebars and said, "Out for a stroll?"

The man next to him snickered.

"Shut your hole, Elwood," the leader said, never taking his eyes off her.

She took a deep breath and smiled. "You're Juggler."

"And you're Becky."

She took the ball cap off and ran a forearm across her brow. "I prefer Rebecca."

Juggler didn't respond.

She replaced the hat and glanced around—no one else in sight. She shifted her weight to one leg to control her trembling, her good hand going to her hip. "I was looking for Johnny."

"So are we."

That sent a chill through her. They were carrying automatic weapons, looked like Uzi Machine Pistols. She'd fired one once, at her father's church camp. She covered her unease with another smile.

Juggler watched her for a long moment then killed his engine, dropped the kickstand and slid off his bike. He dug in a saddlebag and removed a water bottle. He walked over and handed her the bottle. With the exception of Elwood, the rest of the riders took the opportunity to break out their water bottles as well.

She took a long swallow, relishing the relief to her parched throat.

"A person could die out here."

That comment almost caused her to choke on the water but she covered it by swiping a hand across her mouth. "Thanks," she said and handed the bottle back.

He accepted the bottle but didn't take a drink. Instead he nodded off in the distance. "There's a shack out that way. I know they party—"

"Johnny's not there."

His dark eyes flicked back to her and he studied her closely. He nodded again. "Figured as much."

She didn't know if it was a smart move or not, but she was afraid that to ignore the guns would look even more suspicious. "Why are you carrying machine guns?" she said, intentionally using a generic term for the weapons and doing her best to make her voice sound matter of fact.

"Target practice."

It didn't take Elwood's loud snort and laugh to identify that as a lie.

Juggler turned and gave the man a hard stare. Elwood's leer melted and he scratched at the back of a hand. The other bikers looked bored.

"Have another drink," Juggler said and offered her the bottle again. His eyes were completely devoid of emotion, gave nothing away, but she got the impression she wasn't fooling him. Did he know about Magoo? How could he? When she took the bottle he turned and walked away.

He gave Elwood another hard look as he passed him. He walked behind the bikes and called out, "Chico." A biker on the far end hopped off his bike and joined Juggler several feet behind the row of bikes. They held a brief conversation. Chico nodded his head and hustled back to his bike.

Chico slapped the man next to him on the shoulder and jerked his head to the side. They fired up their bikes, spun around and headed back the way they'd come.

Juggler watched them until they were out of sight then walked back and rejoined her. He took the water bottle, a short sip and screwed the cap on. "Sent them to see if Johnny's behind us. There's another spot up ahead he might be. We'll check it out. You ride with me." He took her by an elbow and steered her back to his bike.

THIRTY-SIX

Despite being a better rider, Wild had only managed to close part of the gap between himself and Johnny, who rode like a man possessed. In front of him, Johnny swung across the double yellow line to pass a string of cars. As he did, an eighteen-wheeler popped up out of a dip in the road a short distance ahead. Johnny didn't back off, didn't duck back into the line of cars but increased his speed even more. The semi driver flashed his lights, laid on his air horn and hit his brakes. The fiberglass cab rose visibly, looming over the low-slung bike. No way was the truck going to get stopped and the road had no shoulder. Just when Wild was sure he was going to witness Johnny being splattered all over the mammoth truck's grill, Johnny cut in front of the lead car with only inches to spare. Then Wild was on his brakes to keep from rear-ending the last car in line whose brake lights flared on and ass end rose up on its rear springs.

When he passed the furious truck driver who was locked in a skid, he could smell the stench of burned brake linings and tires ground to their cords. One retread exploded sending alligator hide everywhere. Filthy gray-blue smoke filled the air. He swung out around the line of stopping cars. Most of the distance he'd gained on Johnny, he'd just lost.

They rocketed past a country store with a pair of gas pumps. He glanced at his fuel gauge. *Shit!* He had less than a quarter tank of gas left—well less. He couldn't stop. He had no idea where Johnny was headed.

They blew right by the turnoff to the campground without even slowing then Johnny took the next highway to the right. A pickup truck made a leisurely left out of a side road which forced Johnny to back off fast to avoid T-boning the dirt encrusted vehicle and Wild regained some ground on him. The bearded driver stuck his head out the window, yelled something at them and flipped them off. Wild ignored the redneck and kept after Johnny.

He was worried about what would happen when Johnny found Magoo. Either one of them alone was more than he could handle in a fight. Magoo was unstable to start with and Johnny appeared to have lost all self-control. No way could he hope to control the pair if they got into it. He could see disaster coming. He needed the club with him. But the club was scattered all over hell and gone. First chance he got he'd call Animal, tell him to get the club together and haul ass over here. Not that they could get here in time to do more than pick up the pieces.

Why the hell had Magoo carried off Becky to start with? What kind of muddled thinking led to this? There had to be more forces at work here. For some reason he couldn't get Sheva off his mind.

Johnny slowed to take a road on the left. Wild took a chance and ran up behind him, slammed on his brakes and with his left boot skidding on the pavement, tires squealing in protest, barely navigated the turn. His bike slid right up to the shoulder's edge, dangerously close to launching him over the high side. Johnny glanced over his shoulder at him and gunned his throttle again. He let Johnny pull away then cut across his exhaust and eased alongside him on the left. He made no attempt to signal Johnny to slow down. Johnny wasn't about to slow down.

They ran side by side for several miles. The road was a narrow blacktop with no centerline. The highway appeared deserted as did the surrounding land. They ran down a hill and through a long curve. Back on the straightaway, he spotted a pair of bikes headed their way, the first sign of life he'd seen on this road. The bikes were too small to be Harleys.

Johnny saw them too and slowed, no doubt wanting to talk to them. Wild moved in front. They pulled to a stop as did the other bikes about fifty feet away. They stared at each other. Something wasn't right. The riders were dressed like bikers but were riding dirt bikes. Hadn't he seen one of them before? The other biker swung what looked like a submachine gun off his shoulder and pointed it their way.

"Oh shit! They're Satans Kin! Look out!" he shouted and wrenched his throttle open, just as the biker cut loose with a burst of automatic fire.

*

At least this time Rebecca didn't have to ride in front of her abductor, which would have been nearly impossible on this bike. She'd have to straddle the narrow fuel tank. But it had other drawbacks. She had to squeeze in tight against Juggler's back to fit on the small seat and wrap her arms around his chest. He wasn't the most pleasant smelling person in the world but then right now neither was she. He led the way with the other three bikes right behind him.

When they passed the dirt road that led to the abandoned shack, she took a quick glance that way—no sign of Magoo. She wasn't sure but what she wouldn't have preferred to see him there given her current predicament. Her movement didn't go unnoticed by Juggler who looked that way too.

She was hit by a sudden wave of depression. Her body ached. Fatigue gnawed at her brain and made it difficult to concentrate. She was sweltering, knew she should pay attention to where they went but her eyelids grew heavier. She had to fight it, had to stay awake and alert. Whatever these bikers were up to it wasn't good. She laid her cheek against Juggler's shoulder, bit down on her injured lower lip, welcoming the pain and watched the unchanging landscape.

They continued on for a few miles and crossed over a river on a one-lane bridge. A short distance later, Juggler slowed and she looked over his shoulder. A wooden barricade covered with reflective warning signs and a large *Dead End* announced the end of the road. A dirt and gravel drive led off to the right and they turned down it, ignoring the *No Trespassing* sign. After about a hundred yards they pulled to a stop. A heavy chain, strung across the road from two poles about waist-high, barred their path. Another sign dangled from the chain's center—*No Dumping by Order of the Quinton Co. Sheriff's Department.* Someone had shot-gunned the sign and it was full of small holes. Faded beer cans and used condoms littered the ground, most of the plastic sheaths sun-baked to a crispy brown. A beaten footpath led around one pole. Juggler eased his bike onto it and they skirted around the chain and back onto the drive.

They rode another quarter-mile then up a steep slope and came to a rest on a small plateau of hard earth. A few scraggly bushes were scattered about. A blowtorch wind swept up loose red clay in small dust devils that danced across the ground. Several large birds took flight as they rolled to a stop. The far end of the plateau was covered with all sorts of trash and several abandoned cars. She spotted a discarded refrigerator lying on its back. With the door missing the fridge looked like a crypt.

There didn't appear to be anyone here. No vehicles that looked drivable, only derelicts. Where the hell was everybody? Didn't anyone live along this road? It was like an episode of the old *Twilight Zone*. She couldn't hear anything other than the howl of the wind and squawks from the birds they'd disturbed. The sun cast shadows across the landscape but the heat didn't let up.

Juggler climbed off the bike and stretched. He took her by an elbow again, led her over to the back edge of the plateau and looked around. A small ravine was partially filled with more refuse and scores of abandoned vehicles, most of them wrecked. The only signs of life were a few more birds flittering about.

The other bikers followed them. Juggler turned to one and gave her a shove in the man's direction. "Don't let her wander off," he said and started to walk away but stopped. "Hold it." He tugged Magoo's phone from her back pocket, removed its battery and flung both into the ravine. He looked back at her pants and his nose wrinkled. He made eye contact and his eyes sparkled with amusement, the first emotion she'd seen in them. "What'd you do, piss your pants?"

She felt her face go flush. "Yes."

"Magoo scare you that bad?"

He knew about Magoo. "Yes."

"Magoo doesn't scare me at all," he said and walked off. He stopped several paces away, glanced at his phone, nodded and slipped it back into his pocket, then gazed off into the distance.

Rebecca was left in the middle of a rough triangle formed by the other three bikers. The two Satans Kin mostly ignored her, but Elwood couldn't take his eyes off her. He paced back and forth in front of her. He looked like a junkie in need of a fix. The back of his cut read *Storm Troopers*. That must have been where she'd seen him before, when she and Johnny visited their camp. What was he doing riding with Satans Kin?

All of them were hot and sweaty, but Elwood was a wet mess, hair plastered to his head, perspiration dripping off his chin. He stank like a pile of moldy, damp blankets. He rubbed his arms, scratched at the scabs on his hands and wiped snot with a forearm. "When we gonna do her, man?" he called out.

Juggler didn't respond.

"Hell, let's have her pull this train."

Elwood took a step toward her and she backed up. She might only have been riding with bikers for a few days but caught the gist of that comment.

"Let's see what ya got there." Elwood reached for her breasts and she slapped his hand away.

"Oh, I'm gonna enjoy doing you, bitch." His mouth curled in a nasty grin revealing rotten, yellow stubs and dark gums. A hand shot between her legs, grabbed hold of her vagina and squeezed hard. She yelped, pulled away and slapped his face this time.

"C'mere," Juggler said.

"What?"

"I said c'mere."

"What for?"

"Got something I need you to do."

Elwood shook his head, mumbled, "Jeez, what now?" and wandered over, rubbing at his cheek where she'd struck him.

The fourth biker trailed behind him.

Elwood stopped in front of Juggler, arms dangling at his side. "Whut the hell you want me to do now?"

"Die."

Rebecca felt like she'd just stuck a finger into an electrical outlet.

It took a moment longer to sink into Elwood's meth-addled brain. Then his eyes opened wide, but before he could move, the biker behind him seized him in a bear hug, pinning his arms to his side. Juggler grabbed a handful of the terrified man's hair and bent his head back. Elwood screamed and tried to struggle free but his scream was cut short as Juggler ran a knife across his throat. Blood spurted in a stream from the wound and Juggler stepped to the side to get out of the way as the biker turned the Storm Trooper loose.

Elwood slapped his hands around his neck in a futile effort to staunch the flow and continued to scream but nothing other than gurgles came out. He stumbled forward a few steps, blood spurting between his fingers. His eyes rolled madly. He swayed, collapsed in a heap, shook a couple of times and went still.

Juggler wiped his knife on the man's colors.

"Oh fuck me," said the biker guarding Rebecca. "Did you see that? He looked like a damn geyser. Did you see that?"

She stared in horror through wide-eyes as a large puddle of blood formed around the murdered man's head and shoulders. The fingers on his left hand twitched. His right foot wiggled. A noise that sounded like someone passing gas came from the gash in his throat. Bubbles formed in the blood still oozing from the wound. The bubbles began to pop. Rebecca felt her stomach roll over. She staggered several feet away, clasped her arms around her belly and threw up.

THIRTY-SEVEN

Johnny wrenched his throttle open in response to Wild's warning. They didn't get far. A hailstorm of bullets struck the front of Wild's bike. The slugs burst his tire, exploded the headlight, blew off a turn signal, punctured the forks and shattered the front wheel collapsing the bike beneath him. Wild spilled off the right side and tumbled to a stop.

Johnny laid his bike down in a desperate attempt to avoid his VP. His motorcycle ground to a stop on its side with a screech of metal, half on the roadway and half on the dirt shoulder. He scrambled to his hands and knees behind his bike, shrouded in dust, and tugged the .357 Magnum out of his rear waistband. He fired at their attackers three times. He doubted he hit either of them at this range but maybe his fire would drive them to ground and buy him some seconds.

Wild lay on his back, his right arm bent at the elbow and wavering in the air. If any of the slugs had penetrated the fuel tank and escaping gas hit the muffler, the bike would quickly become an inferno. He had to get Wild clear. He crawled over, seized Wild under the armpits and dragged him off the blacktop and into the ditch to put them below the roadbed. Wild's eyes were open and he grimaced in pain—he'd been hit at least twice. Blood leaked through a hole in the thigh of his leather chaps and another stained the left side of his T-shirt.

There came the sound of running and Johnny started to raise his gun.

"Don't try it, mano!"

An attacker stood on the shoulder above them and pointed a small machine pistol at them.

"Drop the gun!"

A second attacker joined the first. That man also held a machine pistol, a wisp of smoke drifting from the end of the barrel. Johnny let the revolver slip from his fingers.

"Hands on your head."

He placed his hands on his head.

The first attacker's eyes flicked to his partner and back. "You stupid fuck! We weren't supposed to shoot them, just let Juggler know where they were and follow them."

"They saw us, Chico," the second man said.

Chico shook his head. "Frisk him."

The second biker slung his weapon over his shoulder, moved behind Johnny and patted him down. He removed Johnny's knife from a belt scabbard and flung it away. The locking pocketknife in Johnny's right boot followed. He picked up the handgun and waved it beside Johnny's face. "Don't you know you could go to jail for this? Convicted felons ain't supposed to carry guns." He laughed, stepped away and shoved the pistol into his waistband. "He's clean."

"Now him," Chico said. "You back up a few steps." He motioned at Johnny with his weapon.

Johnny started to stand.

"Stay on your knees! Scoot back."

Johnny moved back. "My man's hurt."

"Shut up."

The other biker knelt by Wild and checked him over. He removed Wild's skinning knife and threw it away. He checked Wild's pockets and rolled him over. Wild cried out in pain.

Johnny started to stand again.

"Stay put," Chico ordered and pointed again with his gun.

Johnny returned to his knees and looked the man in the eyes. He was going to kill this cocksucker. One way or another, this piece of shit was going to die.

The second biker checked Wild's back pockets, felt around his belt, then stood leaving Wild on his stomach, lying on his right arm. "Knife's all he had."

"Get some rope from my saddlebag and tie him up," Chico said.

The second biker climbed back onto the road and hurried away.

"I need to help my man."

"You need to shut up."

The biker returned with a short length of rope. Johnny held his hands out in front of himself. The man bound his wrists together and stepped away.

Chico glanced at Wild and back at Johnny. "You move over there," he said and motioned with his weapon.

"I—"

"Move!"

Johnny got to his feet and took several steps to his left.

"Back on your knees."

He knelt again.

"What about this one?" the other biker said, looking down at Wild. "Want I should finish him off?"

"No!" Johnny yelled.

"You don't do nothin'. You already done too much. I need to think."

"I don't know, man. He looks pretty wasted."

"You just keep him quiet."

Wild let out an anguished moan and tried to pull his wounded leg closer to his body. His assailant kicked him in the ribs which caused Wild to scream and double up.

"You son of a bitch!" Johnny hollered.

"You shut your mouth and keep it shut!" Chico shifted the gun to his left hand, dug his phone out of a pocket and glanced at it. "Shit, no service." He stuffed the phone away and nodded at his partner. "You may need to ride back and get Juggler."

"Where's he at?"

"A dump, end of the highway to the right." A sneer came to Chico's lips and he looked Johnny in the eyes. "We got that little bitch of yours. She one hot momma. Can't wait to get a piece of that ass."

"You bastard." Johnny got to his feet. "You touch her I'll—"

"You'll what?" Chico laughed, took a step back and switched the gun back to his right hand. "Maybe Juggler let you watch."

Johnny started toward him.

"Don't!"

The man's partner took a step toward them and pointed his gun at Johnny as well. "We'll do her good, man." He laughed.

Johnny turned to face him. The man grinned nastily.

On the ground behind him, Wild pulled his left leg closer to his chest and his right shoulder rolled further under his side.

*

Rebecca had never been this scared. She'd witnessed a murder. No way would they let her leave here alive. Her heart pounded in her chest, her body trembled, her legs and knees felt weak. She wanted to flee, but her feet felt rooted to the ground. A wave of dizziness swept over her and she felt faint. She couldn't give in to that. Pass out and she might never wake up. She took several deep breaths and tried to force her terror down. She had to think. That they hadn't already murdered her meant Juggler was keeping her alive for some reason. She had no idea what that purpose was, but until it was fulfilled, they probably wouldn't harm her—at least not too badly. She had some time.

She looked around. To try and run away was pointless. There was nowhere to run to. To beg and plead for her life was just as useless. And she had nothing she could offer them in return for her life that they couldn't simply take from her if they wanted it. If she was going to live, she was going to have to fight.

With that realization, an unexpected calm settled over her. She'd fought Magoo and won. Wrong term—win. Hank Carter, the former Marine and deacon in her father's church, had told her that when your life was on the line there was no winning or losing. There was only dying or surviving.

To survive, she needed a gun.

The three Satans Kin were carrying Uzis and God alone knew what else. But Elwood hadn't been carrying a machine pistol. She tried to remember how he was armed. A handgun, an automatic, she'd seen the handle protruding from his waistband. What had become of it? She tried to visualize his murder. The biker who held him, when he'd shoved Elwood away, he must have tugged the gun loose—it was in his hand. What had become of the handgun since then she didn't know. Most likely the biker still had it. It didn't matter. She wanted one of the Uzis.

Right now, only Juggler was on the plateau with her. He'd sent the other two bikers into the ravine to hide Elwood's body. He'd said he didn't want the corpse attracting a flock of buzzards and some asshole wandering in to find out what had died. He stood about thirty feet away, his head bent over his phone, texting. She looked around for a rock big enough to do the job. She didn't see any appropriate stones but spotted something better. A few strides away a rusty tire iron lay on the ground. It'd probably fallen out of one of the wrecks. If she could get it and slip behind him… she took a step toward it.

"Stay put," Juggler said.

He hadn't even looked up from his phone. "I wasn't going anywhere," she said.

He didn't respond.

She licked her lips and glanced at the steel bar again. "I need to pee."

"Do it in your pants again."

Bastard! She was a lot nearer to the tire iron than he was, just scant feet away. But to make a dash for it would give her intentions away. At best, she was going to get one chance, and surprise was the only advantage she had. She had to find a way to get closer.

She heard voices. The other two bikers climbed back out of the ravine.

"Get rid of that garbage?" Juggler said.

The lead biker nodded and ran a sweaty forearm across his brow. "Found an old Yugo. Cage still had all its glass. Stuffed his ass behind the seats. Ain't no one gonna look in a piece of shit like that." They continued over and stopped near Juggler who continued to text. The biker who'd spoken gave her a long, hard stare. It was the same man who'd held Elwood while Juggler slit his throat.

"Insurance policy," Juggler said without looking up.

The man's brow wrinkled as he struggled to grasp Juggler's meaning.

Rebecca got it. She was insurance to lure Johnny in—bait. She also understood the concept of insurance. When a policy was no longer needed, you cancelled it. She edged a foot closer to the tire iron.

Juggler shook his head and put his phone away. "Chico should have—" He jerked upright and raised his head. "Is that gunfire?"

The biker next to him cocked his head and listened. "Don't hear nothin' but the fuckin' wind."

Juggler looked at the other biker who shrugged and said, "Wind rattlin' something?"

Juggler looked at her.

She didn't say anything. She'd heard something, could have been gunfire—very distant gunfire if it was.

"Bring her over here," he said to the biker who'd been guarding her. "But first, get rid of that tire iron she's been eyeing."

God damn it!

The biker walked over, picked up the tire iron and slung it into the ravine then escorted her over.

"I'll keep you close at hand," Juggler said. He turned to the other biker. "Stash that extra bike somewhere it won't be seen. We'll pick it up later."

The man turned and walked away. When he did, Rebecca spotted the grip of Elwood's handgun protruding from his rear waistband.

THIRTY-EIGHT

Johnny was seconds away from charging one or the other of his tormentors despite their guns, when Wild rolled onto his back. Wild's right arm came up, there were several clicks, and something flashed in his hand. The nearest biker turned toward him and Wild lunged, sank the blade into the man's abdomen and ripped straight up. The man screamed and reflexively triggered off a burst of gunfire into the air.

Chico yelled something and let loose with his own burst, firing from the hip, most of which went into his dying partner. Wild was also hit and knocked flat. The rest of Chico's gunfire went high as Johnny slammed into him. The blow knocked Chico down. The Uzi flew from his hands. He hit the ground hard, tried to scamper to his hands and knees, but Johnny was all over him.

Interlacing his fingers, Johnny smashed his bound fists onto the back of Chico's head several times, forcing him flat. He seized the man by the hair, shoved his face into the dirt and pushed down. Muscles straining, up on his toes, boots slipping in the loose grit, he was going to smother the bastard.

Chico's arms flailed, tried to latch on to Johnny, beat against his leg, clawed at him.

Johnny's feet slid out from under him and Chico managed to turn his head to the side.

The sharp outcrop of a granite boulder protruded through the ground just to their right. Johnny swung them that way and drove Chico's face into the granite stone with all his might. Chico's scream was cut short by a sound like an over-ripe pumpkin being dropped. Again and again Johnny smashed his attacker's face into the stone.

Chico's struggles ceased and his body went limp. Johnny sat back on his heels breathing hard. He let go on the man's hair and stood. Blood was splattered all about. He rolled Chico over with the toe of his boot. What was left of the Satans Kin biker's face was unrecognizable. He turned and stumbled over to where the others lay. Wild was still conscious, his breath coming in short gasps. Blood blossomed on his cut, just above the right pocket, staining his vice president patch. The other assailant was dead as hell, on his side, his guts spilled out in a steaming, grayish-blue and red mass that stank like shit.

Johnny knelt and went to work on the rope that bound his wrists, used his teeth. The biker had tied his hands with a simple knot. He was able to work enough play into the cord that he could worm his left hand out of his riding glove and pull free. He shook the binding off his other hand. He checked his phone—no service. He took off his cut, peeled off his T-shirt and ripped it apart. He folded a piece, slipped it under Wild's cut and pressed it tight against the shoulder wound. He folded another strip and pressed it against the side wound.

"No," Wild said, barely audible. "Go on… go get her."

Johnny glanced around helplessly. To abandon a brother in need was the foulest thing a biker could do. But what could he do here other than watch Wild die? He looked at the body next to them and pulled the knife out of the corpse. It was a butterfly knife.

"Took it... off Sheva."

"I'll get rid of it." Johnny wiped off the blade on the dead man's pants, folded it and stuffed it down the middle finger of his riding glove. He balled the glove up, shoved it inside his other glove, wrapped them with the remains of his shirt and shoved them in his pocket. He put his cut back on and stood. He took his revolver, along with a spare magazine of ammo for the Uzi stuffed in the rear waistband, off the dead man. He also took the man's phone. He picked up the Uzi, ejected the magazine and replaced it with the spare.

He paused for another look at Wild. "I'll get you help, brother," he said and left.

The bikes hadn't caught fire. His Harley lay on its right side, flat against the shoulder of the road, sunlight reflecting off the chrome forks. He dropped the kickstand and put the bike in gear. He'd turned it off when he'd laid it down. He sat against the edge of the seat, faced away, and grasped the handlebar and rear fender. The sun-scorched metal blistered his hand. He ignored the pain and pushed backwards. His boots skidded in the loose earth. He dug his heels in. Sinews stretched to the limit, body trembling, he let out a deep howl from the center of his being and stood the Harley on its tires.

The bike was scraped down its side. A rear view mirror had torn off and a foot peg bent. He climbed on. It took three tries to start the bike, but when it fired up, it sounded good and he roared off.

It was a couple of miles before he came to another rise high enough to get cell reception. He slid to a stop and took out the dead biker's phone. He hesitated, but only for a moment. What the hell, he'd already violated one of their unwritten rules, and there was no way the club could get here in time to do Wild any good.

"Oh my God! Oh my God!" he yelled, trying to sound like a frantic civilian when the 911 operator answered. "There's been a shooting out on Desolation Lane, five or six miles off the highway." He listened for a moment. "I don't know—some biker. He's all shot up and bleeding to death. He needs help." He listened again. "That's right, Desolation Lane, six miles in." He listened once more. "Why do you need my name? No, I don't want to get involved. Send help." He disconnected.

He took his own phone and scrolled the numbers. He found Animal's number and dialed it on the other phone. There was no answer. "C'mon, goddamn it, answer." It rang twice more before he got the out of service area recording. He checked to see if he'd dialed the number correctly. He had. Why was he getting a recording? Who else was with Animal? The prospect, Ronnie. He found Ronnie's number and dialed it, again on the other phone. It rang, several times. "C'mon, answer it." The phone continued to ring.

THIRTY-NINE

Rebecca watched her captors. She managed to ease a couple of yards away from them. Juggler punched in a number on his phone and held it to his ear. His eyes narrowed and his jaw clenched. "Need to hear from you," he said and disconnected. He never gave much away, either with his body language or when he spoke, but she got the impression things weren't going the way he wanted them to. His hand sank to his side.

"Want me to check on 'em?" the biker beside him said.

"No."

She heard footsteps and a shadow grew on the ground next to her. The biker, Juggler had sent to hide Elwood's bike, walked by to rejoin them. She took a quick step behind him, snagged the butt of the automatic in his waistband, whipped it out and moved backwards several strides. He slapped at the seat of his pants with both hands, turned around and searched the ground. Then his eyes came up and his mouth fell open.

She held the gun in her left hand, placed her cast under her wrist for support, and thumbed the hammer back. Blood rushed through her veins and she fought to hold the automatic steady.

For a long movement nobody said or did anything. Finally, "You need to rack the slide if you intend to shoot us," Juggler said.

Her breath caught. *Shit!* Could it be… no. He was trying to trick her. "I'm sure Elwood did that—when he loaded it."

Juggler snorted.

She swallowed. "If you don't think so, try and take it away and we'll find out."

The corners of his lips curled into the slightest of smiles. "I'm not going to take it from you, he is." He nodded at the biker she'd taken the gun from.

The man's eyes flicked to Juggler and back. His tongue darted between his lips and his face paled. "We can rush her."

"You lost it, you get it back."

The man took a deep breath, rolled his shoulders and stepped forward.

"Don't! I'll shoot!"

The man hesitated and started forward again.

She squeezed the trigger. *Click.* "Damn it!" She pawed at the slide with her cast, tried to grasp it with swollen finger tips. The biker sprung forward and backhanded her across the face. His blow sent her spinning to the ground. She landed on her side and lost the gun. It bounced several feet away. She started to crawl toward it.

"Fuckin' bitch," the biker said and launched a kick at her ribs.

She managed to rise up so that the toe of his boot went under her but he still caught her hard enough to cause her to cry out and flip her over onto her back. The man raised a foot to stomp on her face.

"Enough," Juggler said.

The man paused, foot hovering in the air and looked at Juggler. "Tried to shoot me."

Juggler didn't respond.

The man lowered his foot.

"The gun." Juggler held out his hand.

The biker picked up the automatic and handed it to him.

Juggler studied it for a moment, then snapped the barrel across the man's jaw, sending him stumbling backwards and dropping him to a knee. Juggler racked the slide, stepped forward and pointed the barrel at the man's forehead.

"No!" The man raised a hand in front of his face as if to ward off the shot.

Juggler whipped the gun to the side and fired three times into the ground inches from Rebecca's head, the blasts deafening.

She screamed and covered her head with her arms as dirt from the bullet impacts peppered her. When no more shots came, she looked up between her arms.

"Like I said, you gotta rack the slide." He thumbed on the safety and handed the gun to the second biker. "She take it away from you, I'll shoot you both."

She uncovered her head and glared at him. Her breath came hot and fast and she knew she was snarling. She spit out some dirt that had gotten into her mouth and rose on her elbows.

Juggler squatted. His hands dangled off his knees while he studied her. He reached out and gently brushed some hair off her forehead. Then he grabbed a handful of her T-shirt and jerked her to her feet as he stood. He studied her for another moment then said, "You've got balls."

*

Clean leaned against his bike and tried to control his fidgeting. He rubbed his chin and stared at the ground. He needed to talk to Ducky. They'd arrived back at the turnout to find both Johnny and Wild gone. Animal said something about Johnny knowing where

Magoo went and roaring off with Wild right behind him. Animal was waiting to hear from them. Clean offered to ride out and look for them, but was told to stay put. He had the uneasy feeling that everything was going to shit.

To make matters worse, Tiny and Moose, the two biggest bikers in the club, rode in. They'd been unable to get a cell signal after they'd checked out their side road, so they'd come back. Animal wasn't sending anyone out again until he heard from Wild. With the prospect, that made the odds six to one—exactly the number of bullets in his gun. But to pull a piece on this crew would be suicide. The first thing they'd do is separate. If he fired at one, the others would swarm him. At best he might get two of them before the others stomped him into a greasy spot on the ground, like a squirrel run over by a semi.

Maybe he could tell them he needed to take a dump. That ought to work. Then he'd have an excuse to get far enough out of sight that he could make a call. He opened his mouth to announce his need to relieve himself when a phone began to ring.

Animal looked at the phone in his hand, raised his head and glanced around. "Whose phone is that?"

Several bikers checked their pockets, shook their heads and looked around in confusion. The phone continued to ring.

"Who the fuck's phone is that?" Animal said.

"Oh," Ronnie said. "Must be mine. Left it in the saddlebag."

"You gonna answer the fucker?"

"Yeah, I guess." He walked over to his bike.

"If'n it's your shack job," Moose said, "tell her you're busy and to hump the bedpost."

"And if it's your mother, tell her I'll see her tomorrow," Tiny said. "And tell her I'll bring a couple of friends."

Ronnie gave them a one-finger salute and dug his phone out. "Yeah?" He listened for a moment. "Yeah, I know who you are, you're—" He listened again. "Yeah, sure." He hurried back. "It's Johnny, but he's talking funny. He don't want me using his name and said to give him the man in charge."

"'Fraid the pigs are listening in," Animal said and took the phone. "You got him." He listened for several moments. "Got it. Desolation Lane, left off the first highway to the right past the campground. How bad?" He listened again. "Motherfuckers! You what?" His brow furled and his lip curled. "Yeah, okay, we're on our way." He handed the phone back.

"Satans Kin shot Wild. He's hurt bad, lying out on Desolation Lane. Johnny called 911."

"He what?" Tiny said.

Animal shrugged. "Said he had no choice. Wild was going to bleed out. Satans Kin got Becky. Johnny's goin' after them."

"What about Magoo?" Tiny said.

"Didn't mention him."

"Man, Magoo wouldn't sell out to no Satans Kin," Dirty Dan said.

Animal shrugged again. "Johnny says Juggler's got Becky."

"Oh, shit."

Clean felt like someone had punched him in the gut. How did that psycho get his hands on her? Magoo must be dead.

"Take Wild's phone," Animal said and gave it to Ronnie. "Get hold of everyone and have them haul their asses back here pronto. When they're all here, bring 'em over. The rest of us are riding. And tell them to watch out for Satans Kin, they're gunning for us."

Ronnie took the phone, opened the directory and hit speed dial.

"Maybe I ought to stay with him," Clean said.

"What the hell for?"

"What if some Satans Kin ride by?"

Animal pondered that for a moment. Ronnie already had someone on the line. "He's got help coming. Let's ride."

"But—"

"Get the fuck on your bike." Animal stared at him as did the others.

"Yeah… okay, I—"

Animal turned and strode away.

The Road Raptors mounted up and blasted off. Clean thought about feigning engine trouble, but Tiny and Moose took position behind him and didn't pull out until he did. He didn't like the looks they were giving him. His only choice was to ride.

*

The pain was bad, but bearable as long as he didn't try to move. Wild lay on his back and watched the sky. It was kind of peaceful. He didn't know how long he'd lain here—hours, minutes—his mind kept coming and going. He hoped Johnny didn't go charging in like General Custer. Juggler was a bad motherfucker and no telling how many men he had with him.

Several large birds circled overhead. He hoped the club would get here soon. Dying was bad enough, but the thought of being eaten by one of those flying shit-bags was sickening.

He figured his time was at hand. At least he'd go out serenaded by the most beautiful music in the world—even if it was only in his head—the sound of a Harley Davidson running wide open. It wasn't until the sound slowed then came to a stop that he realized he wasn't imagining it. Had Johnny come back? He couldn't have rescued Becky already.

Boots crunched on the ground and drew nearer. Maybe it was St. Peter coming to give him a lift to the Pearly Gates, where they'd quickly place him on a Slip-N-Slide to Hell. More likely it was another Satans Kin biker coming to finish him off. A shadow fell across his face and he had to blink several times to bring the face into focus.

"Wild… what the fuck?" Magoo said.

FORTY

Johnny stopped on the one-lane bridge. The sun was low on the western horizon. He had maybe an hour, hour and a-half until dark. He doubted Juggler would wait that long. The Satans Kin Sgt at Arms was too smart. At some point, Juggler would figure out something had happened to his men, cut his losses and disappear into the desert. The clock was running and Johnny was on his own. Even if he had time to wait for the club, they'd never make it past the pigs that would be swarming the ambush site behind him.

He removed the bundle from his pocket, peeled off the tattered remnants of his shirt and pitched it over the side into the water below. He shook the butterfly knife out of his glove and threw it upriver as far as he could. The knife was heavy and would sink straight to the bottom. With luck, it would never be found. The gloves went over the side. Last, he popped the battery from the cell phone he'd used and flipped it over the side. The phone he flung downriver. He heard it splash. The current should carry it further away.

There would be no slipping back past the ambush site on his Harley, not cross country. And there would be no waiting the pigs out at the dump. This was a dead end and sooner or later the cops would get around to checking it out. He didn't want to get caught with the dead man's cell phone especially with the record of the 911 call on it. Surely by dark a cop would show up. That didn't matter. If he hadn't rescued Becky by then, the pig would be retrieving their bodies anyway. He gunned his bike and rode on. So far he hadn't passed anyone on the road.

He'd screwed up badly, riding into an ambush. He'd probably gotten his vice president killed, an unforgiveable mistake. There was only one place Magoo could have gone. If he'd been thinking straight, he'd have been here an hour earlier. If Becky died because of his incompetence, he'd never forgive himself. His chest tightened and his mouth went dry. He shook his head—couldn't think that way. Things were going to get bloody, and he couldn't afford any more fuck-ups. He pushed his concern for her away and let his anger take control. *God damn Ducky and Satans Kin*. He was going to kill Juggler, along with whatever scum rode with him. He hoped Ducky was one of them.

He slowed where the blacktop ended, turned onto the dirt road and let his Harley idle. The tracks of several dirt bikes were partly visible in the loose dirt and sand, but so mixed up that he couldn't tell how many bikes. There were enough of them for sure. At least there were no car or truck tracks. He eased on down the road, moving slowly to keep the noise down.

At the chain, he stopped, killed his engine and dismounted. Not knowing how much farther it was to the dump, he'd leave his bike here and proceed on foot. He paused to listen. Nothing... but the sound of the wind and the faint call of birds he could see in the distance circling. His stomach sank—buzzards.

He unslung the Uzi, released the safety, stepped over the chain and broke into a trot. Gravel crunched under his feet, sounding like the footsteps of an elephant. He moved off the roadbed onto the hard-baked earth. That was better. After a quarter-mile, the road cut sharply up and disappeared over a small rise. He moved several yards to the left, crept up to the edge and flattened himself against the ground. There was a faint, pungent, almost metallic odor in the air. He raised his head for a quick look and got a face full of dirt as the wind whipped up. He ducked back down, cursed and swiped at his eyes. The wind howled over his head, a regular Santa Ana—hot and dry. He probably could have ridden his bike all the way here, and no one would have heard him.

When the wind dropped for a moment, he chanced another look. It was the dump. About a hundred feet away, three dirt bikes were parked. Several paces past the bikes, near an abandoned junker, stood Juggler, along with two other Satans Kin… and Becky. He ducked back down. Thank God, she was still alive. Keeping her that way was going to be the problem. There was no cover between him and them. They'd see him long before he got close.

Ten yards to his left some scrub brush grew at the crest. He moved slowly, alert for the sound of rattles. He didn't hear any. The snakes had enough sense to stay out of this heat. The brush provided cover, and he was able to take a longer look. Juggler stared at his phone, shoved it into a pocket and paced about. Everyone else watched him. A rusty, metal carcass of an abandoned flatbed truck rested on its axles some thirty feet from them. He could use that for cover to get closer. He'd need to move another fifty feet or so to his left to put it between them and him.

He slid down the rise to more solid ground and scampered over. Just as he started to climb back up, a flash of sunlight reflecting off chrome caught his attention. He froze. About ten yards away, lay another dirt bike, concealed by a bush. *Fuck!* He looked around but didn't see anyone. He moved toward it, walking in a squat, his machine pistol sweeping back and forth in tandem with his eyes.

The bike was dusty and showed signs of hard use. But it was in far too good condition to have been here long. The wind hadn't even had time to erase the tire tracks or footprints leading away from it. The footprints led back toward the rise. God damn it. Becky didn't know how to ride. Even if she did, she couldn't with her cast. That meant Juggler had three men with him. Where the hell was the third one?

There was no point in delaying. He crawled back up the rise and waited for a strong gust of wind to obscure vision and drown out the sound of his footsteps. When one came, he slipped over the edge and keeping low, hustled up to the truck. He knelt beside the cowl of the derelict and swiped sweat off his forehead. He had no plan—was winging it. His heart pounded in his chest and his breath came fast. He looked around again. Where the hell was that other biker?

Becky cried out.

Both doors of the truck were missing. He jerked up and looked over the seat. Juggler had Becky by an arm. And he had his knife in his other hand. Shit!

Johnny jumped to his feet and ran around the front of the truck.

*

The half dozen Road Raptors raced past the campground turnoff. Animal pushed them hard. Clean had managed to drift to the rear of the pack but both Tiny and Moose kept glancing at him in their rearview mirrors. What the hell? Was he under suspicion? No way could he drop out unnoticed.

The pack slowed to take the next right and he slipped his cell phone out of his pocket. He couldn't call, but maybe he could send Ducky a text. The bikes accelerated onto the highway and he took a chance—two quick words, *they know,* and send. He shoved the phone back into his pocket.

On they ran. Any minute he expected to be met with a hail of gunfire. He doubted that pockmarked freak would worry about who they were shooting.

Animal hit his brakes, skidded and veered off the highway onto a blacktop. The club followed. They raced along for several miles then up a small hill. At the crest, Animal slammed on his brakes and slid to a stop. The others did the same. Clean slipped his phone out of his pocket and glanced at it. The text had just gone. But would Ducky be able to receive it?

Animal stood astride his bike, and everyone stared down the roadway. The road ran down the hill and straight for about a half-mile before entering a curve between two smaller hills, the pavement there heavily shrouded in shadows. All sorts of red and blue lights reflected off the far side of the hills. "Pigs!" Animal said. "Everyone get clean."

The bikers removed knives, handfuls of pills, small packets and flung them into the scrub brush. Somewhere behind them came the faint warble of more sirens. It sounded like an entire army of cops headed their way.

Animal turned to face them. "We're probably gonna get busted. We don't know shit other than someone called to say we had a man down. Don't mention Johnny." He turned back and led them on.

Clean dropped to the rear of the pack again and chucked the phone away. He hated to part with it, the phone was one of the newest models, but it'd have a record of the text he'd sent. The Saturday night special followed. If he could have stayed with the prospect, he could have put the gun to use. Now all the gun would do is buy him prison time. He wondered what Ducky would do when he received the text—if he received it.

FORTY-ONE

Rebecca struggled to break loose from Juggler's grip. He held her by the arm, just above her cast. Her swollen hand throbbed and bolts of pain shot up her arm as she twisted about. Her heels skidded in the dirt as he drew her closer. Her heart pounded, breath came in gasps. He had his knife out. He was going to kill her.

"Don't think your old man is going to show," he said and shook his head. "Guess you're not worth the effort."

"You son of a bitch!" she screamed and went for his eyes with the nails of her free hand. He blocked her with a forearm, pulled her off balance and swept her legs out from under her. She fell but was jerked up short by the arm he still clasped nearly wrenching it from its socket. She yelped in pain.

Dust swirled about them, and she caught a glimpse of movement out of the corner of her eyes. It was Johnny! And he had a machine pistol.

"Freeze!" Johnny said and stopped a couple of yards away.

The other two bikers froze. Juggler didn't. In a lightning-fast move, he yanked Rebecca up in front of him and pinned her tight against his body, left arm wrapped around her. The blade of his knife went to her throat.

"Don't," Johnny said. "I'll kill you."

"Sure," Juggler said almost cheerfully, "but your old lady dies first. I'd take that deal. Bet you won't."

"Turn her loose."

"No."

Johnny licked his lips and shifted about, his gun moving back and forth between Juggler and his men.

Rebecca couldn't believe this was happening. In a movie, this was the point where Johnny would suddenly whip the gun up for a quick head-shot, one bullet, bang, right between Juggler's eyes. Then he'd pivot and drop the other two. But that was in the movies. If he tried that here, they'd probably both die—her for sure. Still, she could see him figuring the odds.

After several moments, Johnny pointed the gun at the other bikers. "Let her go, or I'll kill them."

She felt Juggler shrug. "Go ahead, that won't save her."

The two bikers looked less than thrilled with that remark.

"Want her to live? Set the gun down and put your hands on your head."

Johnny didn't reply, appeared frozen in place. A strong gust of wind sent another swirl of dust between them. Rebecca's stomach sank and she felt hollow. Things were spinning out of control. Johnny had screwed up. He should have come in firing. She had to do something to help him. She'd stomp on Juggler's foot. The shock might cause him to loosen his grip enough for her to duck loose, leaving Johnny a clear shot.

She held her breath, raised her right leg and tensed her muscles. But Juggler sensed her intentions and hefted her off the ground. She tried anyway but couldn't reach his foot. Her legs kicked wildly between his, unable to connect with anything. The edge of his knife bit into her throat and a trickle of blood tracked down her neck—a warning to stay still. She ceased her struggles.

Juggler sighed. "This sucks. Either shoot or drop the gun." When Johnny did neither, "Gonna count to three. If you haven't put the gun down by then... she dies. One... two..."

Rebecca closed her eyes and gritted her teeth. She'd be damned if she'd make this bastard's day by pleading for her life. Oh God, she hoped it would be over quick.

"Th—"

"All right." Johnny laid the gun down and put his hands on his head. "Let her go."

The other two Satans Kin quickly unslung their weapons to cover him.

She felt Juggler's hot breath on her ear, and his lips brushed her earlobe. "Whatta you think he'd do if I went ahead and slit your throat," he whispered. "Could be good for a few laughs." For an instant she thought he was going to do it, then the knife whipped away and she was sprawled at the other biker's feet. Her hands went to her throat, felt all around for blood and a gash, but except for the nick, he hadn't cut her.

"Hang on to her," Juggler said and sheathed his knife. "And tie his hands together."

Johnny held his hands out in front.

"Behind his back."

One of the bikers stepped behind Johnny, removed the .357 Magnum and handed it to Juggler who checked the safety and stuffed the gun in his front waistband. The man bound Johnny's wrists tightly together.

"Put him on his knees."

The man kicked Johnny in his calves, dropping him to his knees.

Juggler picked up the Uzi Johnny had been carrying and inspected it. "Guess this explains why Chico isn't answering my calls." He handed the weapon off. "Hang it over the handlebars of my bike. What about Wild?"

"Dead," Johnny said.

Rebecca couldn't suppress a gasp.

"Disappointed in you, Johnny." Juggler shook his head. "Should have pulled the trigger, killed the bitch and me both. How the hell did you ever get to be president?"

"Let her go. She can't hurt you."

Juggler snorted. "Don't know her very well, do you?" He looked around and wiped sweat off his brow. "Jesus, it's hot. And this fucking wind. You know people actually live in this shit?"

Rebecca stared at him. The son of a bitch was enjoying himself, running his mouth to drag out the agony. Johnny should have pulled the trigger. They were dead anyway.

Juggler glanced at the other bikers, then back at Johnny. A smile curled his lips. "My brothers have had a rough day. Not as rough as Chico's and Rudy's, but I think they deserve a bonus." He moved behind Johnny, seized a handful of his hair and placed the edge of his knife against Johnny's throat.

"No! Don't kill him," Rebecca cried and lunged toward them. The biker behind her jerked her back by her hair.

"Oh not yet, wouldn't want him to miss the show. You're the star. Wannabe actress gets the role of a lifetime, with a grand finale. How are you at dying scenes?"

His men snickered.

"She's all yours. Throw her over the hood of that heap and have fun."

One biker grabbed her by the wrists while the other took her ankles. She yelled and tried to struggle free as they lifted her off the ground. They raised her over the hood of the derelict car and slammed her down on her back, knocking the wind from her lungs. The hot metal scorched her flesh through her sweat-soaked shirt. The biker released her legs and unfastened her pants. It was the man Juggler had pistol-whipped earlier. His pig eyes glowed, his jaw swollen and discolored. Drool leaked down his chin from injured side of his mouth. She tried to kick him, but it was a feeble effort that he easily blocked with a shoulder. He tore open her pants and pulled them down to her ankles.

"Leave her alone," Johnny bellowed in impotent rage and tried to pull loose but Juggler held him tight.

The biker ripped her panties off. He dropped his own pants, grabbed her behind the knees, jerked her legs apart and pulled her toward him. She yelled in violated fury.

*

Few things in the world can match the man-made thunder of a Harley-Davidson suddenly wrenched wide open. Seventy-four cubic inches of heavy metal insanity let loose to run amok. The wind swung back and with it came an ungodly roar, exploding into their senses like a hammer blow. All heads spun toward the far edge of the plateau, just in time to see the red Panhead literally leap over the edge, both tires off the ground. The bike slammed down and streaked their way, an impressive feat of one-handed riding. The other hand clutched an Uzi Machine Pistol pointed between the ape-hangers. Magoo's long hair streamed back from his head, his beard plastered to his bare chest. His vest billowed. A grimace of what could be either pure hate or pure joy twisted his features.

Juggler reacted first, sheathed his knife, shoved Johnny away and wrestled the Uzi off his back. He held the gun at shoulder level, took aim, and was knocked on his ass by Johnny who recovered and dove into his legs.

The would-be rapists released Rebecca and tried to get clear. The man at Rebecca's feet stumbled to the right and tried to pull his pants back up. The man at her head stepped to the left and attempted to unsling his weapon. He didn't make it. Magoo ended that biker's outlaw career with a shower of 9mm bullets. He swung the gun toward the other biker. The Uzi jammed. He threw the gun away and steered his bike at the man.

Still trying to get his pants up, the biker looked up to find a third of a ton of extinction bearing down on him. He released his pants, swung his Uzi around and squeezed the trigger as Magoo raised the bike onto its rear tire and ran right over him. The man screamed and died as the rear wheel crushed his skull. The bike careened out of control and slammed down on its side sending Magoo tumbling off.

Juggler's legs were tangled with Johnny's who kicked at him, trying to smash a knee, his balls, anything. They rolled across the hard earth, struggling, grunting, cursing. Juggler managed to get loose and sprang to his feet. He swung the butt of his machine pistol at Johnny's head, caught him with a glancing blow that knocked Johnny flat. He glared at him for a moment to be sure he was down, then turned and took several steps away.

Both of his men were down and not moving. Neither was the bitch who still sprawled lewdly on the hood. He looked for Magoo. He couldn't find him. A thick spray of dirt enveloped the crash. The bike lay on its side, rear tire in the air and still turning. He tried to peer through the dirty haze and swung a couple of more steps to the side.

Magoo rose to his feet amidst the swirling dust like an apparition.

Juggler raised his Uzi and took aim.

Magoo started toward him. "You... sum of bitch," he bellowed and swayed.

Juggler hesitated and lowered his gun. Two dark-red flowers bloomed—one on each side of Magoo's leather cut. Magoo dropped to a knee, struggled to get up and continue forward.

"Hell, don't need this," Juggler said and laid the gun down. He pulled his knife out and made a come-on motion with his other hand. "C'mon, Magoo. I'll put you out of your misery."

"You... you motherfucker!" Magoo fell again, got back up and staggered to within a couple of yards of Juggler. The two men glared at each other. Magoo swayed from side to side. He let out a bellow and charged.

Juggler easily side-stepped Magoo's rush and slammed the knife handle down onto the small of Magoo's back as he went by, knocking him to the ground. Magoo hit hard, managed to get his hands and knees under him but could rise no farther. He trembled and spit out a mouthful of blood. He shook his head and tried once more to stand.

Juggler stepped over and straddled the wounded man's back. He gripped Magoo by the hair, forced his head back and slit his throat. Magoo reached for his neck with both hands but couldn't stem the flow of blood. Juggler held onto Magoo's hair while he convulsed beneath him. Magoo tried to grasp Juggler's arms, smeared them with blood. His hands began to waver and dropped to his side. Juggler released him, and he collapsed to the ground. His body shook a couple of times and went still. Juggler bent forward and wiped off his blade on the upper rocker of Magoo's cut.

A steady wind continued across the plateau. Juggler straightened up and glanced around. No one else was about. There were no sounds of any additional bikes, only the howling of the wind. Magoo must have been alone.

He stepped away. His men were definitely crow bait. Johnny's bitch hadn't moved either. One arm hung half off the hood to her side. Most likely she'd caught some slugs as well. The windshield behind her was spider webbed and there were several bullet holes visible. "I told you he didn't worry me!" he shouted at her still form.

The only one left moving was Johnny.

FORTY-TWO

Johnny struggled back to his knees. His head pounded, his vision blurred and tinted red, framed with jagged streaks of lightning. He shook his head to clear it and nearly blacked out. He fought to get control. His ears rang. Off to his side, Magoo lay on his stomach, sightless eyes wide open. Blood seeped from Magoo's neck into a growing, dark pool.

Juggler walked over and stopped a couple of steps away. "Well, that certainly was exciting," he said. "Leaves me one hell of a mess to deal with."

To Juggler's left, several yards behind him, Becky lay on the hood of the car, her bare legs hanging over the grill, unmoving. A vile coldness took hold of his soul. He looked at Juggler. "You... bastard."

"Not me," Juggler said and feigned hurt. "My folks are married. I think it's terminal." He laughed. "I am the spawn of the American dream—house in the suburbs, two incomes, three mortgages, one-point-four kids, strokes, heart attacks, limp dicks and Depends in their future. Reservations for two at the happy, fucking Alzheimer Retirement Home B and B." He laughed again.

Johnny was ready to tell him to shut the fuck up and get it over with when... Becky sat up. *Run,* he wanted to yell at her. *Run! Save yourself before this crazy fucker sees you.*

Juggler prattled on. "Bet you didn't know I'm a college boy. Football scholarship, Division One, started as a freshman even. Along the way I earned a BS in Business Administration with a 3.8 grade point average from a major institution of higher learning. That's BS as in bullshit. After four years of working my ass off, I'm qualified to be a manager trainee at fucking Walmart. Make dear old Mom and Pop proud." He spit on the ground.

Becky slid off the hood and struggled to tug her pants up one-handed.

Johnny tried to keep his eyes off her and focused on the lunatic in front of him.

"I played Pro Ball, was on my way to being named to the Pro Bowl squad. Hell, I might even been rookie of the year. Fame, fortune and all the pussy I'd ever want awaited me." Juggler paused, looked thoughtful and shook his head. "Blew out a knee. Life can be really shitty at times, can't it?" He looked back at Johnny and his brow wrinkled. "I can see I'm boring you with my life history. Sorry. Afraid Magoo ruined our entertainment."

Becky got her pants up and started their way, her face blank.

"Why don't... you fuck off... you psycho piece of shit," Johnny said, trying to keep Juggler's attention on him. He could see where Becky was headed. He needed to buy her a few more seconds.

Juggler's eyes turned cold. "Guess it's time to send you on your way. I really wanted you to watch what I had planned for your old lady. Those two idiots were just the opening act. I was going to handle act two. But now it looks like it's just you and me. Don't worry, if there's any life left in her, I'll take care of it."

Becky knelt and picked up the Uzi, Juggler had laid down. She stood and pointed the gun at his back.

Something in Johnny's expression must have alerted Juggler. Or maybe he sensed Becky's presence. His eyes opened wide. He grabbed at the revolver in his waistband and spun around, just as she pulled the trigger.

The machine pistol bucked madly in Becky's hand, sending bullets everywhere.

Johnny threw himself straight back in a desperate attempt to get out of the way and felt, more than heard, a bullet zip past his face. He flattened himself against the ground, head tucked against his chest. The hammering of the Uzi seemed to go on forever even though it couldn't have been more than a couple of seconds before the magazine emptied.

He raised his head and looked. Becky's left arm dropped to her side and the gun tumbled to the ground. She slumped down, pulled her knees to her chest and buried her face in them.

He jerked his head around to look for Juggler and was hit with a wave of nausea. His mind spun. Lightning flashed again around his eyes. He gagged and swallowed down a surge of vomit that scorched his throat. He gasped for breath. He needed to get to his feet. Juggler had hit the ground too. He had to get to the bastard before he could get back up. Maybe he could fall on Juggler's throat, drive a knee into his windpipe—something.

He clambered to his feet, staggered several yards to the side and nearly fell. His mind screamed to go one way—his body went another. He lurched forward, moved in a wide arc like a damn golf ball on a green. *Please don't let him get up! Please, please, please!*

He stumbled to a stop by the inert figure. Juggler would not be getting up. Becky's fusillade had gone everywhere—high, low, right, left, into the ground, the sky—but not all of it. Juggler had picked up a couple of new pockmarks in the left side of his face. He had no right side anymore. Juggler no longer had a jaw either. Johnny wanted to spit on him, but couldn't find the saliva.

He turned away, staggered over to Becky and dropped to his knees before her. "Becky... Becky."

She raised her head. He expected to see tears but there weren't any. Cold, green eyes stared at him. Something flashed deep inside them—hatred, disgust? "Get me out of here," she said, voice flat. "Get me the hell out of here."

"I will," he said. "I will. But first, we need to clean up a few things. And get our stories straight."

FORTY-THREE

The sun set behind them as they pulled to a stop on the bridge. Johnny threw the handgun she'd seen him take back off Juggler into the dark waters below. Rebecca had no idea why and didn't have the energy to ask. It was all she could do to hang onto him, her mind on hold. The gun hit with a splash.

Another sound intruded into her consciousness. In the distance a helicopter rose into the sky. The sun's dying rays reflected off its sides and blades. It was a touching bit of beauty in a day of ugliness. The MedEvac chopper looked like a multi-colored bird taking flight.

They rode on and passed a trio of squad cars headed the other way, their warning lights flashing. The last driver in line hit his brakes, made a quick U-turn and fell in behind them. The cop matched their speed but made no attempt to pull them over. He turned off his emergency lights. A move she found foreboding.

They arrived back at the ambush site to find the place swarming with cops, both CHiPs and the county sheriff's department. Red and blue lights strobed giving the scene a surreal appearance, like a bad nightmare. Headlights stabbed into the night. Flares littered the roadbed, their toxic clouds hanging heavy and close to the ground. The stench of burning sulfur and idling car exhausts was nauseating. The patrolman behind them surged right up to their rear tire, threw on his emergency lights and squawked his siren once.

Johnny hardly got the bike stopped and the kickstand down before they were hauled off and cuffed. She cried out in pain when one of the deputies twisted her injured hand behind her back and fastened the metal handcuffs. Johnny cursed him and tried to break loose. A pair of deputies slammed him against the side of a patrol car.

Several Road Raptors, who'd been sitting off to the side under armed guard, jumped to their feet and tried to intervene. Everyone yelled. Threats were tossed about, shotguns waved in faces. The county sheriff and a highway patrol sergeant stood toe-to-toe and yelled at each other over who had jurisdiction.

An EMT attendant, scarcely bigger than Rebecca, walked over. "You hurt?" he said.

"My right hand, I think I broke it again."

The attendant turned her around and shined a penlight on her hand. After a couple of moments he grunted and turned the light off. "You want to take the cuffs off her so I can get a better look at her hand?" he said to the deputy who'd cuffed her.

The man didn't respond.

The attendant sighed. "Frank," he said to the sheriff, "have your man uncuff her."

"What for?" the sheriff said.

"Says she broke her hand."

"Probably why it's in a cast."

"Says she broke it again."

The sheriff stared at him.

"C'mon, you got your whole force here, and there must be twice as many highway patrol. She's not going anywhere."

The sheriff stared for a moment longer then nodded at his man. "Search her and stay with them."

"I already searched her."

"Well search her again, damn it," He turned back to the CHiP sergeant to yell at him some more.

The deputy patted her down—he'd already removed the small wallet she carried from a front pocket along with her apartment keys and some change—found nothing additional, and uncuffed her. The attendant led her over to the ambulance and they climbed in. A moth entered with them and fluttered about. The attendant batted at it then took her hand in his. Under the bright lights of the truck interior, her fingers protruding from the cast looked swollen and discolored. "How'd this happen?" he said.

"I tripped and fell."

His eyes flicked up to hers. "Right, there's a regular epidemic of that going on."

Well she had. "I also scraped my knee." She straightened out her left leg. Dirt and dried blood were caked around the tear in her jeans.

The attendant shook his head and checked her over.

Another squad car arrived, and with its siren piercing the air, forced its way through and stopped by the sheriff. A highway patrol captain got out and another heated argument ensued. Eventually the sheriff spat on the ground at the captain's feet, called him an asshole and walked away. Johnny was moved from a sheriff's department car to a CHiPs'.

The captain wandered over and looked in. "What's with her?" he said and nodded toward Rebecca.

"Looks like she re-broke her hand." The attendant climbed out and stood next to the captain. "Cast will need to come off and her hand be reset. Other than that, abrasions, bruises, a little dehydration, over-exposure to the sun—nothing serious. I can transport her to the medical center, or you can have one of your patrolmen do it."

"You do it. I'll have one of my men ride with you."

The sergeant who'd been arguing earlier with the sheriff hurried over. "Captain, Corporal Rodriguez says we got four more dead bikers at the dump. No live ones."

"Wonderful. Get him some backup and a crime scene vehicle. And call for a K9 unit. I want that dump searched. I'll be down there as soon as I get this straightened out." He turned back to Rebecca. "You know anything about that?"

"Talk to my lawyer."

The captain snorted. "Get someone to keep them company," he said to the sergeant.

Rebecca was transported to the hospital. A patrolman sat across from her and watched her closely as though he expected her to morph into Hannibal Lector any second. No one said anything. The attendant appeared to have dozed off. When he shifted some in his seat, Rebecca said, "I saw a MedEvac."

His eyes opened. "Second time today I had to call for one. Miracle that man was still alive with all the blood he'd lost."

"Did you get his name?"

"I believe I heard some of the bikers call him... Wild?"

At the hospital she was fast-tracked through the ER. Her hand reset and a new cast put on. Then she was turned over to the California State Highway Patrol.

A patrolman placed her in the back of a squad car. Her wrists had been carefully cuffed in front, the right bracelet around her forearm above her cast. A seatbelt was fastened over her, the harness trailing off over her shoulder. The door automatically locked. A heavy, metal screen separated her from the driver. She was in a cage, inside a cage. An acrid stench of dead fries, urine and vomit wafted around on the chill air, stirred by the AC cranked to the max. The cheap air freshener, shaped like a Christmas tree, flapped from the rearview mirror and added to the overall foulness. No doubt part of the stink came from her jeans. She hoped it would wash out along with the stains. They were new jeans and even with the rip in her knee, she couldn't afford to throw them out.

The trip to the Highway Patrol station took the better part of an hour. The patrolman didn't say a word, the silence broken only by an occasional burst of static or some garbled chatter from his radio. She gazed out the side window at the dark landscape passing by. She felt like she was drifting through a dream—the whole thing with Juggler and the other bikers, unreal, the details fading. She closed her eyes and tried not to think.

At the police station, she was subjected to a strip search conducted by a pair of female officers wearing latex gloves. An act she found humiliating, having never undergone one before. Her outer clothes were confiscated and she was given a dingy, gray pullover and pair of trousers to replace them. They gave her a pair of thongs for her feet. "No stripes?" she said.

"You'll get them soon enough," one of the women said.

She was photographed and fingerprinted. Ink stained her new cast. Then she was placed in an interrogation room that was cold enough to hang meat in and had an overpowering odor of Pine-Sol. Her rights were read to her. After that she was left to sit by herself. It was a move intended to intimidate her before they began the interrogation. Johnny had warned her about their tactics.

She had no idea how long she waited and had fallen asleep sitting up when the door opened and a pair of detectives entered. They took a seat across from her and identified themselves as detectives Smith and Kelly. "You been read your rights?" Detective Smith said.

She blinked her eyes in an attempt to focus and tried to clear the slumber from her head.

"I asked if you've been read your rights?"

"Yes."

"Do you understand them?"

"Yes."

"Do you waive the right to have an attorney present during questioning?"

"No."

Detective Kelly snorted. "There's an admission of guilt."

She stared at him for a long moment. He returned her stare with a glower. She looked back at the other detective. Only then did he sigh, shake his head and glance at his partner. "Kelly... do you mind?" he said. It was all she could do not to laugh. They weren't good actors. Their timing was off.

"Do you have an attorney?"

"Yes."

When she said nothing else, "Can we have his or her name?"

"I don't know his name."

"You don't know your lawyer's name?" Detective Kelly said.

"Club attorney."

Detective Smith folded his hands in front of him and leaned forward. "Ms. Spade, I'm going to be very direct with you. We have seven dead bikers."

They must have found Elwood—or Wild had died.

"You are in some serious trouble here, as an accomplice if nothing else, and facing considerable prison time."

"Thirty years minimum," Detective Kelly added. "On each count."

"I know you're not some cheap biker babe," Detective Smith continued, "but rather a young woman who's made some bad choices—

none worse than putting your faith in that biker club's attorney. Like you said, he's the club attorney. He will do what's best for the club. If that means selling you out, he'll do it. I urge you to reconsider. You don't want to talk to us... that's your right. But you need your own attorney. If you can't afford one, let the courts appoint you one—an attorney who will represent your interests, not the club's."

She thought that over and looked for the catch. The cop was trying too hard to sound sincere. They didn't give a damn about her. It was an attempt to separate her from Johnny—put her at odds against him and the club. *Bastards!*

"Will you at least consider that?"

"No."

"You have any idea what a women's prison is like?" Detective Kelly said, leaning toward her. "Those dykes will take one look at you and go nuts. You can expect to be raped several times a day. They'll use broom handles and won't be too concerned about which hole they stick 'em in."

Detective Smith didn't sigh or contradict him this time. When she didn't respond, he said, "If the club attorney should get you released, what do you think will happen then? I'll tell you. The club will murder you to keep you quiet."

She didn't bother to point out that if Johnny wanted her dead, she wouldn't be here to start with. She faked a yawn and said, "I have nothing further to say until my attorney gets here."

They moved her to an empty holding cell and left her by herself. It was cold in the cell, the AC here on overdrive too. The highway patrol must have quite the budget. She sat sideways on a bench bolted to a wall, pulled her knees against her chest and rested her chin on them.

She had no idea how dire her situation was or wasn't. Johnny had warned her if she told the cops what had happened they'd arrest her for murder. Then go out for a beer with their buds and brag on how they'd solved the crime. Instead, she was to tell their attorney she'd fainted when Juggler cut Elwood's throat and when she came to all the killing was over. Johnny would spin the story so Magoo and Juggler got all the blame. By claiming she was unconscious, she couldn't contradict anything he said. Johnny had wiped down the gun she'd used and placed it in Magoo's right hand after rolling him onto his back. He used what remaining water he could find to scrub her left hand and arm, then dirtied them back up with mud and a bit of oil leaking from a bike. If anyone asked, she was to tell them she put Magoo's spare shirt on after she'd revived.

Johnny said it didn't matter if the pigs believed them or not. Without witnesses they couldn't prove a damn thing. Just keep her mouth shut and let their attorney do their talking.

He'd given her a part to play and she would. She wouldn't think about it anymore.

A strange calm settled over her and she felt at peace. What she found most surprising was her complete lack of remorse for what she'd done. Rather than shame, she felt a perverse pride, glad she'd killed that son of a bitch Juggler. She pondered her future. If she didn't end up in jail, she'd continue to chase her dream of becoming a successful actress. She loved to act. Would Johnny remain a part of that future? That she would have to give some thought—without the emotions that tended to cloud her judgment.

*

She gave her statement with the club attorney by her side, delivered exactly how he'd coached her, then answered the questions he allowed. She paused for several seconds before answering each inquiry, kept her answers short and direct. The detectives tried to trip her up by re-wording the same questions but her lawyer would butt in and instruct her not to answer that question as she already had. They did ask her about the shirt she'd been wearing. She did her best to look puzzled, as if, *what did that have to do with anything?* "I put it on after I came to," she said. "Got it out of Magoo's saddlebag."

Near the end of the interrogation, Detective Smith asked, matter-of-factly, if she knew what had become of Elwood's body.

"My client has no knowledge of what became of Elwood's body," her attorney answered for her. "She was unconscious at the time."

Detective Kelly snorted. "They found him in an abandoned Yugo," he said, his eyes locked on Rebecca's. "Bikers got no class at all."

She held his gaze, kept her expression neutral and her mouth shut. It was a stare-down that was finally terminated by her attorney who announced, "That's it, we're done here."

The lawyer told her she'd done good and not to worry. The police had nothing on them. He'd move that they be either charged or released. She was returned to the holding cell.

FORTY-FOUR

Rebecca jerked upright, her feet going to the floor, eyes wide open. She'd nearly fallen asleep, stretched out on the bench, when something one of the detectives had said came crashing back into her consciousness. She felt dizzy and chills that had nothing to do with the temperature in the holding cell. Her throat went dry, her breath became ragged. She felt like she was going to hurl. Her earlier confidence replaced with a sense of impending dread.

If the club attorney gets you released, the club will murder you to keep you quiet.

She'd passed that off as a cheap attempt to scare her. Johnny would never hurt her—or would he? What if he had no choice? Bikers were as paranoid as her father. And paranoia knew no bounds. She needed to think this through.

The club would not believe that Magoo and Juggler had killed each other anymore than the cops did. Like the police, they'd figure Johnny killed Juggler. The club wouldn't believe that she'd been unconscious throughout it all, either. They'd know she witnessed everything. A few months ago she'd watched a documentary on prosecuting attorneys. The show claimed that the majority of convictions resulted from one of two reasons. Either the perpetrator confessed to the crime, or someone ratted him out, for reward money or as part of a plea bargain. Johnny would never confess to murder. If he was to go down, it would be because someone ratted him out, and there was only one person who could do that.

Early in their relationship, Johnny had explained to her that when the club was faced with a potential problem, they'd hash it out in church and then vote on a solution. No one brother's vote counted for more than any other's, be he the president or a biker who'd just been awarded his patch earlier in the meeting. Majority ruled and the vote was binding. What if the club viewed her as a threat that needed to be removed? They might even act without Johnny knowing in a misguided attempt to protect him.

Her stomach rolled and she hurried over to the toilet set in a corner of the cell. She'd decided to break off her affair with Johnny. She wasn't cut out for this biker lifestyle. She wanted to be an actress. But to end her affair with Johnny now might well prove to be an act of suicide.

*

An hour later she sat in her cell, legs tucked beneath her, arms tight around her chest, her mind a complete quandary. Should she stick with Johnny and trust he could convince the club she posed no threat? Or was her best hope for survival to confess to the police and see if she could work out a self-defense plea? It would mean giving up Johnny, but that would work to her favor. No doubt Johnny was the one they really wanted, not her. But then what? The club would be after her for sure. Would the police protect her? And what about her career—she'd have to leave LA. She couldn't even discuss this with her lawyer, he was the club attorney. Maybe she should have listened to the detective—had the court appoint her a lawyer. But court appointed attorneys were shit.

The door to the cell block clanked open and footsteps approached her, the heels clacking on the tile floor. "Spade," one of the female cops called out. "You got a visitor." She stood and walked to the middle of her cell.

The last person in the world she expected to see stopped in front of her cell and scowled at her. He wore a light gray, double-breasted, hand-tailored suit and black wingtips, polished to a high sheen. His full head of sandy hair, now going heavily gray, perfectly coifed, not a strand out of place. His dark eyes burned with an inner fury.

"You've got five minutes," the guard said and walked away.

"Whore of Babylon," the man said just loud enough for her to hear.

"Hello, father. Come to break my jaw again?" She hadn't meant to say that, but in the shock of seeing him, it slipped out.

"Blasphemer."

That's what he'd said to her before hitting her five years ago. He'd have a hard time reaching her now.

For a full minute they stared at each other. Then she shook her head. "How—"

"One of the brethren from my on-line gospel works here. He made the connection and contacted me."

Right, the bi-weekly Wrath of God Salvation Hour with internet access.

"I came to see for myself what sins you have committed." He shook his head.

"The only sin I committed was being in the wrong place at the wrong time." When he made no comment, she said, "You came all the way from Missouri?"

"I've been holding a revival in Anaheim. Something a dutiful daughter would have known and attended. Honor thy father sayeth the Lord thy God."

And what about thy mother? Your wife. What's your God say about her? She resisted the urge to snap back and took a deep breath to steady her nerves. So he'd been in Anaheim—he'd have to driven all night. Probably flew over on the ministry's Lear jet, *The Angel of the Lord*. He used the jet all the time. He also used lawyers, high-priced, good lawyers, with contacts all over the country. "Come to go my bail?" she said in an effort to lighten the tension.

He didn't answer.

She licked her lips and gave him a nervous smile. "I've been working hard on my career, father. I'm going to make it as an actress."

His face grew red but he remained silent.

She took a deep breath and swallowed. It galled her to have to ask him for help, but he looked like her only chance to get out of this mess. "Father… Dad… I'm kind of in a bind here. I could use your help."

"Repent! Confess your sins. Beg forgiveness."

"I'm not sure that will work with the police."

"Not with the police. With God! It's your only path to salvation. Confess your sins. Accept your punishment. I can offer you nothing else."

Heat pulsed through her veins, her muscles quivered and her heart pounded. *That's it?* "How about a lawyer? A good lawyer, one I can trust. You can afford it… and I'll pay you back, however long it takes. I will make it as an actress. You'll see."

If possible, his features grew even harder. He shook his head—once.

"Why you hypocritical son of a bitch. You stand there in your two-thousand dollar suit and tell me you're not going to do anything for me, your own daughter?"

"You chose your path. You reap what you sow."

"This isn't a bible class, stop quoting scripture. This is real life. I need your help. I'm begging you. Help me, please."

"Jezebel. Harlot. You're no daughter of mine. I cast you out." He turned and walked away.

She ran to the bars of the gate, gripped and tried to shake them. "You bastard! Fuck you!" she screamed at his back as the guard let him out and the door slammed shut.

She walked back to the bench and slumped down. *Why the hell am I trying to prove anything to him?*

FORTY-FIVE

The detectives released Rebecca right after cutting Johnny loose. They returned her jeans and shoes but kept Magoo's shirt allowing her to keep the gray pullover. No doubt Magoo's rancid tee had gunpowder residue all over it and they were hoping to use it for evidence.

She left the building. It was early evening of Memorial Day. The American flag flew at half-mast, flapping listlessly in the hot breeze. Several flower arrangements sat at the base of the pole, their blooms wilting, leaves drooping. Johnny stood on the parking lot surrounded by club members who shook his hand, patted him on the back and hugged him. They led him over to his bike. The lawyer must have gotten his motorcycle released from the impound lot.

Two patrolmen loitered outside the door, smoking and watching the scene in the lot below. "Best steer clear of that crew, little lady," one of them said in his best John Wayne drawl. The cop rested one foot on the edge of a concrete retaining wall, forearm laid across his thigh. A cigarette dangled from his fingers. His partner snickered.

Her temper flared and she started to say something but caught herself. What if someone in the club saw her speaking to them? Instead, she descended the dozen steps to the curb at the edge of the parking lot. She took a deep breath of fresh air and watched Johnny do a slow walk around his battered bike. He gave no indication that he was aware of her presence. No one took any notice of her. Her muscles tensed and her heartbeat increased.

After several long moments, Flo wandered over and stopped on the lot, which left their eyes on the same level. "So... how'd it go?"

"They took my mug shot, fingerprinted and strip searched me. I was grilled by two detectives and locked in an icebox of a holding cell. I was threatened with thirty years imprisonment and warned not to leave the state."

"And you were expecting what?"

"I wasn't expecting anything. I've never been through this before. I'm fine."

Flo studied her through pale-blue, expressionless eyes, arms folded across her chest. It was impossible to tell what the woman was thinking. Shouldn't it be obvious that she hadn't ratted Johnny out or they wouldn't have turned him loose. That is... unless maybe she'd agreed to become a snitch. She felt her heart beat even faster. "How's Roxy?" she said to change the subject.

"They had to remove her spleen. She'll be okay."

"And Wild?"

"He's fucked up—was shot three times. Last I heard he was in surgery, listed in critical condition." Flo was silent for a moment. "Wild's tough. If anyone can pull through he will."

Rebecca nodded and watched Johnny climb on his bike. "Satans Kin?"

Flo snorted. "Assholes roared out about an hour before dark yesterday. Fled for their home turf I guess."

Another bike pulled alongside Johnny and stopped. A wave of

heat flooded through Rebecca's body as she recognized who was on it. She stood straighter to see better.

*

Johnny checked over his controls to make sure the pigs hadn't sabotaged them as another bike pulled alongside of him. He looked over to find Clean there, a simpering smirk on his puss. Clean was bitch-packing Sheva. Sheva stared at Johnny through wide, bright eyes. She gave him a nervous smile and leaned his way, ready to switch bikes in an instant. He ignored her. "Whatta you want?" he said to Clean.

"Gonna need someone to ride alongside you."

"Won't be you."

Clean's smile faded.

"Johnny?" Sheva said and reached out a hand to him.

"Get the fuck back in your place. Take her with you," he said and turned back to his controls.

Clean hesitated, then turned his bike and rolled back to the pack.

Once they were gone, he turned and looked over the club. "Animal!" he yelled and waved him forward. Animal gunned his bike up to Johnny's and stopped. "You're acting vice president until Wild gets back."

"He'll be back."

Johnny nodded and continued to fiddle with his controls, checking them over and over, delaying as long as he could. The weekend had been a disaster. They had one dead and two in the hospital, one of whom wasn't expected to recover. They were at war with Satans Kin and the pigs were hot to hang at least Juggler's death on him. He was pretty sure he'd cleaned up the crime scenes enough to at least muddle any forensic evidence to the point it couldn't convict either Becky or him. But if the pigs turned up a witness—a hunter, Boy Scout leader on a hike, or with his luck, a fucking prospector leading a mule loaded down with crap—they were screwed. Just a witness who'd testify that Becky had Magoo's shirt on prior to the killings could hang them.

He knew Becky stood on the curb behind him but he couldn't bring himself to face her. He'd fucked up. Trying to rescue her he'd nearly gotten her raped and murdered. She'd had to kill to save his sorry ass. How could she ever want anything to do with him again? He lit a cigarette, just to have something to do.

FORTY-SIX

Rebecca watched the exchange of bikes, not sure what was going on. Equally unsure what she should do, she looked back at Flo.

"You can ride back in one of the trucks if you want," Flo said. "We'll make room for you."

"Why the hell would I do that?" Rebecca said, too fast and too loud but she couldn't help herself. Was this some sort of test, or a trap maybe? She leaned forward and got in Flo's face. "I ride with my old man."

She pushed past Flo and started across the lot. Her path led her past Clean's bike.

"Fuckin', bitch," Sheva said. "You'll get yours."

Rebecca spun around and shoved Sheva off the back of Clean's bike. Her movement was so quick and unexpected, Clean didn't have a chance to compensate for Sheva's weight shifting and it took his bike over with her. He was barely able to do the splits and jerk his foot out of the way to keep from ending up under it. "What the fuck?" he yelled.

Sheva screamed. She was pinned under the bike and the hot exhaust pipe seared her leg right through her pants. A pair of bikers walked over and helped Clean stand the bike back up. Sheva grabbed her right calf, squirmed on the ground and continued to holler. A couple of women hurried over to help her but pulled up short when Rebecca glared at them. When Sheva looked up, Rebecca spit on her. Then she turned to Clean and said, "Sorry," in a tone of voice that was anything but.

She walked on, careful to keep her expression neutral and her gait to a casual stroll. If bikers respected anything, it was strength and toughness. It was all so clear now, like one of those cheesy scenes from an old movie where a ray of sunlight burst through the storm clouds to fall on the heroine. She controlled her own destiny. She was the president's old lady. Nobody was going to move her out or scare her off.

How ironic, it looked like a confirmation of her father's prophesy. She'd only been kidding herself. She could have become as successful an actress as Meryl Streep or Julia Roberts and her father would still consider her nothing but a whore. The only thing that would change his mind would be to come crawling back, begging forgiveness for trying to live her own life. Then become a good Stepford wife for a member of his congregation that he'd choose and churn out a passel of kids to be indoctrinated into his hate-filled brand of Christianity. Well fuck that. She'd rather be dead.

Would her father have risked his life to save hers? No. He'd leave it up to the proper authorities to rescue her, gone off and written a sermon about it—two sermons, one to cover each possible outcome. She had no doubt as to which sermon he'd devote the most effort to.

But Johnny had risked his life for her. More, he'd refused to harm her, preferring to die with her rather than to sacrifice her to save his own life. She couldn't suppress a small smile. Not a smart choice on his part, but that told her everything about his feelings for her. No, she'd never repay his devotion to her by selling him out, even if she ended up in prison. Logic be damned. Sometimes you just had to trust your emotions.

She had no intentions of giving up her dreams. Yet to dream, she had to be alive. So she'd become the toughest, bad-ass biker babe in the club. It would just be another role to play, a stone cold bitch, although she'd be playing for much greater stakes. But she'd discovered that the highs that came with risking your life were greater too. She'd never felt more alive than she did right now.

Johnny pivoted on his bike to see what the commotion was. Their eyes met. His lips, which had been set in a straight line, twitched and then curved into his full-blown grin that she loved so much as she stopped beside him.

She plucked the cigarette from his mouth, took a long drag on it, then flicked it away. Without a word, she took her place on the back of his bike.

THE END

ACKNOWLEDGMENTS

I want to start by acknowledging my wonderful wife and life partner, Wanda, who has put up with me for all these years and encouraged me in my quest to become a published author. I couldn't have done it without her support.

I want to thank the gifted author, Les Edgerton, for his guidance through several of his online boot camps as well as for the single best piece of writing advice I ever received. I'd be remiss if I did not also thank all those budding authors in Les's boot camp for providing invaluable critiquing and assistance.

Many thanks to Heather Luby and Jordan Oakes, Continuing Education writing instructors at Meramec Community College. Thanks to the Pen Gangsters writing group: Cortez Byrd, Amanda Heger, Heather Luby, Laura Schmidt and Stephanie Stempf and to members of my current writing group, Dave Bommarito, Dana McAuliffe, Laura Schmidt and of course, my wife.

Thanks to Jennifer Gibson for her wonderful cover design and to Jamie Wyatt for his professional layout and guidance.

Finally I want to thank my editor and very dear friend, Bill McShane.

This book would have not been possible without all of your assistance.

Made in the USA
Monee, IL
01 August 2022